Night of the Dragon

Dragon

Eyes of Midgard Book 2

Lee Dawna

LeeDawna Books, Inc.

First edition

Cover design by Premade Ebook Cover Shop

https://www.premadeebookcovershop.com

ISBN 978-1-949192-32-2 (paperback)

ISBN 978-1-949192-29-2 (ebook)

Published by LeeDawna Books, Inc.

https://leedawnabooks.com

leedawnabooks@gmail.com

P.O. Box 824, Aurora NC 27806

~

For all those carrying unseen burdens. May you find light in the darkness and strength in the magic of hope.

~

1

Sean

My throat is raw, the putrid taste of vomit still clinging to my lips. The violent torrent of convulsions was my body's feeble attempt to rid itself of whatever the red-haired witches broke open inside of me. That molten inferno—wild and untamed—that their chanting called forth. Unleashed. Gelby told me the Völva line is powerful, and with the strength of his family's own magic amplifying the witches', the Vasilis would finally be able to figure out what kind of spell was placed upon me. Instead, they dug too deep. Drew too much. Pulling until they awakened the fire within me. Until it tore free and turned on them, consuming everything in its path.

I blink, each reflexive dip of my eyelids showing me flashes of what happened inside the Völva circle. Forcing me to feel my insides ripping apart all over again. To shudder over that spot within my core where the fire originated. A place now feeling like the deep root of a raging beast. I shift my weight, still on my knees, kneeling too closely to the acrid, steaming pile of black vomit in front of me. I swallow the lingering bile and crawl in the opposite direction. There's no time to sort through the agony of what it felt like to become a walking inferno. No time to worry about how such a thing is even possible or about how those who were meant to help me took me inside their coven house and unleashed a horror that massacred them. If any of the witches survived, those Völva can thank Keela for their lives. If they don't die in the battle now raging around us.

Blue thunder streaks across the smoke-filled sky, shaking the ground as Rohan and Gelby once again shoot their electrifying magic into the swarming, writhing lines of vampires trying to surround us. To *slaughter* us. This was an ambush. Yet another terrible thing that would have been avoided if those overgrown elves hadn't forced us to come here to begin with. But with the Vasilis, it's their way or their way. No debate. No other options. Anyone who questions them gets to hear them lecture about how the Vasilis are blessed by their god, Odin, and therefore the rest of us are expected to fall in line. Something my unspooling insides keep doing the opposite of.

I stay on my hands and knees, steering my sweat-soaked body toward the chainmail net that's holding down the thrashing form of what was once Haldir. He's no longer the muscle-bound rival I was certain to fight. No more a man at all. He's beast and rage. Ready to destroy everything in his path. Same as me.

I reach the wall of chainmail, my heart pounding a deafening rhythm. I use its relentless drumming to tune out the cries of anguish around us. To muffle the storm of emotions whirling inside of me. From chest to limb, there is only room for the driving lead of determination. I dig my fingers down into the ground, clawing through earth, the soil caking under my nails as I shovel through grass and dirt, desperate to unearth the sleek metal spikes edging the net. A week ago, I would have been petrified by Haldir's transformation. Disbelieving of what my own eyes just witnessed. Today, his ability to shapeshift is only one more thing I have no time to focus on. I need him free from the net that's keeping his fifty-ton dragon subdued. Not for my own safety or even his. This is for Keela. Haldir is my only shot at saving her.

I yank at the harpoon-like tips of the net, taking in the enormity of the trapped beast. He's covered in small interlocking plates that are sealed underneath thick, ruddy-red leathery skin. His textured hide wraps underneath the dragon's belly where vertical rows of opal scales distort what little light is reaching his underside. He shoves his wide, spike-studded feet into that small amount of space underneath him, but his massive tree-trunk legs are pinned low against the leathery sides of his body, going nowhere as the dragon pushes upward. The rows of spikes running up his back, jutting out thicker and wider like rows of jagged teeth, clank against the metal of the net above him. Haldir lets out a roar, his steel-rending claws ripping chunks out of the earth beneath him. "Cut the net!" I yell at him.

Haldir opens his oversized mouth and a breath of his dragon's fire coats my skin. I may not have a hide of impenetrable armor like his, but it appears I'm immune to fire. The same as earlier when I killed the witches—not a hair is singed. "Nice try," I shout, the sound of my voice mixing with roars from the battlefield. "If only your witches were as fireproof as I am."

I shouldn't gloat, but the Vasilis family has turned my life into a living hell. Something Haldir seems poised to continue doing despite the fact that I'm trying to save him. He unleashes a torrent of flame directly into my face. I blink through the onslaught, resolve coursing through me as I continue to dig and claw my way underneath a spike. Hesitation means death. For us. And for Keela. Haldir knows it too. He might be taking his anger out on me, but there's a frantic urgency in the way his leathery wings are trying to beat against the chainmail, the spikes lining the bony implements of the bat-like wings rendered useless. Whatever indestructible metal this net is made of, the dragon can barely move let alone free himself. Not even the blanket of obsidian spikes wrapped around his regal throat or the crown of jagged obsidian spears on his head are capable of releasing him from this prison. As magnificent as Haldir is to behold, this chainmail has left the jaw-dropping beast utterly helpless.

I dig faster but the harpoon tip I'm working on only burrows deeper. I flinch. Magic. Everything around me is full of magic. Even my own body. And I can't control any of it. Haldir lets out an ear-splitting roar, tossing his bony, spiked head as far left as he can, flames leaking from his nostrils as the angry dragon fights the magic-infused metal. I follow his line of sight to where a small group of the Völva I accidentally set fire to are losing their battle with the vampires. Between me and the bloodsuckers, I don't know what will end up being left of these red-headed women. The witches being attacked by the Vampir is at least a confirmation that even though this ambush happened on Völva land, these women weren't behind it.

I look beyond those being overrun to where three witches stand hand in hand, chanting. All around them, vampires writhe on the ground, screaming in pain. The tightness in my chest eases a bit. I don't know the witches, but I do know that I don't want to see any more of the Völva die today. Not by anyone's hand. Especially mine.

Haldir thrashes. The end of the spike I'm working on digging free vibrates, the whole harpoon-like tip slipping through my fingers to once again burrow itself deeper into the ground. "Stop moving!" I shout, glaring up at the terrifying beast with two thick bony protrusions growing from the corner of each slitted eye. The sharp protrusions sweep into the air behind his head and give little doubt as to the fact that every inch of Haldir is built not only to protect the dragon, but to kill. And he can't utilize his potential to do either of those things unless I free him. "There's some kind of magic on the net. The more you thrash, the deeper the spikes go, so knock it off!"

He turns and sends a wave of fire rolling over me. It batters against me as if *I'm* the one covered in a layer of too-thick leather. "Save your attitude for Arsenious. The Fae king is here, and that's who Keela is going after." I point a mud-crusted bloody hand in the direction I last saw her go. "So help me dig you free, and then let's go get our girl because I'm looking forward to kicking your overgrown lizard tail for her later."

I shove my hand under the net, pulling up so I can work on the harpoon tip from the inside as well as the outside. Up until now, I wasn't sure Haldir could understand my words in his dragon form, or if he'd even bother listening to me if he could. It appears that he can, and that even without being remotely calm, he's willing to listen to reason.

The dragon angles his snout away from me, smoke mixing with red-hot embers as he exhales, each forceful breath proving just how ticked off the dragon is. Yet he shows me that his lizard skull isn't as thick as it looks by reaching one obsidian-clawed foot toward the edge of the net, keeping the rest of his body still as stone. He curls his toes under, the claws ripping through earth while the stillness in the rest of his body keeps the harpoon-tipped ends of the net from digging farther into the ground. "That's a good lizard," I taunt, thankful that whatever magical spell was put on me has me immune from his dragon's fire because once he's free, I don't want him to hold his emotions in check. I want him to rain holy hell down upon this land until Keela is safe. Until she is away from all of this death and destruction.

I dig down into the ground right along with Haldir, tugging on the harpoon until it breaks free of the earth. I wrap a fist around the bottom of the spike and slide forward to the spot of the next harpoon. With one last flick of his talon, Haldir unearths the second harpoon, shooting a blast of fire over my head in victory. Or maybe to rub in my face how quickly his claws removed that spike now that he knows what the game is. "Show off," I mutter. "I might not have dragon strength but your pathetic little flames still can't hurt me."

He growls from deep in his chest, careful not to disturb the net above him. I point to the spike I'm working on and he digs it up, being sure to breathe soot into my face while he does. "Good boy," I continue to taunt, flipping the heavy chain metal up, putting my body between it and the ground, and hoping with everything I have that these harpoons are only spelled to dig into earth, not any surface they happen to touch.

Haldir moves on to the next spike and I have no choice but to use my back to hold the freed section of net off the ground. Haldir unearths the next harpoon and another foot of net releases its burrowing hold on the ground. I shove myself forward, gathering all the pieces against me to keep the net's edges up above the ground. "That's good, dragon boy. Work on the next one. We're almost there."

Haldir shoots a breath of steam over me and I'm almost grateful for the cleansing. I've never considered what war smells like, but now the coppery scent of death mixed with sulfur and ash is something I'll never forget. And Keela is out there in it.

I feel the next foot of net giving way. I pull up with all of my might, jamming my bloody fingers into the chainmail as I gather the metal, keeping the edges safely off the ground. Haldir digs faster. Deeper. I'd give anything to roll back time and find myself falling onto all fours, hot vomit the color of tar spewing out of my mouth, because, back then, Keela was beside me. Safe. Whole. Untouched by the monsters swarming us now. "Hurry," I urge.

Haldir huffs, lowering his massive neck. His eyes lock on mine, the promise of violence etched in every reptilian fleck of color within those leathery slits. With no more warning than that, he lunges, the hundreds of tiny spikes lining his snout rending through clothes and flesh as he forces himself underneath me. He thrusts upward, crushing me between his lethal face and the heavy, unyielding links of the metal. Pain flares through my body. Thin, warm streams of blood trickle down my face, arms, legs... "Stop!" I shout. There's no way Haldir's head, let alone his entire body, can fit through the space between me and the ground. Even if he pushes so hard that I'm shredded by the net and left in pieces.

The dragon doesn't relent. I grip the tangle of net tighter, voice strained with a mix of anger and desperation as I try to unwedge myself. Try to get out from under the metal and away from Haldir. "Stop!" I yell again. "Kill me, and I drop these spikes! Then you'll never get out of this net!" His snout bucks upward. I brace for the slicing impact, turning my face away from the biting chainmail...and fall. Slamming into...legs. Human ones. Haldir brings his knees up, both of them connecting with my chin. I roll to the side, the net heavy as it slams down against my back. "The spikes!" I shout, but Haldir is already gone. The net must have kept him from shifting back to human. All he needed to thwart the net was to get a part of himself outside of its magical barrier.

I scrabble away from the chainmail, kicking and shoving until I'm free of it. I don't know if it's only spelled to contain dragons, but I don't intend to find out. I shove to my feet and spin around. Haldir is ten feet away, murder still etched in every line of his face. Pulsing from still-slitted eyes. I lift my hands in front of me. "Your fight is not with me. *Yet.*" His neck begins to elongate and his body... My lungs constrict, no oxygen moving in or out as Haldir's torso expands. Contorts. His powerful dragon form taking shape right before my eyes. Dreki. That's what his family called him. Keela is Vampir. Gelby, Rowan, and Bishop are Álfar. And Haldir is Dreki.

Haldir's colossal body swells and grows until he's towering stories above me. From his back, enormous wings unfurl, stretching wide as the dragon throws back his boulder-sized head and lets out a mammoth roar. Fire and ash shoot into the sky. I don't move. Standing my ground even as his giant clawed feet stomp down into the earth, sending tremors through the compound. Haldir can stomp me into nothing just as easily as he can skewer me on any one of his many obsidian spikes, but I don't fear the impossible beast. A part of me wants to bow to him. A part that has no doubt that I am looking at the King of Dragons.

His stocky legs fold against his powerful body and I brace for the impact of his killing blow, but the bend in the beast's knees is yet another thing I shouldn't know how to recognize. The King of Dragons is getting ready to launch into the air. "Not without me, you're not," I mutter, putting all the strength I have left into my legs and running straight for the dragon.

2

Haldir's leathery wings beat down toward the ground. He's already airborne but the tips of those wings are close enough. I dig down into my smoldering core and leap, cursing as my hands, slick with sweat and blood, slide over the leathery membrane. My toes hit the ground and I grind my teeth together, running along below the dragon until I get a fist clamped around the single bony protrusion at the tip of Haldir's wing. My body goes vertical and I hold on tight, gripping this patch of bony real estate like it's my last hope, because that's exactly what it is. I already know enough about Haldir's feelings for Keela to know that the man behind the skin of the dragon can be easily persuaded to forsake all others in an effort to rush to her side. To keep her from fighting in this battle alone.

Haldir's wings reach their apex, falling back down again in a flapping rush of choking wind. I use the downward momentum to overcorrect the arc of my flailing body, thrusting sideways to sprawl myself across the span of the massive wing. Haldir banks hard, but the leathery texture of his wing grips my clothing and I use the thick, bone-like veins of his wing to tuck my feet in tight while my hands curl over the edge of the wing, holding on for dear life as his wing dips low, forcing blood to rush into my head.

In one fluid motion, Haldir's wings rise again, his legs tucking against his body and his massive head swinging side to side, a stream of flame spewing from his gaping maw, incinerating every vampire in its path. I curl my bloody fingers under the lip of his wing and shimmy myself toward his back, peering down at the ever-distant swell of burning earth below us. Now that he's joining the fight, I don't know if Haldir cares that I'm still hitching a ride. All I know is that the dragon doesn't care whether or not I fall. I whisper a prayer into the wind and stretch a hand toward the next bony protrusion. There's no easy way to get from Haldir's wing to his back. I could either inch my way over to where the wing meets the body and then climb up through the rows of shark's teeth that line his back, or I time the beat of his wings and jump. Either way, I'm exposed out here on his wing, and I don't want my body weight affecting his wing's ability to maneuver in the heat of battle.

I work my way across the wing and wrap my palms around two razor-sharp spines jutting out of where his wing joins his body. "You could at least install some hand grips that don't resemble knives," I mutter, holding tight as the dragon soars across the battlefield, leaving a trail of scorched earth behind us. I ignore the rivulets of blood spilling down the spines and haul my legs up and over, pushing upward until I can reach the first big row of jagged teeth-like spikes lining his back. They pierce my skin as I crawl over them. Slice as I'm forced to shove both hands and feet down in between them to keep myself from flying off his back.

I bend forward like a slinky and make my way over the next jagged row. Haldir banks left, swinging his massive head to spew dragon fire down onto a circle of vampires surrounding an enormous black wolf. An Ulfr. That particular Ulfr being Liam. Head of the MacKenzie pack and my best friend's dad. The wolf howls up at us, acknowledging thanks before dropping his head and running to the aid of the light brown wolf. His daughter, Leah. I look away. In the short time I've known that magic is as real as dragons, what hurts the most is knowing that the MacKenzie family has lied to me my whole life. Not only lied, but kept secrets. They all betrayed me. Even Collin, my conveniently missing-in-action best friend.

I reach the center of Haldir's wide back and turn toward his head, aiming for the ring of obsidian spikes that cover the Dreki's neck. "There!" I shout as I reach them, dropping down to tuck my legs into the space at the base of the spikes. On the other side of the complex, Keela's black hair fades out of sight, shadows engulfing her as she races across the battlefield. The shadows gather around her and then shoot away as if she splintered them, sending them slicing through the air like a thousand tiny sickles. Any Vampir in their path is beheaded. Bodies dropping all around her while Keela's stride never breaks. Never slows. Her daggers are heat-seeking missiles, always hitting their mark as she speeds toward the wood line at an inhuman pace. Because she isn't human. She's a vampire. Just like those attacking us. Only, none of them are as fast as she is. None of them are commanding shadows the way she is. Keela is an angel of death. One showing no mercy as she slaughters hundreds of her own kind.

For every Vampir Keela puts down, though, two more seem to take their place. They race from the woodland all around us, their numbers growing despite their casualties. Despite the almighty power of the Vasilis that I keep hearing so much about.

Haldir swings his head, incinerating a line of Vampir armed with throwing spears. I scramble up his neck, using the spikes as hand and foot holds as I crane my neck to look for the source of the net that was blasted over him earlier. I don't want Haldir getting trapped under one of those again, especially with me on his back. I don't see anyone attempting to aim a net at us, though. All I see are bodies, flashing blue lines of magic, smoke, and blood.

I tuck my knees against two spikes and lean forward, shoving my hands in the collar of spikes around his throat as I shout into the rushing wind. "Go for Keela! We have to reach Keela!"

The dragon huffs and gives his massive wings a strong flap, gaining speed as I give thanks for the shapeshifter being able to understand human speech while in this form. Keela's dark hair glistens amid the carnage below us. Mid-stride, she throws her twin blades. I don't watch their path as they hurl through the air. All I care about is reaching her. "Keela!" I shout as we close in. She's running for a portal. I push harder against Haldir's spikes, wedging myself in tight and wrapping one arm as far around his neck as I can while I loosen the other and shift to the side. I lean to the left, stretching my free hand down. "Get closer! I'll grab her!"

Haldir's wings flatten to his sides and his massive body dives for the ground. For Keela. A man steps out of the portal behind her. He's tall and slender, with messy dark hair the color of Keela's and skin just as pale as hers. "No," I whisper as he steps to her side, a red gem at the base of his throat catching the light as he speaks to her. "No!" I shout the word this time, Haldir's roar drowning out my own warning. Heat soaks through my bones. I throw the force of the building inferno into my shout. "Keela!" Her head snaps in our direction, her eyes meeting mine. She heard me. In all of the noise and chaos, above the clamor of Haldir's roar, Keela heard me call out to her.

Haldir tilts and I stretch my hand down farther. One more heartbeat and she'll be in my grip. She lifts her hand...and places it into the waiting palm of the Vampir beside her. "No!" I shout, but it's too late. Between one frantic heartbeat and the next, she disappears. Gone into the portal with the man, the doorway between here and wherever she is now blinking out.

Haldir slams into the spot the portal was just in. The place where Keela was just standing. Light flashes over my shoulder. I crank my neck, catching sight of fire licking across my bare arms. Above me, an eight-legged white beast with the body of a horse spreads its feathery wings, casting shadows over us as it soars toward the battle. On the beast's back is Bishop, his whole body a faint blue glow as electricity courses around him, tentacles arcing out from a massive crystal staff clutched in his meaty grip, radiating in every direction as if he's a live wire and the staff is concentrating his sizzling magic. The bolts skim over the ground, incinerating the Vampir on contact.

Behind Bishop, another horde emerges from the portal. This one formed by men and women I now recognize as Álfar because they have the same look as Rohan, Gelby, and Jofir. They don't look like any elves I've ever heard of. They look like gods. This must be the Vasilis army, and they're mounted on the backs of majestic beasts with shimmering crimson feathers covering their wings. The sleek bodies of the mounts are covered in iridescent scales that shift from ruby red to molten gold in the sunlight, but the fiery splendor of the creatures' avian grace is broken by the long pointed beak that glows red, flickering like a distant star.

Haldir lets out blast after blast of fire, setting everything in his path aflame. I jump from his back just as another light flashes bright white. Haldir runs headfirst into it and disappears. I hit the ground, rolling head over shoulders, dousing the flames my own body is causing to burst from my arms. I spring to my feet and run for the spot where I last saw Keela. "Stop," a voice commands. Powerful and fierce.

I swing around. Bishop is standing beside his winged beast, the creature's eyes glowing as red as the man's. I look behind me at the patch of empty ground. "Keela. She's gone. She was here and then she…" I turn back and meet Bishop's sinister eyes. "She went through a portal. How do we reopen it?"

"We don't," Gelby answers, he and Rohan, bloody and worn, walking up to stand beside their father. I glance behind them. Leah and her dad are back in their human form and Monique is kneeling on the ground beside Bonnie…Beatrice, the head of the Völva coven. A woman I might have…killed.

I look around at the rest of the battlefield. Bishop and his reinforcements wasted no time putting an end to the battle. The few remaining Vampir are running back into the forest, being chased by the freshly arrived Álfar army. Too little, too late. I meet the eyes of each Vasilis in front of me. "Keela went into a portal with some guy. We have to get her back."

Rohan steps forward. "He is Fae, Bishop. The Völva confirmed it."

I shake my head. "No, I think the guy was Vampir. He looked a lot like Keela."

Gelby folds his arms over his chest. "Rohan is talking about you."

I gape at him. "Me? No, I'm not Fae. But Arsenious was here. Keela saw him and she was going after him. We have to find her before he hurts her." I move toward them but a blue wall erupts between them and me. I pound on it. "What are you doing? We're wasting time! We have to find Keela!"

Red vines of electricity run from Bishop's eyes, down his face toward the cruel set of his lips. "Keela is with her king, and you, Sean Winkle, are with me." A surge of power bursts out of his crystal staff and slams into my chest. I fall backward. Into darkness.

3

Collin

"Are you sure about this?" I ask Lance for the third time.

He toes the volcanic rock covering the ground in front of us, a stark contrast to the moist floor of the dense woods we traveled through to get here. "This is exactly what my father said his grandfather described. Jagged black rocks covering the entire surface of the land, remnants of an ancient lava flow." He sniffs. "And where the stench of sulfur still seeps from the hundreds of fissures underneath."

I scan the distant rise of the dormant volcano that once fed this land with the lava now broken and brittle at our feet. Its peak is shrouded in the clouds but the landscape between here and there is shrouded only by the occasional curl of steam rising up from the fissures like mist dancing off the surface of a hot spring. I glance off to our right where Ethan, Mark, and Nathan are waiting for my signal. Instead of traversing this harsh terrain in our wolf forms, I've decided our human bodies with heavy boots spelled to stay on our feet is the best way to move forward.

Despite the fact that we'll be totally exposed once we cross over into the desolation of this place. "Let's just hope your great-grandfather wasn't delusional about what they found here."

Lance huffs. "Greaty G made up one little story and now everyone wants to dump on him."

"Your *Greaty G* accused Odin of trying to steal his soul. *To Odin's face.* Forgive the rest of us if we question the other stories your long-dead family member told. He nearly got all of the Ulfr kicked out of Midgard."

Lance sighs. "Yeah, I know. The old wolf went a little batty near the end, but the MacKenzie pack made nice with the Vasilis and now we all bow to your dad." Lance jabs an elbow into my ribs. "So stop complaining. If it wasn't for my crazy family, you wouldn't have the best beta in Ulfr history."

I catch Mark's eye and nod, giving him the signal to lead the others forward because Lance is right. After his great-grandfather called a meeting that included the heads of all the Ulfr families as well as Bishop and his top elves—wherein Greaty G claimed Odin was a psychopath who not only made a blood oath with the likes of Loki, but demons who crawled into Greaty G's bed at night trying to steal the old man's soul—my family took over.

According to the stories told by my own great-grandfather, the Vasilis were ready to color all of us as traitors. When Odin himself materialized in the room, Bishop was the only one who wasn't stunned by the god's arrival. Lance's family immediately began apologizing for his great-grandfather's outlandish claims, and when the old man refused to apologize himself, Odin took Greaty G's life and then appointed *my* great-grandfather as their alpha, effectively stripping Lance's family of their own lineage by forcing them to fold into the MacKenzie pack. Since then, they have spawned many strong wolves but no alphas. Lance is one of their strongest members, and when the time comes for me to step into my father's place as alpha, Lance will be at the top of my list for beta. Appointments we're both hoping won't happen for a very, very long time. "Let's go find ourselves a Seidr. And she better be a hot seer because I didn't come all this way to have to flirt with an old crone."

Lance moves ahead of me, out into the desolate landscape. "Ethan has sacred offerings in his bag just so you *don't* flirt with the Seidr. We want her to help us, not kick us out because our leader can't stop drooling on her like some house dog salivating over steak."

I sweep out beside him and move cautiously over the unforgiving terrain. "You guys are just jealous that my alpha energy gives me first dibs. All the sacred baubles in the world can't compete with my natural, dominating, lust-in-a-bottle alpha musk."

He groans and despite the unexpectedly long journey that's left us all tired and increasingly uneasy over the lack of communication with our pack, a smile itches at my lips. If we find the seer who is rumored to live somewhere in the shadow of the volcano, maybe we can finally find this ancient artifact that the Fae who hired us couldn't give us a description of. They said the mystical object they sought was created by the gods and held immense power that only the Fae themselves could harness. Like my dad, I'm sure that claim was a lie. But when both the Seelie *and* Unseelie Fae contact you within a week of one another, paying handsomely whether we find their artifact or not, you take the job and go for the bonus chest of jewels that will be awarded if we successfully retrieve the object. Our only choice will be whose bonus money we want, and we're not above leveraging that fact to milk the Fae for as much as we can get.

I just hate that I missed Sean's first week at Merrymont. I had a lot of things planned for him. Like how to ease him into the fact that I'm not human and he's been surrounded by supernatural beings his whole life. Instead, I pulled him into the middle of a supernatural hive and then Leah, of all people, was put in to replace me as head of Sean's detail. I can only hope she's keeping her promise and leaving Sean alone so he can enjoy college life.

Nathan's low whine bites through my depressing thoughts. *Sorry*, he mouths when I cast him an irritated glare. He points at the low dancing curl of steam rising from the smallest of cracks beneath him. It's thicker than before and the air is turning more acrid. "We need to steer clear of the fissures."

Lance grunts. "Tell that to her."

"Who?" My head whips around, catching the tail end of a wave of long brown curls dashing through the jets of billowing steam suddenly exploding from fissures across the entire landscape. I growl. "I guess your Greaty G forgot the part about the witch having booby traps?"

Lance sighs. "Seidr. Not witch. If you want to flirt with the old bat, then you better spend your time getting her profession right because if she still looks that good after all this time..." He lets out a low whistle. "Game on. May the best wolf win."

I signal for the others to fan out. "Let's catch ourselves a seer."

Lance circles away, all of my wolves spreading out so we can trap and push the Seidr to a central point. Her kind is extremely rare and they're powerful, but not in the way a regular witch would be. A Seidr's magic is mental. They can sense and see things the rest of us can't. Many of our elders claim that the original Seidr was created when each of the gods dropped a splash of their blood into Urðarbrunnr, the Well of Fate. Not for the purpose of creating another living being, but each one of the gods seeking out the all-knowing wisdom of the Norns—those sisters who tend to the spring-fed waters of the well. They draw from its depths to nourish the roots of Yggdrasil, the tree that gives life to the cosmos. And those same three goddesses of fate draw water from that well to shape the destinies of all who live within the worlds given life by Yggdrasil.

I move forward, keeping an ear tuned to the advance of my wolves. The Seidrs might not be physically dominant but they're smart. When the first one slipped from the waters of Urðarbrunnr, the Norns lost their minds. They manipulate life, they don't create it, and therefore the three goddesses accused the gods of conspiring to overthrow fate itself. The gods denied meddling even though most of the stories told about them prove just how meddlesome they are. They also refused to execute the Seidr. Instead, they scooped her up and took her back to their realm. To Asgard. Soon after, the Seidr escaped, hiding herself from the gods and escaping each thread of cursed fate that the Norns still weave for her today.

In the span of her eternal life, the original Seidr has managed to procreate with other kinds, passing on her cunning and power to her offspring at varying levels of strength. Some say the Seidr is the creator of the Changeling grift, not the Fae. True or not, I don't really care. Whichever child this is and no matter who raised them, all I care about is our intel being right. If this Seidr is as powerful as Lance's great-grandfather whispered about, we can finally finish this mission and get back to our normal lives.

Ethan's deep wheeze draws my attention. The stench of sulfur was already overwhelming and now that the fissures are activating, the air is becoming toxic. We won't be able to stay here long. My eyes are already watering and I can feel the tightening in my chest. The others will succumb before I do, but I'm not willing to risk their lives. I let out a demanding howl and my pack sprints forward. Even in our human forms, the Seidr can't outrun us.

Loose rock shifts under our feet, but it's the rock scattering from underneath the girl's rushing feet that gives us the direction we need to close in on our prey. The sulfur is ruining our heightened sense of smell and the searing steam from the fissures clouds our vision, but this secluded, barren valley gives up its secrets to those of us with the predatory ears of a wolf. The girl is heading straight for the volcano.

We close in and I allow my wolf to rise, vision sharpening and claws elongating as a dusting of coarse charcoal hair covers my arms. The others do the same. We don't anticipate a fight from the Seidr and we definitely don't want to hurt her, but there's a very good reason why so few ever seek them out. Speaking directly to a Seidr is as dangerous as trying to journey to see the Norns. None of them give up their information freely. There's always a price, and sometimes that price is your life.

"We're close," I tell the others, voice barely audible even to my own ears, but I know my pack can hear me, and I know they're as determined as I am to secure the information we need to finalize this mission.

Their movements synchronize to mine as we near the steep, sloped walls of the towering volcano. Here, around its base, patches of gnarled vegetation twist up through the blanket of rock, proof that nature will find a way, no matter what. The bones tucked around them like garden edging and the ones crafted into bizarre ornaments that dangle from piles of rocky outcroppings littering the side of the volcano, are not. The outcroppings themselves aren't even natural and if wasn't for the set of piercing green eyes looking out at me from behind one of them, I wouldn't believe that anything not deserving of death lived here.

My wolf brushes a shuddering shoulder against the bond that links our souls as one. I run a comforting mental hand over the spot. The graceful cascade of curls falling over the girl's shoulders makes for a beautiful picture, but I feel the pulsing instinct of danger hidden behind that pretty face. Whatever comes next, I won't be letting my guard down with her. "Stay behind me, and stay alert," I order the others.

Lance moves one step behind on my right, Nathan copying the motion on my left with Ethan and Mark flanking both of them. This girl doesn't look old enough to possess the wisdom of a Seidr but after coming all this way to find her, I can only hope the story passed down through Lance's family about having encountered a powerful Seidr in this land are true. I straighten and let my alpha shine through as we approach. The girl doesn't move. Doesn't flinch. Beside her, the outline of a door is cut into the mountain itself. A clever hiding spot that we might not have found had she been fast enough to get inside before we reached her. "We're not here to hurt you."

"We won't even have to huff and puff and blow your house down now," Mark adds with a what I know is a big dumb smile without even looking at him.

I growl in warning. He huffs. "What? My little sister loves that fairytale."

Ethan groans. "The wolf doesn't win in that one, dude."

"It does in my version," Mark mutters.

The girl's head cocks sideways and I run a hand down my face. If Dad hears about this, he'll back Leah as alpha over me. I step forward and try again. "I'm Collin, and these idiots are trying to tell you that we brought gifts. Offerings. We need your help, and we can pay." I motion Ethan forward and he begins to unpack the offerings.

The door beside the girl opens. Slowly. A faint light flickers from within, the thick scent of spice and incense drifting toward us. "Come in," an ancient voice calls. My eyes flick to the girl's. Her face is pure stone. The voice is coming from within the volcano. "I've been expecting you, heir of Liam." It speaks again, drawing my attention back to the door. "If you want to save your pack, Collin MacKenzie, put down your weapons and leave the others outside with Zara. She will guard them, as she does me."

4

Sean

I grip the bars of my cell. The last time the Vasilis let me walk out of their prison, I knew there was a chance I'd get locked up in here again. I just didn't expect it to happen so soon. Then again, instead of days, it feels as if years have passed since I was freed from this place where the jailer is a flesh-eating dwarf who looks more like Santa's little helper than any of the other Vasilis do. *If* you turn Santa's cute little toy makers into demonic nightmares with razor blades for teeth.

At least I'm not alone this time. Haldir is trapped in Alberich's magical dining room dungeon with me, one cell over and, from the sound of things, still in his dragon form. I rest my forehead against the bars, standing silently at the front of my definitely not-big-enough-to-fit-a-dragon cell, listening and watching as the roaring, thrashing, fire-breathing Dreki breaks all of Alberich's rules of silence. The monster hasn't yet come to devour the dragon, though. Maybe that's one of the perks of being a Vasilis. You can be imprisoned by your own family, but the Vasilis won't let their prison master eat you. That, or Alberich is afraid Haldir will roast him before the hammer-fisted dwarf gets anywhere near the Dreki.

When Haldir disappeared from the battlefield, I assumed someone opened a portal to let the dragon go after Keela. Never would I have imagined that his family trapped him in their dungeon. Me? Sure. But one of their own? When Bishop blasted me and my body dropped through the portal, my back slamming into the achingly familiar floor of this cold cell, I was more shocked by Haldir's presence than my own unfair sentencing.

Haldir's roar once again vibrates through the mountain of stone that is our prison, managing to rattle every bone in my body without so much as making these bars creak. My teeth grind. His fiery assaults have turned the stagnant underground air into a potpourri of sulfur and the walls are now painted with scorch marks that flare over the ceiling and spray down the hall as far as I can see in either direction. All for nothing. When he first started to rage, I thought Haldir might free us. Now I know his dragon's fire is as useless against this magical jail as the squirming, lazy thing inside of me that refuses to so much as let a single flame sprout from any spot on my body.

I pace away from the bars. Haldir isn't a true Vasilis. He isn't Álfar. He's Dreki. An orphan the Vasilis took in. Bishop raised the dragon to be *like* one of his own sons, but Haldir isn't his son by blood. Now that I've seen all of them in action—seen Bishop's army and heard their battle cry mix with their victory shouts as they mercilessly slaughtered every remaining Vampir—I understand more than ever how different Haldir and Keela are from Rohan and Gelby. No matter how Keela and Haldir were raised, they are no more Álfar than I am. And two of us are in prison while the other is...who knows where.

I run my blood-crusted hands through my hair, ignoring the fact that the cuts along my palms are all healed now. I might somehow have magic, but I'm not a fairy. Or a too-tall elf like the Vasilis. I'm not a dragon, vampire, or even a wolf. This *thing* inside of me isn't my own. Up until I met Keela and her now dead boyfriend, proof of my ordinary humanness was all around me. Evidenced by me spending my whole life trying to fit in with the unflawed perfection of the other people in Richlands. The seemingly immaculate Collin and his siblings, his cousins...nearly all of the residents of my former hometown. People I now understand are Ulfr. Or Völva. Or probably some other kind of supernatural that I've never heard of before.

I touch my face. The day I met Keela, I felt a murderous flicker in my chest when Aether's hands were on her. It did feel as if flames were licking against my ribs but...the fire exploding from my body...the healing...the increased tolerance for pain...that all came *after* Aether punched something into my chest. This is all his fault. He probably gave me enough magic to end up with one of those impeccably flawless appearances too. The only thing he didn't give me was enough power to rip a hole through this prison. And instructions. A little guidance would have been nice.

Haldir rakes his steel-rending claws over the unbreakable bars, the trapped Dreki launching yet another useless assault. He would have fit in perfectly in Richlands. Muscled physique. Stronger than he looks. And I bet he's never had a pimple a day in his life. A lot of good that otherworldly charm is doing him now.

I stomp back to the front of the cell. His dragon fire crashes over the walls of the narrow hallway, and I tighten my fists around the bars, bracing as his roar rumbles through the rock beneath my feet and over the ceiling above us, so powerfully this time that I'm sure the dark stone is going to collapse, burying both of us alive inside this mountainous world of Álfar magic. A world that shouldn't exist.

I beat my head against my fists. What good is it to have this power if I can't use it? My life is already ruined. My parents are dead, my best friend is a liar, and even if I didn't mean to, I've murdered innocent women. Witches, but still... Even if I hadn't missed the start of college, I wouldn't be able to go now. To pretend that life is normal enough for something as mundane as a college education. Worse than all of that, even though I know it shouldn't be the most devastating part, is that I can't rescue Keela while I'm stuck inside of this prison cell.

Maybe I'll get lucky and she'll save me. Again. Because she's the only reason I got out of this cell the last time, and the way she behaved in the car before we entered the coven house... My feelings for her might be caused by her vampire allure but what she expressed for me is not. I close my eyes, picturing Keela placing her hand into that of the dark-haired stranger. The Vampir king. *Her* king. Anger blooms in my chest, followed by the welcome burn of fire. It strengthens my bones, the marrow boiling. Hardening.

I grip the bars harder, the magic I now wield thrumming through my veins. Pulsing into every dark corner of my body. My jaw clenches, mind fixed on the image of the vampire king. His hand resting on Keela's shoulder. Fingers trailing over her neck. His head dipping toward her face while his mouth seeks hers. Images I've never seen, yet ones that are as clear as if I'm in the room with them. Watching them.

The *thing* inside of me rises up, like an eye blinking open to see what I see. When the Vasilis first tortured me, I felt it move. Grew stronger as it released a little of its strength. What I experienced then was nothing like the surge of burning power I felt spew out of it when the Vasilis combined the strength of their elfin magic with that of the Völva. Nothing like what I feel now.

A shout rips from my throat and my hands blaze. Brighter and stronger than they did at the witch compound. I jerk away from the bars...away from the dark metal turning to liquid underneath my palms.

My breath shallows, a gasp sticking in my throat as I inspect the bars. Where my fists had surrounded the metal, the bars are melted clean through. "Hal?" I swallow, watching as the bars begin to reform themselves right before my eyes. I wrap my fists around them again. "My Dreki fire melts the bars. That's what I have, right? Dragon fire, like you?"

He doesn't answer. Probably because he's still in his dragon form. I tighten my fists on the bars and try to melt them again, this time imagining fire boiling up from deep within me to torch the bars completely. Hal roars, sending my teeth clanking together. I groan. "Yeah, I get it. You're a big bad dragon. Now shoot your fire at the bars and get us out of here!"

His roar fades into the deep huff of a man. "What do you think I've been trying to do? The bars won't melt. The Vasilis magic is too strong."

I close my eyes and think of Keela. "You have to be in your human form to get the fire concentrated enough. I'm focusing it into my hands and it—"

"I already told you that I've tried my fire," he growls. "It doesn't work. No magic works against that of the Vasilis. Odin himself blessed the Álfar."

I tug on the bars, willing my fire to ignite again. "Odin didn't do a very good job then because I'm telling you that I just lit my hands on fire and melted these bars!"

His chuckle is anything but friendly. "Then do me a favor and melt mine."

I remove my hands and inspect the bars. Nothing this time. Not even a little melted dent. "You're the dragon. Focus your lizard spit and get us out of here."

"There is no *us*," he snarls.

I slam my hands back against the bars. "I've already saved your tail once so when I get out of here, don't count on me to do it again."

Haldir snorts. "If you're melting the bars, it isn't because of Dreki fire. You may wield something similar, but you are not Dreki. You stink."

I focus my anger on the bars. "Right back at you, dragon boy."

He sighs, the sound of it echoing down the hallway. "I'm not insulting your smell. I'm telling you that you smell different. Before the witches took you into their circle, you smelled human. Now you don't. But you do not smell of Dreki either."

I sniff at my armpit. No matter what Beatrice told the Vasilis, or what any of them choose to believe, I am not Fae. I can't be. In addition to my flawed human existence, I'm nothing like Arsenious or his recently deceased son Aether. In looks or demeanor. "I'm not Fae."

Haldir groans. "I never said you were. You smell like nothing I've ever smelled before, including the Fae. So I don't know what you are, but I do know my brothers will not allow you to escape our territory. If you are capable of escaping this prison, which I doubt, you will not get far. And when they catch you, we will find out what you are and what you're hiding from us."

My turn to snort. "We? Your brothers, and the guy who's supposed to be your dad, sent you to prison. I don't think there's a *we* where they're concerned."

Silence spreads between us. I keep working on the bars, getting nowhere. Haldir's voice cuts through my frustration. Low and calm. "When I am enraged, I often lose control of my dragon. He can't be reasoned with. In the heat of battle, my rage is beneficial. Afterward..."

I move closer to the wall that separates us, choosing two new bars to focus my energy on. "Your family sent you to a prison where the head guard eats the prisoners, for a time-out?"

Haldir draws in a noisy, annoyed breath. "Alberich will not bother me, and my brothers will release me when I am calm. Something your presence isn't helping with. All I can think about is taking you up on your offer to fight for Keela. I will end you, and then I will go after her on my own."

I close my eyes and envision her with Haldir. His face fades, replaced with that of the vampire king. His blood-red lips smiling as they move so very close to her own. My fists burst into flame. The bars begin to melt, reforming under my palms just as quickly, transitioning from solid to liquid and back to solid again. A wicked smile cuts across the face of the *beast* inside of me. I can't see it, but I can feel it. "I'll make you a deal, lizard-breath. I'll get out of here, go get Keela on my own, and then come back and let you give *ending* me your best shot. But you have to stay in human form. That's only fair."

He chuckles. "Fair or not, after Keela is back, she will not let me kill you. If Bishop allows it, I will end your life before Keela returns to us."

My fire dies out and I remove my hands from the bars. "She's coming back? Without our help, the vampire king will let Keela go free?"

Haldir goes silent. My hands shake. "Is that a no? The king *won't* let Keela go?"

Haldir takes another deep breath, this one less laced with annoyance. "Keela is powerful. Because of that power, many years ago, Abhartack, the Vampir king, demanded that Keela be sent to him in Dökkbraek, the realm of the Vampir. Bishop is the High Álfar of Midgard, though, and Abhartack has no authority here. Therefore, Bishop left the decision up to Keela. She chose to remain with the Vasilis. Abhartack was not happy with her choice, or the fact that Bishop even gave her one. There is...*was* nothing Abhartack could do about it, though."

My heart sinks. "Does that mean Abhartack now has leverage? He can keep her? Will he hurt her?"

Rohan and Gelby appear in front of my cell. They both look worn. Gelby, in particular. Instead of his otherworldly perfection, there are dark circles under his eyes. "Abhartack will not be quick to harm one single hair on Keela's head. She is immune to compulsion and more powerful than any of his other Vampir. As one of his kind, he should be able to command her, but he cannot. That makes her both valuable to him and a threat. She knows this, and she will do whatever it takes to stay alive."

I wrap my fists around the bars, keeping my eyes on Gelby's as I remember Keela placing her hand into that of the king. How one second her eyes were on mine, and the next, she was gone. My palms ignite and the bars begin to melt. Gelby's face pinches. "Would you stop doing that?" He moves forward, lifting his hand, weakly placing it on my bars as if the motion itself is taxing.

I move my hands to the bars he's touching, wrapping my fists around the cold metal just above where his hands are splayed. "Let me out of here, and I'll stop."

Rohan's jaw flexes. "You can force our magic to work overtime, but you will never deplete it."

Blue vines scurry under Gelby's skin. "There is magic all around us, Sean Winkle. I draw it from the very air I breathe. You may intend to allow me no rest, no time to replenish, but I will *always* maintain enough magic to expend against the *Fae*."

"Save your magic," Haldir grumbles. "The boy is not Fae. Not fully, anyway."

Gelby releases the bars. "That doesn't mean he isn't our enemy."

I glare at him. *And* Rohan. "Up until you took me to the witches, I thought I was human. For all I know, I still am. You people are messing with me and that's the reason I have this fire in my hands!" I wiggle my fingers and then clamp my palms back around the bars. "Thanks, because now that I have this power, I'm not going to stop attacking anything or anyone until I have Keela back. Understand? If that makes me your enemy, then so be it."

"That'll be enough." A low-pitched voice crawls over my skin. I cringe as the sound scrapes against my eardrums, more grating than nails on a chalkboard. The shadow behind Rohan moves. No, not a shadow. A man. He's thin and hunched, his color so dark he must be made of the night itself. His almond eyes are solid white, his movements quick and spiderlike. He thrusts forward. Rohan and Gelby step aside. The man's lip curls up in disgust, his white eyes fixed on mine. "Bishop is not happy with the boy who challenges his family's magic. No, no, no," the shadow-man hisses. I recoil from the sound but the shadow pushes ever forward. "Then let us see his bones, I say." His big eyes blink and eight round balls float to the surface of the milky almonds. Eyes within eyes. Refracting. Studying. As if he really can see inside of my body, down past my soul and into my bones. His curled lip twists into a sneer. "Naughty, tainted blood you have, but your bones will tell us no lies."

My cell door clicks open. I back away but there's nowhere to go. I can't even hide in the darkness. Gelby snaps his fingers and my entire cell lights up, he and Rohan following the spiderlike man inside. "Do not fight them." Haldir's voice travels from the confines of his own cell into mine. "The dark one is Pete. He is Bishop's shadow, and what he does to you *will* hurt."

5

For once, I wish Gelby hadn't cast light in the darkness of my cell. I'd rather not be able to see the menacing kaleidoscope of eyes housed in the face of the now-named Pete. I press my back against the cool stone of the wall separating us from the Dreki. My new best friend. "Hal, remember how I got you out of that net? Well, I seem to have lost my fire so how about you get me out of being ripped apart by midnight man?"

Rohan glares at the wall, as if he can see through it and straight to Haldir. "Pete is Seiðmenn. A mare raised by a powerful witch. He is gifted as a seer and devoted to all Vasilis. Therefore, he stays close to Bishop, to warn us when an unhinged Dreki is about to start a war with the gods themselves."

Haldir snorts. "If not for Jofir, you'd be in a cell right along with me, brother."

Gelby pulls a jewel-studded dagger from thin air and hands it to Pete. "With or without Jofir, Rohan is never reckless, and whether or not you know your heritage, Sean Winkle, even the faintest trace of Fae in the midst of our house is a threat. One we will not allow to continue."

Pete moves forward and I hold up my hands. "Wait, if you're some kind of seer, shouldn't you know that I'm not Fae without cutting me open? Or at least be able to tell them that I'm not a threat? I only came to their house to begin with because I was drawn to Keela. I think I'm her soulmate. The way Jofir is Rohan's."

Gelby snaps his fingers and two vines of sizzling blue magic bind my wrists. "It is Keela's nature that drew you to her, and it is her inability to compel you that attached her to you. If the plan was to endear yourself to our family through Keela, you and whoever you're working with miscalculated." He nods to Pete. The man's spindly arms reach forward, grabbing my left elbow. I try to yank free but Rohan waves his hand and every part of my body freezes. Pete drives the blade of the dagger into my forearm, burying it hilt-deep. Driving down until the tip of the narrow blade pierces my bone. I shout, sucking the sound back in when Pete's grip tightens, his eyes flashing bright yellow, those round balls of starlight circling and scattering. His mouth opens and a waterfall of noxious mist rolls over his lips, down his chin, and all the way to where my warm blood is seeping out from under the base of the hilt.

I clamp my mouth shut, transfixed as my blood beads and runs along my skin, filling invisible grooves until my forearm looks close to how Beatrice looked after she'd held my hands in the witch circle. Only instead of looking like a sausage that's been cooked too long on a spit, my skin isn't broken. It's painted. In my blood. Like a mural etched into my skin with invisible ink, now revealed through whatever magic Pete possesses.

I look to Rohan. His eyes are narrow, his jaw set in stone. Gelby is the same. They're both watching my blood as it fills in every invisible groove on my skin. I stare at the angular designs. The sharp, intersecting lines. "What are these? What is he doing to me? And why can't I feel the pain of his blade anymore?"

Pete rips the dagger from my arm and I shout, feeling the slicing pain of the blade the same way I did when he first jammed it into my arm. Bile rises in my throat. Pete lifts the blade to his mouth, his pitch-black tongue darting out to taste my blood. "No," he hisses, eyes dimming as he sniffs the tip of the blade that was lodged in my bone. "No, no, no!" He hisses again, dropping the blade and scrambling backward. Away from me. "You are not right!" he screeches, his almond eyes fading once more to pure white. "You are wrong. You are not here. You are too many!"

I take a step forward but Rohan intervenes, a flick of his wrist summoning a gust of wind strong enough to slam me back against the cell wall. "Too many what?" I yell at the retreating Pete, my ire rising. "I'm too many what? Because I'm sure as hell *here*! And you're the one who's *wrong*, for stabbing me!"

"No!" Pete's voice screeches from his mouth like an army of ants yelling all at once. "No, no, no. He isn't him. Inside he is wrong. *Wrong*. Wrong, wrong, wrong!"

Sizzling blue vines matching those still wrapped around my wrists snap in the air around Rohan and Gelby, the two of them poised to strike. The thing inside my core shifts. I look down at my forearm. The blood is seeping back into my skin, disappearing just like the stab wound. I look back up at my captors, icy fear settling deep inside of me. Deeper than the swirling mass of fire that's now stoked and ready to be unleashed. This power might be my only chance at freedom, but the way it exploded from my chest before... The way fire erupted over my skin, hot and thick, unburning to my own flesh yet deadly to the Völva... I can't risk incinerating Keela's family. Or risk them incinerating me. I have to figure out another way to survive. Because I don't care what Gelby says, what she and I feel for one another is real. Magically, mystically, illogically real.

Keela

Two Vampir move across the lawn below my tower window, their bodies cast in a haze of crimson shadows from the blood-red aurora glowing and shimmering across the sky above us, stretching out farther than even my keen eyes can see. Across all of Dökkbraek—the dark realm of vampires. A place little is known about. Even the streaks of blood aglow in the sky are something of myth. Many speculate it's the blood of some ancient beast who sustains the Vampir. Others say it's merely light colliding with particles, while even more say it's magic born of the Vampir king himself. That when Abhartack brought his people to this land millennia ago, he claimed this dark, frost-covered land for his people by pouring his own blood into the sky, where it would forever feed them. Where it would forever be a reminder to outsiders that what lives in Dökkbraek is death.

I close my eyes. Listening to the cold, dry wind whistling through the deep canyon off to my right. I once heard a rumor from a Vampir whose throat pulsed under my fangs. He said that deep within the twilight forests of his homeland, perched high on the edge of a cliff, was a fortress carved from the mountain itself. Dark stone whittled away, leaving Draugrkeep in its place. It seems the Vampir spared no detail in what he told me about the dusky land where Abhartack and his horde have been hidden away. Protected. Safe. With even the wind whipping past the cliffside fortress promising to deter the most skilled climbers from attempting to breach the walls of Draugrkeep from below. Should they even be so lucky as to find the entrance to Dökkbraek to begin with. Books and scholars all say the same thing. Dökkbraek lies beyond the reach of the World's Tree, past the convergence of realms, existing in a place that draws power not from Yggdrasil, but from a twisted root of Hel. One that feasts on the souls of the dead.

I climb onto the wide ledge of the window, crouching just inside where the bay of translucent panes are latched together. I push them open and let the wind rushing from the chasm sing to me of its depth. Its width. This land, for good reason, is one few have ever sought to enter. One that fewer still have ever returned from.

I turn my attention to the darkness of the frosty forest beyond the castle. The unyielding darkness of this land cloaks the Vampir. With their speed, strength, and predatory ability to see in the night, they can move with stealth to strike their enemies. Fast and unheard. Unless their enemy is me. Lucky for them, I have no plans to escape. Yet. If Abhartack does not return soon, I'll give myself a tour of his land. Starting with the source of the icy whispers now scratching their way into the breeze offered up to me by the forest, where towering, frost-dusted trees shimmer like a sea of crimson jewels. I tune my hearing to their words, listening even to what the silence of the leaves is saying. From my perch, I now know the location of the Vampir guards making rounds across the lawn and through the forest. Their hearts do not beat as mine does, but I can still hear them. *See* them. Shadows in the darkness. I monitor their speed. Their patterns, even though they're desperately trying not to have any. And I smell their fear. It thickens the very air around me, potent and undiluted.

A smile threatens to lift the corner of my lips. I may not know how long I've lived, but I do know I'm older than most Vampir. They know it, too. Our strength increases with age and I do not need them to be standing in front of me to know they are terrified to find out just what I'm capable of. The guards will engage me if I launch myself from this gilded perch that teeters on what feels like the edge of the world, but those Vampir are as certain of their own deaths as the trees are of their desolate life.

I pull the panes of the window closed and set the latch back in place. One hundred enemies, I can survive. A Vampir swarm, I cannot. All it would take is five hundred of them to end me, and I can sense thousands of Vampir around me. Dökkbraek is a nest teeming with numbers far greater than anyone has ever speculated. Unfortunately for them, even with their startling numbers, the side they chose today was the wrong one. Whether I end up dead or not, the Vasilis will come. When they do, no Fae alliance will save the Vampir.

I slide off the windowsill. Vampir are known for their brutality, but they are equally known for their neutrality. Each of them must understand that a reckoning will come. So it's curious that Abhartack has suddenly made this move, and even more curious that he's chosen to allow me into the midst of his nest knowing that blood slaves are against the treaties. As Vasilis, I am sworn to uphold those agreements. Yet the cavernous room Abhartack ushered me into betrays the treaty; it's lavishly adorned with comforts the Vampir do not need for themselves.

Unless brutally extreme, we are not affected by temperature so the furs of grays and browns covering the floors and the ones layered across the bed with stacks of crimson pillows piled high against the stone-whittled headboard are not for the harbingers of death, but their prey. Those humans whose coppery scent wafts up from the forest floor, hanging on the guards as it does Abhartack himself, clinging like the perfume of freshly sprayed cologne.

The scent of human blood is laced into the fabric of the velvet loungers on my right and misted over the black finish of the intimately small table set for two where a cape of dark fur rests over the back of a marbled chair. That would be the seat given to the human, and it is Abhartack whose scent occupies the other. His scent permeates this entire room. My fangs ache, pains of hunger tracing along my abdomen. Outside of Abhartack, the smells of blood inside this room are stale compared to what's coming from the forest. From *inside* the castle beneath me. But it is no secret that I need to feed more often than most Vampir and after expending so much energy in battle, even the stale smell of blood is appetizing. As is the scent of the king.

I ball my hand into a fist and shut out the sudden wave of thoughts that will not serve me. Humans are most certainly not my only source of food, but they belong only in Midgard. Nowhere else. Especially not *here*. There is a reason Bishop weaves magic and supplies humans with bedtime stories that make them believe that instead of an Álfar army riding their flame-nosed steeds, what they really saw in the sky was innocent reindeer pulling a jolly old man's flying sleigh. That his accompanying *elves* were nothing more than tiny, harmless toymakers. Bishop delivers this magic each winter, erasing the memories of what the humans saw of our world and keeping their minds impressionable for whatever other stories they may need to be told, because humans are weak. They cannot fend for themselves or survive against the supernatural forces of the worlds. Therefore, it is the job of the Vasilis to keep them from being enslaved, tortured, or outright slaughtered. With Bishop's magic, the humans remain blissfully unaware.

Knuckles connect with the bronze door behind me, sending a sharp metallic ping reverberating through the room that's carved from the same dark stone as the castle itself, hewn and whittled until each intricate detail took shape. From the swirling designs framing the windows to those that protrude like shelves along the far wall. The patterns are reminiscent of runes, but these are curvier. Older. Just like everything else about this cliffside monstrosity. It feels ancient. And it is much nicer than where my family will imprison Abhartack. If I do not kill him before they come for me.

His knuckles rap against the door again. Softer this time. I open my senses. Searching. If he means to earn my favor with this show of politeness, he has severely underestimated me. I willingly came to Dökkbraek and brokered no objection when he led me into Draugrkeep, but only after he made the choice to attack my family. To side with the Fae against the Vasilis. That's all that matters. He's a fool if he does not already know that. But at least he's smart enough not to broadcast his emotions. Unlike most of his guards.

I face the door and wait for the king's patience to run thin. Bishop says he does not know why I have command over the darkness, why it bends to my will. I don't understand the reason I have this power either, but I do understand the resolve of a life that is forced to live, day after day, a shell of a thing. They are the same as me—those pieces of things that live within the darkness. Spirits. Energy. Power. *Force*. All yearning to be seen. *Felt.* Even here, in Abhartack's own nest, I feel them gathering around me. Waiting for the command of their conduit. Me. The creature happy to give them shape and form. So long as they do my bidding.

The door clicks open, the coppery scent of fresh blood filling the room as Abhartack enters on silent feet, his eyes spilling over the shadows swirling around me. He is tall. Slender. With dark hair like mine, and skin just as ghostly pale. But he is not afraid as he crosses the room, holding a goblet of still-warm blood. "I hope I'm not intruding?" He places the cup of blood on the table, pulling out a chair. "I am ashamed that I had to run off so abruptly earlier. I hope you won't hold our hasty meeting against me for too long. I do not wish to suffer the silent treatment where you are concerned. Nor do I wish to see you starved." He motions for me to sit. "I'm sure you can understand why I could not allow anyone other than myself to deliver your meal. But I have no doubt that you are starving. So please, sit. Drink."

I refuse to look at the blood. Instead, I keep my focus on his assessing eyes. "Blood slaves are against the treaties of Midgard. Humans *are* Midgard. You cannot enslave them. According to the power given to the Vasilis by Odin himself, for this and your other ill-thought-out offenses against the Vasilis, I find you guilty. Abhartack, king of the Vampir, you will meet with the rule and judgment of the Vasilis. And it will be painful."

Shadows bleed through his eyes, blotting out all color until there is nothing but darkness. Under his skin, shadows swim like eels, slithering over flesh and bone, writhing across his face and down his neck. He lifts a hand, watching as he twirls shadows between his fingers. My chest heaves. His black eyes dart back to mine, a smile curving up over his elongated fangs. "Surprise, mi Dauði. You are not the only master of shadows. And you will soon find that I have little patience for the rules and judgment of the Vasilis. If you continue to cling to Bishop, you will die."

6

Sean

A gust of wind surrounds me on all sides, a vortex holding me in place. Rohan's face is as solid as ever but it's the tense curve of his shoulders that has me backing down, relaxing my own shoulders in a fake show of defeat. One that has no impact on Rohan. His tight posture doesn't ease. He's still poised to attack, and his voice is edged with a demand that tells me he fully intends to follow through on what his body is promising if I don't give him an answer he deems acceptable. "Why didn't you tell us this before?"

Dread coats my tongue. I never told these torture-happy people about Aether planting his fist in my chest because right after it happened, Keela's Fae boyfriend was murdered. With the way his body was found, I'm fairly certain I didn't kill him. But I *did* want to. At least, the burning beast inside of me was calling for Aether's death. The one that showed up *before* Aether put his fist inside of me. Something I'm not really prepared to talk about. Especially with the Vasilis.

I meet their rigid faces, Gelby's own posture no less threatening than Rohan's. "I told you that I saw Aether portal onto your front lawn. I left out the part about him hitting me because at first, I wasn't sure it happened. I remembered the sensation of his fist going inside of me but then I woke up surrounded by all of you, and you told me I'd hit my head."

I give them time to admit this is their fault. At least in part. But of course, their convictions are immovable where I'm concerned. I shrug. "When all of the crazy stuff started happening, I was trying to sort out what was real and what wasn't. But then you threw me in this cell and started torturing me. Then you let me out and forced me to be tortured by witches. And now I'm back in your prison." I keep my voice steady, speaking normally instead of yelling at them like I want to. "All of the weird stuff started the day I first saw Aether. *And* all of you. Up until then, I was normal. Human. Weak compared to dragons and magical elves. Even Liam MacKenzie told you that was true. But here I am, in your dungeon being tortured *again,* with you asking me questions that I *still* don't know the answers to." My throat constricts. "I'm being accused of things that I don't know anything about, and none of you believe me when I tell you that I'm not a threat to your family. Even when you know that I *only* came here because of Keela. And when you know that I'm only still here because *you* won't let me leave." I lift my still magically bound wrists. "I kept the full details of my interaction with Aether to myself because you've been threatening me from the beginning."

Gelby's hand glows bright white. He shoves his sleeve up, revealing the scar running the length of his arm. The scar from where he merged with his wand. From what he told me, each Álfr is born with magic, the strength and manner determined according to their heritage. The wands and the enchantments they are imbued with only amplify the elf's inherent magical abilities. He walks toward me. "Do not move."

I drag in a breath. "I don't intend to. Because I'd rather let you bring Pete back in here and have him cut me open to see what's inside my chest than to keep being forced to live in this cell. I'm done fighting with you. All I want is Keela. And you know that's true."

Gelby moves forward. I was hoping my honesty would keep them from doing anything else to me but the Vasilis are determined to remain on my enemies list. So be it. They seem to have already forgotten that their torture tactics didn't work last time and that I'm stronger now because of it.

Gelby plants his glowing palm against my chest. "Do not fight me."

I mock his glare. "I wouldn't know how to even if I wanted to. Just remember that, so far, pumping your magic into me has only gotten you a torched lodge, a bunch of dead witches, and a whole lot of disappointment. *None* of which is my fault. Until I met all of you, I was *human*. Remember that."

Gelby's eyes narrow. My skin warms underneath his palm and I brace for the pain of his magic, but there's only a little pinch as his magic swirls out of his palm and burrows inside of me. Painless. I stare into his eyes, watching the shock of emotion run through him. Gelby Vasilis isn't used to anyone being able to stand against the destruction of his magic. He isn't used to anyone possessing a power that rivals his own. Even without knowing anything about this new world I'm living in, I can see the truth of how powerful I am reflected in the widening gape of Gelby's shock. I only wish he would believe that I'm as shocked by all of this as he is. I can't even figure out how to tap into this power so I can get it to work for me. To protect me and buy me time. It feels sentient. Alive. But only sometimes, and never with any real intent to do what I tell it to do.

Rohan steps up to his brother's shoulder. "Well?"

Gelby's jaw ticks. "Same as before. I can't detect his magical signature."

"I vote for cutting him open," Haldir rumbles from where he's leaning against the frame of my open cell door, Gelby's magic powerful enough to finally let his *brother* out of prison. "I don't think he's a threat to us, but I'd still like to kill him."

Gelby pulls his hand away from me. "The boy *is* the one who made that suggestion."

Magic sparks in the air around Rohan. "Dissecting him is definitely looking more and more like our best option." He moves forward, magic sizzling and popping. "Tell us again exactly what happened when you encountered Aether. Leave no detail out or I'll flay you myself. Nose to groin."

I cast my gaze to Haldir's unreadable face. Despite our threats, I thought we were building...a nonlethal coexistence. "What I've already told you is all there is to tell. Believe me or don't. I'm not going to keep repeating myself."

Gelby and Rohan share a look. I huff out a sarcastic laugh. "Let me guess, you don't? Surprising, seeing how fair and understanding you've been up until now."

"Arsenious recruited the Vampir!" Rohan shouts. "We thought he was standing against us because his son was taken, and possibly *murdered*, in our territory. But with what you're just telling us *now*, there may be more to the attack."

Gelby tugs his sleeve back down. "Arsenious came for Keela, that much is clear. How you connect to the Fae is not." He turns away, the man of pure midnight practically oozing out of the wall across from my cell. "Pete, have you ever heard of the Fae being powerful enough to...make a Sean Winkle out of a mere human?"

Pete's white eyes bore into me. "Fae cannot make him as he is. You must take him to the Norns."

Haldir springs up straight and the tension in Rohan's shoulders doubles. I blink, and the midnight-man is gone. "Norns? What are Norns?"

Rohan turns on his heel and bumps into Haldir on his way out of my cell. The Dreki fixes on the wall behind me with a look that says his mind has traveled somewhere else. I hold my magically bound wrists out to Gelby. "Doesn't seem like anyone really wants to go see these Norns, so how about you let me go and once I find Keela, I'll come back and we'll sort everything out?"

A spark of orange breaks from his fingertips and wraps around my throat. "Ignorant pawn or agent of the Fae, the Norns will reveal all. And then the *Vasilis* will administer your fate." He flicks a hand at the wall Haldir is still staring at. Then, just like before, a blast of magical energy sends me falling through a portal.

***

Gelby

I finish stowing my portion of Sihoma's loaves of sabem bread into my pack. She compiled smoked meats and mixes of dried fruits and nuts for Haldir and Sean Winkle, but for the Álfar, the specially imbued bread is what will best sustain us on the journey ahead. It is what fed us during the devastating years of the long war. But back then, it wasn't Sihoma who made loaves for Rohan and me. It was our mother. The warm and powerful Álfr who gave birth to us. Some days, if I close my eyes tightly enough, I can see her face. Her smile. Hear her laugh while chastising her rowdy sons for whatever childhood foolishness we got ourselves into. Foolishness that ended when the war started. When there was no longer time for fun and games. A sudden turn in the tide of our lives and one that seems to be rising again.

I buckle my pack closed. Rohan enters the kitchen looking just as worn as I do. For many reasons, this day has been worse than most, and we're each fighting our own internal battles. For me, no matter how hard I try not to, all I can see is blood pouring from my mother's chest. Spitting from her mouth. Her delicate wand of ash wood tumbling from her hand. It took me too long to realize what happened to her. Too long to understand what the bone-chilling howl echoing through the mist-shrouded mountains had been. It wasn't until her feet lifted off the ground that I noticed the spiraled horn she was impaled upon. Noticed the dark fur covering the hulking body of the Skarthorn rising behind her. Most of them are hard to miss because of their size, the largest ones standing at twelve feet tall, but the one that killed my mother was young. It was barely taller than me. Still, as it rose from all fours to stand on its two hind legs, it took my mother's dying body with it.

I don't exactly remember what happened after that. Somehow, the creature was dead and my mother was bleeding out in my arms. No one could save her. Bishop tried. For longer than even Rohan and I thought was sensible. But the poison that coats the horns of the Skarthorn is stronger than the darkest of magics. And it spreads quickly. My mother's own healing magic couldn't slow down her fate and it was impossible for any of the rest of us to do anything. Despite the armor our mother wore, the Skarthorn pierced her heart, pumping its poison throughout her whole body. She never had a chance and the rest of us barely escaped with our lives that day. The Skarthorns are cunning. Intelligent. Capable of setting traps to ambush their prey. In the long war, *Álfar* were their prey. Compliments of the Unseelie Fae who unleashed them upon us. The same Fae it appears Sean Winkle is involved with.

I send my pack sliding across the counter with a bolt of magic and then flick my fingers to whip the next pack forward. Rohan leans on the counter. "Conserve your magic, brother. Bishop cannot be swayed to send reinforcements with us or to allow us to postpone. He's ordered that we leave at daybreak."

I stuff Haldir's pack full of supplies and consider not making one for Sean Winkle. My magic is nowhere close to depleted but I am strained for the first time in centuries. Rejuvenation has been lacking ever since the attack at the Völva lodge. At first, when the flames burst from Sean's body, I thought the witches had betrayed us. Then I realized it was Sean who was killing *them*. Then the Vampir attacked, and it is not lost on us that the presence of Arsenious among them is no coincidence. The Unseelie have been our enemies since before the war. "If Bishop will not bend, does that mean he's keeping the rest of our army here because he fears another attack from the Fae? Or because he intends to seek retribution without us?"

Rohan rolls his neck, working out the tension that's been building since Jofir arrived. His *mate*, who is now in the middle of what we both feel is the start of another war, even though neither of us has outright said those words. "Our father, the mighty Bishop, believes our talents are best spent guiding the hu—Sean, through the land of the Norns. *Since we already have a rapport with the boy.*" Rohan groans. "I told him our *rapport* isn't a good one, but Bishop insists. As does Jofir. She refuses to stay behind. I tried to tell her that the journey will not be a pleasant one, that the dangers the Norns will test us with are designed to exploit and *kill*. Still, she will not be deterred."

I flick my fingers, drawing another pack across the table to me. This one for Jofir. Rohan is right that the Norns will not let us pass easily through their lands. No one knows that more than Haldir. We once went with him to seek out the Norns so he could get answers about his parents. About Keela. We didn't get any. The Norns starved us. Made us walk up the sides of endless mountains. Sent all manner of beasts against us. And in the end, they separated Haldir from us.

He has never talked about what happened to him while he was gone. All we know is that the well was suddenly before us and when we approached, Haldir was there but the Norns were not. We waited but they would not come. An absence that meant they had found Haldir unworthy and would not answer a single one of his questions. In his rage, Haldir shifted and blew fire down into the crystal waters of Urðarbrunnr. The next thing we knew, we were each back in our own beds. It took us more than a month to be convinced that we were actually back in Midgard and not stuck in the land of Norns, living some kind of simulated experience. "If Bishop would allow it, you know I would take your place so you could remain here with Jofir. Complete the mating ceremonies."

Rohan's weary eyes meet mine. "Bishop won't allow it. And he will not allow us to take any others with us because now that the Vampir king has made his move, Bishop intends to seize control of the Ulfr, the

Völva... The Vampir could have only entered the compound if they had help. Bishop is first going to find who helped them, and then he intends to annihilate the Vampir."

My magic thrums along my skin. "Then the war has begun."

Rohan lifts off the counter. "It has. And Bishop believes Sean is a powerful tool. It is up to us to find out if he is meant to fight with us or against us. If the Norns give any indication that he is against us..."

My magic flares. "We kill him."

7

Keela

Exhilaration. Unease. They crackle and splinter, feathering over my bones and breaking along my spine. Abhartack is like me. He has command over the shadows. Only, his control of the darkness is different. He doesn't draw from what's all around us the way I do. I know this because instead of fighting me for control, the king is pulling from that which is already within him, bringing the darkness to the surface of his skin and unleashing it through his hands. My pulse quickens. The king smiles. I form a dagger in my palm. Abhartack's broad smile deepens, his fingers curling as a blade of his own making takes shape in his hand. One that is familiar to both of us. It was my preferred blade on the killing field at the Vólva compound where his horde attacked.

He closes his fist, the form of the weapon disappearing, the darkness seeping back underneath his blanket of snow-white skin. "Now you know another fact about me." His voice is as smooth as his movements, his long-fingered hands removing his suit jacket while his attention remains fixed on me. He drapes the jacket over the back of a chair, and I don't stop my eyes from snapping to the display of muscle pressing against the crisp fabric of the long-sleeved shirt the crimson king is wearing. Abhartack is a delicacy. And I am hungry.

I send my shadows scurrying back from whence they came. It's bad enough that the display of the king's rare power excited me. Paired with his lean, muscled physique, my hunger has me willing to let my body be as pliable to him as his impressive shadows. A shuddering thought. I press my eyelids together in a forceful blink. Instead of being superior to this king the way I have always been to every other Vampir, Abhartack is my equal. That makes him far more dangerous than even Bishop knows. "Do any of your other Vampir control shadows?"

Abhartack chuckles, eyes returning back to their normal, stone-matching obsidian as he rakes them over me. "Our gift is shared only between the two of us, as I hope many other things will be." He begins to unbutton his shirt, the jewel at the base of his throat glowing as his long, nimble fingers move over his unblemished skin. My mouth waters. The king walks toward me. "If you must take your sustenance from a vein, then you will take it from mine. I do not yet trust you with the *free* people of Dökkbraek."

I resist the urge to rip the jewel from his throat. To sink my teeth into the soft, pale skin at the base of his neck. To know what he feels like beneath me. What his dark power *tastes* like. I shut off my senses. This cannot be...Vampir cannot affect their own kind. Unless they are me.

I dart to the table and lift the rapidly cooling goblet of blood, pouring it down my throat. "If your intent was to starve me into submission, you've chosen the wrong tactic. I've gone much longer without food."

He walks back to the table with an affirming grunt. "You have certainly gone through much worse than what I have unintentionally inflicted upon you today." I narrow my eyes on him. The corner of his mouth ticks up. "My method was crude, and I have no doubt that you would rather rip out my throat than feed from it, but my intentions are pure and us getting acquainted with one another is long overdue." He pulls out the chair the fur is draped over. "Will you consent to us having a civil conversation?"

I don't allow myself to look at the veins in his neck. One cup of blood is not enough. It isn't *nearly* enough. I pace away from Abhartack, conjuring the memory of being held on Sean's lap. His hands. His mouth. My chest warms, calming the rising lust for the king and his blood. It is Sean's neck I want to feed from. *His* body I want to wrap mine around. All I want from Abhartack is answers. He must know where the power we share came from.

I face the king. "We have no need for civility. Your hasty retreat earlier was so you could once again conspire with those who hold your allegiance." I let the corner of my mouth tick up, matching his rapidly fading smirk. "Don't bother denying it. I'm well acquainted with the stench that is Arsenious. The same stench that now mingles with every other odor clinging to the air around you. Take me to your faithful partner and I will be *civil* enough when his blood spills across my lips and down my throat. The Fae king is sure to be as delicious as his son ever was, only much more satisfying." I pace toward Abhartack. "Because when I am finished with your partner, I will be holding Arsenious's decapitated head in my fist."

Abhartack touches the red gem at the base of his throat, as if he knows of my thoughts from only moments ago and might remove the necklace for me himself. "The stories told about you do not do you justice, Keela *Vasilis*. I only hope you take me up on the offer to be your buffet because whether or not I give you someone else to feast upon, I am certain that I *alone* am capable of quenching your thirst." His eyes roam over my features. "Throughout these many centuries, my life has had little need of anything other than what can be found in Dökkbraek. But now that you are here, I find that I am finally content. Do you know why? Can you *feel* why?"

I keep my face blank, hiding my emotions from both body and essence. I will not let him know that he has an effect on me. Whether my rush of emotion is because his allure is also like mine or his appeal is only a flaw of my own hunger, Vampir do not respect weakness. This king needs to know that he will find none in me. "If these words are your attempt at flattery, I will spare you the chore of launching yet another attempt. Your actions this day have announced your allegiance and sealed your fate. After I take the life of Arsenious, I will settle the issue of your allegiance to the Fae king. Unless you'd prefer I settle your issues now? Because that can be arranged."

Abhartack disappears in a cloud of shadow, reappearing directly in front of me, his coppery breath tickling over my face. "Your voice is as lovely as you are, but your words are a shame to hear. We will have to work on remedying that." His head dips low and it takes all the willpower I have to force my body to stay firmly in place. His lips curve into a sinful smile, as if he knows how badly my traitorous body wants to lean forward to meet his. I extend my fangs and hiss in warning. The king's smile only broadens. He lifts a tentative hand into the small gap of air between us. "May I?"

I stiffen, my fight draining away as I study his hopeful eyes. He wants to feel my chest. My heartbeat. This isn't the first time I've had this request but unlike every other time, something tells me I will not regret giving this moment to Abhartack. An uncomfortable part of me *wants* him to touch me. Other than Sean Winkle, I've never wanted any particular person to touch me. I've wanted to *be* touched, and I've found plenty of willing participants, but they have all served to satisfy *my* needs. This feeling of needing the touch of one specific person is new. The feeling of wanting to satisfy *their* needs disturbingly more so.

I give the slightest of nods. The thought that Abhartack could be strong enough to force his will upon me runs through my mind, but the instant his hand moves forward, palm resting reverently against my breastbone, I do not regret the decision to let him touch me. Compelled to do so or not.

His lips part, eyes going distant. Unfocused. The heel of his hand moving with the steady rise and fall of my breast as he both listens and feels the way I am different from him. From all Vampir. "Remarkable." The word whispers past his lips.

Seconds pass, feeling like hours as the solid presence of his hand remains steady against me. I do not pull away. Or dare to make a sound. I like the feel of him against me. Compulsion or not.

His head shakes, as if he's forcing himself out of a daydream. His hand falls away, his dark hair sliding across his forehead as he steps backward, eyes darting to the window before coming back to rest upon mine. The ruby at the base of his throat bobs. "I have heard many heartbeats...can hear the steady drum of yours from so far away...yet I have never felt anything quite like it before." His gaze drops to my chest. "A beating heart inside of a supposedly dead thing."

I close the distance he's put between us. "I feel no more dead than you feel alive."

Another one of his alarming smiles breaks across his handsome face. "Indeed. Which is precisely why you are here. I *did* leave you earlier in order to finish conducting business with Arsenious, but you will soon learn that little is as it seems." He paces away from me again, glancing back at me over his shoulder. "Like you, Dökkbraek is a paradox. A place where death and life intertwine. The night within this realm holds secrets darker than any abyss. Come. Sit with me. Let me tell you what you have been missing out on, Keela *Vasilis*."

He motions to the chair he pulled out earlier but I remain where I am. I may want to do more with him than have a conversation, but I will not roll over and beg him to pet my belly. "No need to sneer the Vasilis name, *King* Abhartack. Your simple acknowledgment of where my allegiance lies is enough."

He inclines his head, rolling up the sleeves of his partially unbuttoned shirt to reveal the smooth skin of his forearms. "I know exactly who you have pledged yourself to. What *you* need to know is that I have no fight with you, Keela, and no allegiance to the Fae. I will explain my involvement in today's events and you will see that for yourself." He crosses the room and sits on the edge of the bed. "First, you must eat. Take all that you want from me, and in any manner you want it." Shadows darken his eyes. "After the way I ambushed you earlier, it's only fair that I offer myself to you. Completely."

An ache forms in the back of my throat. It's all I can do to keep myself rooted to the floor beneath my feet. Abhartack's blood would be...powerful. Filling. *Electrifying*. I yearn to taste it. Yearn to enjoy every pale inch of him. He smiles, as if he knows exactly what I'm thinking. "It is evident that you are starving, and these are my private quarters, Keela. We will not be disturbed. Inside this room, I am at your full disposal."

His words strike an unnerving cord. "This is your *room*? Killing room? Blood slave room? Keep-the-Vasilis-isolated-in-a-tower-cell-so-they-don't-know-where-you've-hidden-Arsenious-in-the-castle room?"

He snaps his fingers and a spark of magic flickers, revealing two doors that were not there before. "Personal bed chambers *room*." He snarls. "I have been fond of this tower since the day I first arrived at Draugrkeep. However, one does not live as long as I have without learning to seal your room to hiding places. The closet and bathing facilities are yours to use, but they are spelled to seal whenever I am not present inside of my own personal and very private room."

I study him the same way he is studying me, each of us attempting to read the other. To anticipate movement. "What happens if I should be inside one of those sealed rooms when you leave?"

He leans back on the bed, propping himself on his elbows. "If you allow me to stay in here with you, we won't ever have to find out."

I turn away from him and walk slowly along a wide, arcing path. "Then you should explain what happens to these rooms when you are dead."

He chuckles. "I admit, I will miss entering my own suite whenever I please, but while you are here, this room is yours. It is safe, and you will face no threats from anyone. Fae, Vampir, or any others." He sits up and fully removes his shirt. "I believe that I can find a way to give you access to all that you require in my absence."

I stop pacing. "I only require one thing."

He waves me off. "Yes, I know your terms, Keela. And I am inclined to give you the Fae king's head. Which surprises you because you do not know me as well as you think you do, and I most certainly do not know enough about *you*." He extends his hand. "We've barely had time to even be properly introduced. I would like to change all of that. There is so much to learn about each other. So much that I want to tell you. I knew that to be true from the very first moment I set eyes on you." The corners of his mouth turn down. "A day that was all too long ago. But we are here now. Together."

I walk across the room to the cavernous closet, pulling out a long black gown with a train of flowing red silk. "I believe the human who last wore this would be disappointed to hear you speak as if I will be remaining here with you."

He tsks. "You have no need to be jealous of my former guests."

I toss the dress onto the floor. "What I am, is Vasilis. You may have walled yourself away from Midgard, but being here in this realm is not a loophole. Blood slaves are forbidden. No matter how well you pamper them."

He gets up from the bed and snatches the dress off the floor. "As you well know, the Vampir rarely engage in the politics of the realms. Which is why, here in Dökkbraek, the Vampir live in harmony with *all* who choose to reside in harmony with *us*."

I give a dismissive snort. "Blood slaves bound to you by compulsion does not make the humans complicit in your harmony."

He moves with predatory stealth, arms extending on either side of my hips, hands folding the dress against my back as he pulls me into him. "Why would I need to use compulsion on humans? I certainly can, but though your personal allure is stronger than most, all Vampir possess that which draws the humans to us. Especially me. Your *king*. Who hired someone with your measurements, who just happened to be a human, to try on clothing so this closet could be stocked for you."

I lift my chin, bringing my mouth within a breath of his. "Is that how you get the humans here? By enticing them not only with your allure, but with shopping sprees? You raid Midgard and sweep them off their feet. Then suddenly, they find themselves trapped here in this dark and cold world. With you. And your nest of Vampir that is *thousands* strong."

The gem at his throat glows, as if the blood-red sky lives within the stone. He straightens to his full height. "I can see that I have failed to properly assess your temperament but despite that failing, I can assure you that I have broken no treaties. The Vampir of Dökkbraek do not keep slaves. Human or otherwise. Everyone in my realm is here by choice, save for you."

"Choice?" I scoff. "Mortals cannot traverse the tapestry of realms. Select few have traveled outside of Midgard and none without the help of those immortals skilled enough to make the journey. And which of those immortals have the ability to navigate their way to your beloved, paradoxical Dökkbraek?"

A wave of anger rolls off him, slamming against me. "Dökkbraek is indeed my beloved. As are all who live within this unique land, including the humans who are as adaptable and determined in this realm as those humans who reside in Midgard. Only, in Dökkbraek, they do not go cold and they do not hunger. The needs of the humans are as important to me as those of the Vampir."

I laugh, a haunting sound even to my own ears, because I feel no humor from Abhartack. No lies. Only truth. "Do not mistake the Vasilis for fools. We may have failed to secure the Völva territory before entering it, but your successful ambush will only ensure no others will catch our guards down again. You have gained no leverage today. No honor. My ear will not be bent to your twisted words. All you have earned yourself this day is regret and sorrow."

He growls, low and guttural. "I have gained a great many things this day, and your people, the *Vampir*, have sacrificed much, so do not stand before me and mock the lives that were given to free you from the shackles of Bishop and *his* kind."

I open my mouth to defend my family but Abhartack grips my chin, his thumb thrusting through my teeth and pressing down on my tongue. "Spare me the outrage of your ill-placed loyalty. My honor is not in question. So it is *you* who should not mistake *me* for a fool. I will not demand that you hold your tongue in the presence of your king, but I do expect civility. I have not harmed you, nor do I intend to." He drags his thumb out of my mouth. Down my lip and over my chin. "I plan a great many things, but all of them you will like."

My heart pounds. I press my palms against his chest. "My civility was not killing you on the battlefield." I call on my shadows for strength, gathering them from the corners of the room so that for once, instead of me giving form to them, they can give shape and life to that which my mind wants but my body does not. Abhartack away from me.

The king does not stop me. Once again does not fight me for control as the shadows blur around me, taking what they need from me so that they can be felt. Alive once more. They move with me, creating illusions as I disappear within them. He follows me, step for step. Shadow for shadow. Two swirling masses of night as he calls upon his own shadows. His chest brushes against mine and I mean to shove him away but the contact ignites a hunger that I cannot control. I launch myself into the arms of the ancient Vampir. Claiming and devouring. Screaming out when the king bites back.

63

8

I stare at Abhartack's bedroom door, fingers absently pressed against my lips. Feeding has never before felt the way it did with the king. His blood is heavy with power but drinking from him only made my hunger more ravenous. Wild. *Vicious.* I drank deeply and so did he, the sensation of his body familiar. Satisfying. *Rough.* Our motions were laced with a deep-rooted anger that made us both despise and enjoy, our ecstasy balanced on the precipice, torn between pleasure and death. I could have killed him. *Should* have. But he too could have killed me. *Should* have.

I study the spattering of blood crusted on the crumpled furs covering the bed. Abhartack and I spared each other for different reasons. I need more information about his involvement with the Unseelie Fae. He needs me for a bargaining chip. With Bishop and the Fae. Our heated blood exchange was only a perk of our unspoken agreement. One that, up until recently, I might have had enough resolve to abstain from. But Sean Winkle's impact on my senses has broken what I once thought was ironclad. I can no longer trust myself to stave off the lust that comes with my need to feed. And though I wish it were not so, I have no choice but to feed often.

In the past, I have fed from Vampir, but this is the first time I've considered how the warmth of our spilled blood stands in stark contrast to our cold eternity. Maybe because I am in Dökkbraek, where there is nothing but endless cold giving shelter to death turned life. Like Abhartack, who is made of stealth, yet exposed by the shadows whispering to me of his approach. Each time his silent feet move upon the tower steps, the shadows scatter, telling me of his speed. His location. But he is not the only one they speak of. In the corner of the room beyond the bed, they gather, coalescing into a form that is burned into my very being. I close my eyes. I do not need them to show me Sean Winkle to remember that it was he who shook me to the very core of my being. Not the king.

"Mmm," Abhartack purrs as he enters the room. "Is that jump in your heartrate because of me? If so, I can tell you that if my own heart still beat, it would leap out of my chest for you."

I blink my eyes open, the shadows melting away and taking Sean with them. Since my time on the Isle of Misery, when I had no other choice but to ration my meals, I have not been truly hungry. Now, it's as if I cannot feed enough. Even with the heady sensation of Abhartack's blood still coating my throat, I am once again growing ravenous. "It seems I have much to learn about the arts of compulsion and allure."

Abhartack's tongue clicks. "What we feel for one another is not because of our inherent trickery. You know that's true, Keela. My natural allure is not a weapon against you, and I have spent far too many years looking forward to the day when our blood would become one to dilute the experience we just shared with *compulsion*."

I watch him cross the room. His figure is striking in a suit as black as the midnight sky. The threads along the cuffs glisten like frost while his messy dark hair brushes against his collar, giving only small glimpses of the pearlescent embroidery that glistens there. At his throat, the red gem is still on display, and underneath his arm is a wide, red satin-trimmed box. He places it on the table, looking up at me with a predatory grin. For a brief second, I think about running to him. Jumping into his arms and covering his mouth with my own, just to see if the barely contained savagery of our last romp could be replicated. "I cannot stay here."

Disappointment hollows his eyes. "The way I brought you to Draugrkeep was unsavory but there was no other way." He snaps his fingers, once more revealing the doors that disappeared into smooth walls when he left me earlier. "In my years of waiting, I have prepared for you, mi Dauði. You may not like the clothing I have chosen for you, but it is a wardrobe fit for a queen, not a prisoner."

I eye the red train of the dress we left forgotten on the floor. It is the kind of dress a royal might wear. A queen. But I am neither. I am death. "Now that we have dined on each other, you believe I should abandon my family for you?" I raise a brow at him. "Are you sure *my* allure isn't affecting *you*?"

He runs a finger along the box on the table, the simple caress a reminder of how gently we didn't bother to touch each other earlier. How gently he might stroke me later, if I answer the desire building in his eyes. "Keela," he purrs my name in a way that makes my insides quake. "I am sure that I have already given you more information than anyone else has ever come close to giving you. And I am sure that you like what you are getting from me, and in every way that I am giving it to you."

He walks toward the bed. "You want more. Because no one else around you comes close to being able to give you what *I* do. What *I* can." He stops beside the bed. "I am confident in what I know. In the things you *should* know. Which is why I will continue to educate you. Because you are no one's prisoner, mi Dauði, and it is time you start making choices for yourself. No one else." He runs his finger along my jaw. "It isn't your allure making me covet you, but I *do* covet you. In a way that has me exposing my people." That finger continues its path, trailing down my throat. "Something that I have not done lightly. You must know that."

I slide away from him, exiting the bed on the far side, glancing at the corner where Sean's shadowy form had been only minutes ago. "Why? What is your end game where I am concerned?"

The king's hand falls to his side. "Information is my end game. For you. Not me. There is a bounty on your head. A significant one."

I shrug. "There is a bounty on the heads of all Vasilis."

His sigh is deep. Vexed. "Yes, but I do not care about *all* Vasilis. So when Arsenious approached me about obtaining you for him, I made a choice. *For you.*" Abhartack shoves his hands into the pockets of his tailored suit pants. "It is for you alone that I chose to enter a battle knowing full well that it would lead to the casualties of many Vampir."

I train my eyes to the lines and edges of his face, looking for the deception that must be there, but I can sense no dishonesty. "Arsenious has wanted to kill me since the moment Bishop brought me into the Vasilis family."

Abhartack's tongue darts across his bottom lip. "I am aware. But despite this not being the first time news of a bounty on your head has reached my ears, it was the first time I truly feared for your safety. The

Fae meant to have you, and Arsenious was not going to stop until he found the alliance he needed. Therefore, I became his alliance. Without hesitation. All in order to secure your safety. A choice I would not hesitate to make again."

I fight the urge to go to him. To touch him. To hold him in a way that feels so opposite of who I am. "The Fae king is weak, so the only safety you should have been concerned for was your own."

Abhartack removes his hands from his pockets. "Perhaps. But in addition to saving you, which you are welcome for, by the way, I was far too curious as to why Arsenious was so adamant this time. Something it doesn't appear that even your beloved Bishop knows. I asked him as much when I sent word to let him know that he is also welcome that I've managed to do what he could not. What he *promised* me he would do."

Confusion grinds through me. "Bishop made you a promise? About me? When?"

Abhartack returns to the table and removes the ribbon from the box. "I disclose this information to you because Arsenious is not the only weak male in your life." The king lifts the lid from the box and sets it aside. "You already know that I came for you, Keela. And that I left Midgard without you only because I wanted to respect your decision to stay with the Vasilis." His voice turns rough. Hard. "A decision that was yours to make, even though it was the wrong one. So I left, but only after I made demands of Bishop. Only after we talked through what we both wanted for you and reached an agreement."

My throat tightens. "What is it that you both wanted?"

Abhartack lifts a diamond-studded necklace from the box. One that resembles his. Only this one has a broad, thick chain and the large ruby embedded in the center of the choker is encircled by rows of diamonds. "Your safety. Your happiness. And, for me, a little more than that."

I watch the dim glow of light refracting off the gemstones. "You should have considered what you want from me before you conspired with my enemy."

The king closes in on me. "Trust me, I did. Many, *many* times."

My body warms but my voice hardens with each spoken word. "You knew you couldn't take me unless by ambush, and on witch ground, no less, being sure any Vasilis present would have to focus on keeping the Völva safe."

Abhartack comes closer, circling me, brushing his arm against mine as he does. "That part was my idea. Rather clever, don't you think? The instant I heard you were inside the Völva coven house I organized our numbers. Five more minutes and I fear we would have missed our opportunity to bring you here. To the safety of Draugrkeep."

I clench my jaw. "How did you get through the wards? The Fae should not have been able to portal onto Völva land, and I highly doubt your arrogance was helpful."

He brushes my hair aside, reaching over my shoulders and draping the necklace around my throat. "I possess a great many talents, and in time, I will show them all to you."

A chill-inducing tone purrs from my throat, the kind of sound that rakes down spines and raises the hair on the necks of my enemies. "Bold words to utter in the wake of your treachery. Give me Arsenious, and maybe I'll allow you to live long enough to exhaust yourself in this foolish effort to persuade me that you possess a talent worth keeping you alive for."

He clasps the necklace in place, fingers brushing against the nape of my neck. My heart skips in an odd way. Not the pounding thud as it quickens at the first scent of Sean Winkle's presence, but in a way that excites me all the same. Abhartack's head dips to my ear. "The best part will be that moment in which Arsenious finally realizes what he's done in aligning himself with me. In that moment, when I ensure the bounty is removed from your head, the Fae king and your deceptive Bishop will finally understand that I alone can do what they cannot."

Despite myself, I lean into Abhartack's caress. "If you sided with the Fae against the Vasilis because you alone can seduce me, you should know that Arsenious is the only reason I'm still here. Give him to me, or I will rip out your throat and the throats of your people. One by one. Until I get what I want or all of you are dead. Whichever comes first."

The king's nose trails along the rim of my ear. "Since the glorious day when Bishop pulled you from the Isle of Misery, I felt your presence. From that day until this one, I have wanted nothing more than to honor you." He shoves me away. "But you are certainly a disappointment. The ignorance you have shown by failing to see with anything other than the coldness of your Vasilis judgment is precisely why I had no choice but to rip you from their clutches."

An odd sensation crawls over me. Reminiscent of a feeling that came over me the first time I set eyes on Bishop. A prodding that urged me to follow the high elf of Midgard as he led me off the Isle of Misery. I have no memory of who exiled me to that island or how long I lived there among the forgotten. All I know is that the others who resided on the island, the few whose lives I managed to spare, called me Dauði. *Death*. The same as Abhartack does now. And I do not wish to follow this king anywhere.

I draw the shadows to me. Abhartack smiles, shadows swirling in his eyes and dancing beneath his skin. "This is why we need true civility between us, Keela. I have shown you some of my power, but I have seen *all* of yours. Because I have watched you for a *very* long time."

His words ring foreign against my ears. Truthfully and painfully foreign. Every word a sledgehammer crashing against a rusted bell of truth housed inside the hollow of my retched heart. I can sense no lie on his breath, feel no deception in the air. But he is a king. A powerful, ancient king. Old enough to find ways to disarm a heart that has only ever beaten with loneliness. "I do not need your honor, and there are many who desire me. I came here only for Arsenious. Not to be draped in jewels or to hear you waste your breath on flattery. And I will not allow you to continue to insult my family."

The king's perfectly sculpted fingers flutter, causing a wave of butterflies to erupt inside of me, their dark wings fluttering underneath my skin until I want to claw it open and remove them. Abhartack's smile is sinister. "I have not forgotten the reason you last placed your hand into mine. So let me be clear. I want you, Keela. In every possible way. My desire for you is at the very core of what happened today. I have tried to draw you to me but despite my most grueling efforts, you have never responded to my influence. But now you are here, and I will *never* be too exhausted to stop persuading you to take your rightful place in Dökkbraek." Abhartack's voice lowers. Deepens. "I did not relish the idea of our meeting happening this way. Despite how badly I want you as part of Dökkbraek, I will never demand that you choose me over the Vasilis. All I can do is speak truth to you. Bishop has taught you nothing. *Will* teach you nothing. You are his tool. His weapon. His *pawn*. He may love you enough to fight for and with you, but he does not tell you the truth. He does not reveal those things that are rightfully yours to know. But *I* will. I will give you the answers you seek and the keys to unlock the truth of what you have never even thought to ask."

I laugh, a sound as hollow as I feel inside. Abhartack might be speaking truth about his desire for me, but it seems more and more as if it is only because he is under my unintentional influence. He could also be pretending, thinking I expect to be fawned over and therefore is adapting his behavior to mimic what he has seen while watching me for the many years he claims to have studied me. To make me believe I have an upper hand that I do not possess. One that I do not need. Under normal circumstances. But these circumstances are anything but normal. This king has rendered me incapable of rational thought. I place my hand atop the ruby now gracing my neck. "You will tell me everything? If I pledge allegiance to you? Fight for and with you? You will give me these mysterious answers if I allow myself to be *your* pawn instead of Bishop's?"

Abhartack's eyes roam over my face. "There need not be allegiances pledged. I *want* to tell you all that I know. To show you the truth of our world." He disappears in a cloud of shadow and reappears in front of me, showing me he's capable of the same things that I am. His knuckles brush against my cheek, hand idly sliding down to where my own hand still rests at my throat. "Trust me," the king begs. "Please? I swear you shall have all that you desire." His lips drop to my bare shoulder. "On my life, I swear that you will have even the darkest desires of your remarkable beating heart." He lifts his mouth to my neck. "Still clinging to the Vasilis or not. Believing what is right in front of your eyes or not."

My heart thunders. He drops his hand to cover it, hard lines of his face softening as he straightens himself before me, shadows disappearing.

"Please, mi Dauði, let us not fight. There is more at stake here than either of our lives alone. Which is why we must go. All of Draugrkeep awaits our arrival. So I am begging you to set aside your biased judgments and thoughts of death long enough to enjoy tonight's festivities. Our people wish to meet you. The great Vampir warrior whose very name, Keela, means *beautiful* in the old tongue."

9

I walk steadily beside Abhartack, the two of us maintaining a casual pace through the halls of Draugrkeep. My eyes are on the ancient runes carved above every alcove, into the walls, and along the floors, but my mind is contemplating the intricacies of fate. Destiny. That which is weaved and intertwined. A tapestry the gods themselves cannot escape. One I've been tightly wrapped inside, even before I ever thought to consider the impact such things have on my very existence. Abhartack speaks with familiarity of Bishop rescuing me from the Isle of Misery. If he possesses the knowledge he claims to have, maybe he knows how I came to be exiled there to begin with. Maybe Sean Winkle's appearance at Merrymont College was a seismic shift that has now made it easy for Abhartack to utter words that are no great secret, yet have those same words still throw me so far off-balance that I'm questioning things I have no business wondering about.

I glance at him. As powerful as the king is, his emotions are pooling around him. Abhartack is either inept at shielding himself from the curious probes of others or he's once again attempting to lull me into believing things that are not true. Though, if the latter is his goal, I'm not so sure he's correctly assessed the impact of telegraphing his turmoil. The complicated mix emitting from him doesn't exactly make me want to fall into his arms *or* into a sense of security. I can only speculate as to whether or not his unrest has anything to do with the human scent growing stronger the farther we travel into the heart of the castle.

Abhartack looks down at me knowingly. "Today has been a difficult day for all of us. Those waiting in the dining hall are eager to be introduced to you, no matter what else you might be feeling from them." His eyes are still brimming with the softness that grew in them back in his room. Over whatever it was that he saw reflected in my own eyes. "Thank you for coming with me, Keela. When you first placed your hand in mine, all I could hope for was a measure of your grace. You have exceeded that expectation and so many others. Yet I fear I have still failed to deserve your benevolence. I was not composed earlier. That is why I ran off so quickly after our incredible feeding. Were you...*are* you upset that I left?"

I huff out a dismissive breath. I've never allowed anyone to curl up next to me afterward. Not even Aether. I fed while we enjoyed each other's bodies and then we went our separate ways. Now my body is reluctant to leave the king's side. The way I want Abhartack is wholly different from the draw I feel to Sean Winkle. Sean is a need. Abhartack is a want. A suffocating, indulgent want. "It is best to keep my enemies close, and you are most certainly an enemy of the Vasilis. A seductive one whose allure might actually outmatch my own, but I do not care when you come and go. You know why I'm here. It is the body and blood of Arsenious that I'm most interested in."

Abhartack turns us down a long, wide hallway that is lined with arched windows. "Then it is my mistake that I ran off to retrieve the gift that I have spent quite some time designing for you."

My hand itches to jump to the gem-studded choker around my throat. "You had this necklace made for me? Not one of the humans you had playing dress-up in the clothing you supposedly had stocked in your closet just for me?"

His laugh is rich and vibrant. "Don't worry, I have learned my lesson where your clothing is concerned. But the crown of jewels around your neck is perfect. I had it designed for you many years ago, mi Dauði. A piece of art as unique as you are."

I tamp down my desire to thank him and turn my attention back to the runes. Most of them are unknown to me. The same as my warm affection for this piece of jewelry. Such things are impractical in Midgard. Too bold. And usually only given by those under my thrall. Which Abhartack is not. Otherwise, he would not have been able to push me away earlier. Those affected by me cannot fight off their attraction. Like Sean, they will follow me anywhere. *Do* anything... "Once again, your compliments are ill-timed. Fail to deliver Arsenious into my hands and all of Dökkbraek will see why Bishop *also* believes me to be an exceptional work of art."

Abhartack's fingers graze mine. "I do not wish to fight with you. Nor do I wish to discuss Bishop with you tonight. I give him little credit for molding you into the spectacular being that you are. And, unlike him, I am trusting that you are a *Vasilis* who can be reasoned with."

I resist the urge to let my own hand caress his. "Bishop harbored no ill will for you until now, so I'm surprised at your open disdain."

The king sighs. "It is not disdain you hear. It is disappointment. Bishop kept you chained and bound by rules and judgments set upon us by those who serve only to use us as pawns in their own selfish games. I will not do that. If you choose to remain at my side, I will teach you what Bishop never would." He slides his hand onto the small of my back, voice low. "If you allow it, I will unleash for you all that you are. Show you what the Vampir *truly* are."

Fit for a queen. I force the echo of his earlier words out of my thoughts, because I will *not* allow it. Being here with Abhartack, inside of Dökkbraek, feels so utterly right. As if I've come home. Be he was not the catalyst that fundamentally changed me. That blame is with the boy even my shadows are obsessed with. I may long to stay in this castle where my every need can be fulfilled by the king, but that is only because I am as afraid of myself as those Vampir gathered behind the doors at the end of the hall are afraid of me. "I may live in Midgard, but I already know what the Vampir *truly* are. I've encountered too many of the beasts in my lifetime and have seen for myself exactly how brutal and savage all of us are."

Abhartack thrusts a hand toward one of the many windows lining the hall, the light beyond it tinged with red, like a dawn full of nothing but warning. "Open your eyes, Keela *Vasilis*. Look at Dökkbraek. Assess what is all around you. The Vampir are creatures of death, yes, but we are not only feared by all worlds sprung to life from the very root blood of Yggdrasil itself, we are *revered*."

I loose a mocking breath. "Feared not by the Vasilis, and revered only in the minds of the Vampir *king* and his hidden horde of monsters."

A snarl accentuates the swift removal of his hand from my back. "Your immeasurable ignorance proves once again that I am right. You do not belong with the Álfar, you belong here, where you will learn to respect your own kind. The elves may be blessed by Odin, but the Vampir are sacred. We share a connection to the primordial forces of creation itself, and *that* is why our place is one of reverence. We stand in the gap between eternal night and living day."

I stop walking. "You think I am so ill-educated that I would believe Vampir are spawn of the Primordial Void, not Loki? That you could bring me here and I would not be able to figure out how you glamoured the humans spilling their blood behind every wall in Draugrkeep? Changing their weak minds so that they do not fear you and your horde?"

Shadows bleed through his eyes. "While Bishop would love for me to be found guilty of compelling citizens of Midgard so he may challenge me for the power this land possesses, the humans who live in Dökkbraek are free men and women, with rights and choices. If they do not wish to be fed upon, they are not." He leans toward me. "And I did not mention Loki's spawn. Do you know the gods themselves have connections to the primordial forces? That they are *gods* because they have manipulated those forces, the same way they have manipulated fate." Abhartack spreads his arms wide, those beautiful shadows writhing like snakes between his fingers. "I will teach you many things, Keela. Like how those Vampir you've been allowed to slaughter in Midgard are the scourge I have banished. Those I have *allowed* to nest there. To eke out an existence like the insignificant gnats they are. Why do you think Bishop has never attempted to alter our treaty? If the Vampir are the blight you proclaim us to be, why allow us the freedoms we have? Why allow *my* Vampir in Midgard at all?"

I shift forward. "As Odin decreed it, no creature created *by* or *from* the gods may be hunted to extinction. Bishop upholds that decree. Which is why you, and the handful of other vampires capable of turning humans into one of you, are permitted to exist. Until those you change into monsters inevitably break the rules. At which time *I* am sent to correct their behavior." I smooth my hands down the front of his suit jacket. "The scourge you allow to escape this dreary castle are never so lucky as to escape *me*."

His shadow-infested hands clamp around my wrists, digging in painfully. My heart thuds. His lips lift, eyes dilating with delight over the sound of the one reaction I cannot control. "There is no need for you to accept my words as truth. I will take you to the human village so you can see for yourself that my Vampir do not harm them. I will show you *all* of Dökkbraek, tell you its secrets, and give you ample time to try again to find an excuse that will save your beloved Bishop from the reproach he deserves."

Abhartack pulls me against him, moving his hands from my wrists to my waist, his shadows vanishing, that earlier softness returning. "We are not cruel, mindless beasts. There are the rogues and those who go mad or find themselves diseased, or *cursed*. Those are the ones Bishop and others have used for centuries to paint the Vampir as you have been led to believe we are. But there is so much more to the Vampir, Keela." His arms slide around me. "You yourself are brutal, but you are no beast. You are logical and cunning, as most Vampir are." He runs his nose along mine. "Do not let your encounters with the few taint your opinion of the many, mi Dauði. Our true nature is not at odds with the laws of Midgard, and I want nothing more than to prove that to you. *Our* people revere you." He pulls away, meeting my stare. "Do not make me regret the years I have spent nurturing that reverence. *Our* people need you, so be nice to them. Or, at least, civil."

He tugs me forward and I keep my gait steady beside him. *Our* people. *Mine*. I toss his words against the boundaries of my mind. Splay them next to the images of the Vampir I've slaughtered. Few with dignity. I've made them suffer as they have made their human victims suffer. Made them want me, and then ripped them slowly apart, my allure too strong for them to fight back while their limbs were agonizingly cleaved from their bodies. I've made them watch me lap their blood from their open wounds and whispered their demise into their ears while they beg me for more. "You are wrong. I am a beast."

The king stops before two metal-plated bronze doors. His fingers twine through mine. "So am I. When need be, we are each capable of unimaginable brutality." The thick doors begin to open. He brings my hand up to rest on the crook of his elbow. "Together, we will be a force unlike anything the worlds of Yggdrasil have ever known."

We. Us. Once again, his words hit a mark inside of me. A familiar one. One I cannot determine the origin of, let alone the weight of what it means. Be it instinct, fate, destiny, or nothing but desire, I keep my hand where the king placed it and move forward with him, passing through the doorway arm in arm with Abhartack.

The room before us is cavernous. Long tables extend end to end, surrounded by plush chairs built of dark wood, their high backs covered with a silver-hued fabric that twinkles under the soft glow of the crystal chandeliers high overhead. They are plentiful, but not even their light reaches the darkest corners of the massive dining hall. This room was meant for a horde, and Abhartack's is currently filling it.

At the king's side, I hold my head high, sweeping my gaze around the windowless hall. Vampir are not the only kind present tonight. There are humans here. Hundreds of them. Tall. Short. Young, old, male, female... They are scattered among the Vampir. In their arms. On their laps. Standing beside them, as still as the stone underneath our feet. I yank my hand from Abhartack's arm, nostrils flaring as I scent the air. There is fear here. Much of it. Coming from both the humans and the Vampir. "What is this?" I hiss, Abhartack's words from only moments ago now dead against the vision before me.

The king's laugh fills the room. He motions to a brown-haired human who is curled tightly in a Vampir's arms. "Merisol, stop clinging to Diakos that way. Your affection for your husband is upsetting our honored guest."

My neck cracks as I whip my attention to his face. To the couple. And then back to Abhartack. "Husband?"

A wave of satisfaction rolls off of him, slamming into my senses. "What? Did I forget to tell you my Vampir are progressive enough that we do not see race as a reason to hinder love? My mistake." He plucks my hand from my side and places it back onto his arm, leaning in close, his lips skimming across my cheek on their way to my ear. "Ignorance is unbecoming, mi Dauði. But do not worry your beautiful little head. I will teach you, and then everything shall be *exactly* as it was always meant to be."

Swollen with confidence, Abhartack turns us into the center aisle, keeping me at his side as he strolls down the length of the table set at an intersecting angle to all of the others. As we pass, the Vampir and humans lower their heads. The king circles the table and takes his place behind a chair gilded with jewels that match the one at his throat. A chair sitting side by side with another just like it. We face the crowd. "Hraesvelgr," the amassed horde reverently utters as one, sending a startling jolt racing through me. The word means Corpse Swallower.

"Gott kvöld," Abhartack responds to his people, speaking the old language again. The Vampir call their king the Corpse Swallower, and he answers them by saying good night.

My throat tightens. Abhartack senses my unease, a smug smile flashing over his lips as he meets my eyes. He leans close, voice low. "Your precious Álfar are not the only beasts who speak the language of the gods."

I force every ounce of coldness I have into my eyes. The king chuckles, a deep, rich sound that echoes through the cavernous room. I snap my attention back to the couple. Merisol is at her husband's side, shoulders tense. Diakos leans over and presses a tender kiss to the top of her head, as if to console the human. His *wife*. His wary eyes meet mine as his king begins to speak, Abhartack's voice projecting throughout the room. "Today has been a challenging day. We have lost many, and we will grieve for them as is our custom. First, I must ask you not to be alarmed by Keela's presence. Though she fought against us this day, she is not our enemy."

I cut my eyes to his. He smiles, sliding a hand up my back and letting it come to rest on my far shoulder as he continues his speech. "As I said to you on the eve of our battle, every war ever fought was based on deception. Greed. Power. We are not immune from those ravages. Those ambitions. Which is why we pick our battles and choose to fight when it is necessary. Not for the cause or rights of one side or the other. We fight for *our* rights."

The room explodes in a deafening roar. Abhartack grins at me, knowing this show of loyalty from his people is impressive. Knowing that as a Vasilis, I will respect their loyalty to their king. "War is coming." His voice booms through the room, his words meant for me as much as his people. "We do not have to prepare for it, *plan* for it, because we are Vampir. We are always ready." His people cheer. Shout. Fill the room with noise that threatens to topple their castle from within.

The blood-red gem at the base of Abhartack's throat begins to glow. I reach up and touch the largest stone set in the center of mine, feeling the warmth of the same type of glow that is emitting from his. Three doors appear along the far side of the room, sliding open to unleash a parade of Vampir and humans alike, all carrying trays of drinks and platters of food. Abhartack pulls his eyes from mine and once again addresses his horde. "Tonight, with our long-awaited honored guest among us, let us feast. For tomorrow we mourn our dead, and afterward, we honor their lives by showing all the worlds of Yggdrasil that the Vampir bow to NO ONE!"

10

The Vampir bow to no one because they fear no one. Except for me. Even through the deafening, pre-dinner roar incited by their king, I can feel the slam of the horde's fear. It pulses through the dining hall, cold and thick, like threads of a spiderweb, bringing me their dread. Their screaming waves of unease. I latch on to thread after thread, sifting through the twisted knots of emotion, only to find myself as the cause of their alarm. I know why I elicit such a response, but I don't understand anything else I'm seeing. At every table in the banquet hall Vampir and humans alike feast together. Some on blood, others from platters piled high with every human delicacy. Beyond them, in every corner, couples nip and tease, promising each other a different sort of meal later tonight. Some of the couples are of the same kind, while others are mixed.

Abhartack shifts toward my chair, his voice meant only for me to hear. "Before you once again begin to deny that such harmony is possible, I must ask that you fairly assess whether or not compulsion is at play here.

Once you are satisfied that it is not, I beg you, for the sake of our people, to endure this dinner with me as if we are not enemies."

I narrow my eyes on him. "It seems you are as ill-acquainted with my temperament as you claim that I am when it comes to your precious Vampir. The only reason I haven't ripped out your throat is because you are the conduit for things I want. Arsenious, and answers."

His hand slides up my thigh. "I believe you want more than that." His fingers dig into my leg. "And threats are beneath you. If you think you can best me, I would much prefer to see you try. Only later, in *our* room, after you have put *our* people's minds at ease." His lips press against my cheek and I feel the tension overlaying the horde ease when I do not pull away from their king. His lips find my ear. "Be angry and disbelieving if you must, but know that when action is needed, I take it. Always and *only* for the betterment of all Vampir. And for you." He leans away from me and motions toward the tables on our right. "Caroline, you have something to offer our guest?"

A rustling of movement gives way to a clear view of a curvaceous brunette in a skintight scrap of leather. Her bright amber eyes land on mine and her already frantic heartbeat kicks into frenzy. She dips into a shallow curtsey, her trembling hands doing their best to steady the silver goblet clutched between her palms. "Hello, I am Caroline. If you are hungry, it will be my honor to feed you." She straightens, casting a glance to Abhartack before lifting her chin as if she is proud to be my prey tonight. "I understand you prefer your blood to still be warm, so I offer to fill this cup for you whenever you are ready." Her knees wobble. "Or I can sit beside you..."

"So that you may drink straight from her veins," Abhartack finishes for her.

My eyes drop to the mounds of her breasts. They're spilling over the top of the barely-there leather that's hugging her body. Her breath hitches, the motion causing those plump mounds to jump. I stand. Her eyes dilate, heart skipping several beats. Despite the brazenness of standing before me, this girl is terrified. And excited. I tilt my head, listening to the way her heart begins to race as I move closer, conjuring my thrall. Her head dips. I run a finger under her chin, lifting her gaze to mine. "Tell me, Caroline, did you choose your own outfit? Or did Abhartack request that you attempt to *seduce* me into drinking from your delectable veins?"

Her forehead creases. "I...um, Abhartack? My king did not request that I do anything. I volunteered. Feeding you is my privilege. I sought the honor and he gave it to me."

I stroke her cheek, scanning her body. "Do all of your king's *honored*, sacrificial lambs wear nothing but revealing scraps of leather?"

Her entire face turns an unflattering shade of crimson. She glances at the prying eyes around us and tucks a strand of glossy hair behind her ear, words nothing more than a whisper in the now hushed room. "I wore this because I wanted to impress you."

Abhartack rises from his seat and removes the cup from her hands, setting it on the table before cupping a palm over both of our shoulders. The gem at the base of his throat glows and the one on mine warms in response. His face pinches, an itch of irritation spreading across his features. "You may now speak freely. The others cannot hear what we are saying, but they can see us." His eyes pierce mine. "So please, Caroline, answer the questions of Keela *Vasilis*, even if they are insulting. She must settle her own mind about what is right in front of her." He gives the girl's shoulder a reassuring squeeze. "Answer honestly and quickly. There are many other matters that Keela must see with her own eyes before settling the matter of being convinced that I have told her no lies. And our time runs thin."

His hands slide from our shoulders, hanging in the air just beyond our bodies while the gem at his throat remains bright. The girl looks around at the curious banquet guests. Hesitant. I rest my gaze on her throat, opening my senses to every whiff of scent and wave of emotion. Looking for the lingering signatures of compulsion while deploying my own. "Why did you say you wanted to impress me, Caroline?"

She smooths her shaking hands over what little fabric there is to her dress, her voice coming out stronger than the uncertainty still threatening to buckle her knees. "I am not a lamb and the king assured me that you would not...*sacrifice* me. Not with him by your side." Her stare darts to him and then back to me. "I came here tonight because my mother...my *adopted* mother, was Vampir. She spoke of you. Told me stories about a forgotten vampire who came from the Isle of Misery only to rise from her own ashes to become one of the greatest warriors ever to live."

I study her features. I can sense no lies. No compulsive signatures on her person save for my own. Caroline slips a small knife from between her breasts, a smile etching her lips. "My mother said that I too could do more than merely survive. That I may not have the strength or speed of the Vampir, but that I could be as cunning and clever as Keela Vasilis. So I've spent my life training to fight and my mother..." Sadness crawls across Caroline's face. "She died five years ago, but I carry on her training. Should the king ever call upon me, I will be ready."

I show no emotion as her story winds its way through me. As I listen to her heartbeat and detect nothing but her truth. Abhartack's compulsion may be too strong for me to break, though, and too well crafted for me to detect. I won't know if my power displaces his as it does with others until I can test the king's strength.

Caroline looks down at the ground. "I know, it's stupid. The king will never need a human in his army. But I thought that if I could impress you…" She lifts her gaze once more. "I thought my outfit would convey confidence. I am not ashamed to be who I am, as my mother told me you are not ashamed to be different in all of the ways that you are. That's why I learned to throw knives the way you do, and I know if my mother was here, she would be right beside me, offering up her veins to you."

Abhartack's fingers brush my shoulder, but I refuse to look at him. This human girl was raised by a Vampir? And *I* am the hero in the bedtime stories she was told? I suppose curiouser things have happened. Sean Winkle for one. "Thank you for the invitation to feed, Caroline. I have rarely received such an honor." I bow to her. "I have no hunger for you, but I should like to train with you one day."

Her eyes fling wide. Abhartack lifts one of Caroline's golden-skinned hands to his blood-red lips and presses a kiss against her knuckles. "Indeed, thank you, Caroline. I now have hope that I myself might find favor with the beautiful Keela Vasilis, even if I have to borrow your outfit to do so."

She laughs heartily, so at ease with the Vampir king. Abhartack's stare whips to mine, his superiority drowning my scrutiny. He lowers Caroline's hand. "Would you mind subjecting yourself to further questioning, Caroline? Keela would like to ensure that you are not under the thrall of any Vampir. Particularly me."

She looks between us, brows furrowed. "Vampir using their thrall on residents of Dökkbraek is forbidden."

He raises a brow at me, as if he knows I have covered the girl in mine. "Yes, Caroline, it is forbidden. But when I told Keela that, she called me a liar." He gives Caroline a charming smile. "The effect of being raised in Midgard. Something your mother saved you from."

I growl. Caroline casts a wary glance my way, her throat bobbing. "I have heard about what happens in Midgard but in Dökkbraek, the Vampir do not harm the humans who live here with them."

"Do not harm?" I challenge, refusing to withdraw my influence over her. "How did you come to be here to begin with if not abduction? Stolen from your home and family to be given another life here." I level my glare on Abhartack. "And all so the Vampir could train you to give them your blood freely."

Abhartack begins to speak but I cut him off. "Don't. I want Caroline to answer."

Irritation flashes across his features but he wipes it away, painting on a relaxed smile as he edges Caroline forward. She glances at him before answering. "I, and almost everyone else I know in Dökkbraek, were born here. My mother died in childbirth and my father fell through the ice when he went out fishing alone when I was only seven. His betrothed, my adopted mother, kept and raised me after his death. She had been in my and my father's life since I was three years old."

My body goes still. Mind racing through everything I've ever seen or heard. Through the many books I've read, and stumbling over what I have learned since entering this crimson-hued world of the Vampir. Abhartack's fingers curl through my stiff ones. He waves a hand through the air and dips his head in gratitude. "Thank you, Caroline. I believe you have more than served your duty to our guest today, and it is I who am honored by your presence tonight." His horde begins to chatter. Some of them letting out sounds of appreciation. The girl looks more embarrassed now than she did earlier, but the smile on her face is genuine. So is the one being offered by her king. "If your mother were here, she would be as inspired by you as the rest of us are."

The horde cheers and I release my hold over Caroline. She folds herself into a low curtsey, exposing yet more of her thighs. When she rises, a pang of anger hits me as her eyes cut to mine. She knows I compelled her to tell her story, but she is most offended over my audacity to question her king. How curious.

Abhartack notes the girl's hostility toward me and chuckles softly as she walks away. He pulls my hand to his arm. "You will find there are many among us like Caroline, those willing to *freely* open their veins to you. But I do not expect you to take my word for anything, mi Dauði. Let us leave now, I promised to show you all of Dökkbraek and I want to do that before your ravenous hunger has me doing things in front of my people that would make even you blush." I pull away but he drags me closer. "I understand your hunger, mi Dauði. And you understand that I am the only blood and body to fulfill you, so do not fight me. Let us go peacefully."

I comply, repulsed at the ache settling into the back of my throat. His is not the only life-sustaining blood that I would enjoy, but I am overwhelmed by a desire to feed upon this king. "I doubt leaving their banquet so early will earn me any favor with *your* Vampir."

He whisks us out the door and down the hall. "Nor will you sitting stone-faced at their king's side, only opening your kissable mouth to interrogate *our* people." He stops us at the crossroads of an intersecting hallway. "Do you ever laugh, Keela? Has anyone ever allowed you to enjoy your life?" His fingers brush my hair from the curve of my ear. "You are remarkable. Not as a weapon, but a being. Will you let me prove that to you?"

The sincerity in his eyes and the pleading in his words… I step away, effectively removing his touch. "Prove it by bringing a half-naked child to feed me in a room where bloodlust is building? Did you tell her to make up that story about her mother or is it true, and you were hoping I wouldn't hear it until after I'd ripped out her throat in front of your people?"

He sighs heavily. "As I told you before, many in Dökkbraek would happily open their veins for you. But I do not trust you alone with *my* people, so if you should ever feed from them, I will always be nearby. To protect them. Tonight was a perfect opportunity to show them that you do not wish to feed from them, though." He leans into my face. "Because you have *me*."

I wrap my hand around his throat. "Caroline was a test, then? To see if I would take the delicious bait, and to see if you were fast enough to stop me from killing her if I did?"

Abhartack's arms form a vice grip around my middle. "It was a test for Caroline. One of her own making. She has never allowed a Vampir to feed directly from her veins before, but she assured me she was willing to give you that option. So long as you didn't try to do anything more than *feed*. But we both know that isn't your style, and we both know that *I* am who and what you want." His lips seize mine, his tongue forcing its way into my mouth. I release his throat and curl my fingers into his shaggy hair. He bites my lip. "Make no mistake." His voice is rough. "The only way I will stomach watching you feed from someone other than me is by first removing their head from their body." He fists my hair and yanks my head to the side. "Or by watching you remove it." His fangs scrape my neck, stoking the already roaring flames of my hunger. He pricks the skin just below my ear. "So you will feast on me and no one else."

Sean

I watch the ravens soaring high overhead, the faint glow of the coming dawn illuminating the iridescent sheen of their sleek bodies. I wonder if they've been outside this window all night. Wonder if my imagining them being connected to me is any more of a delusion than the rest of what I've experienced since meeting the Vasilis family. The presence of the birds could be a coincidence, or I could be right about them watching me. Guiding me. I first saw Keela after following the flight of a raven who nearly scalped me while I stood on the front lawn of Merrymont College. The next day, I only found her house again after following the flight of a raven that swooped low in front of my truck. Now the birds are here, outside of this bedroom window in the Vasilis house. And not for the first time.

If I were free to leave here on my own, I'd leap out the window and beg the circling birds to once again lead me to Keela. "Please," I whisper to them from behind the glass of the same room I was brought to after the first time I was released from their prison of torture. "Find her. Let her know I'll come for her as soon as I can."

"Talking to the shadows?" Gelby asks from my open doorway. I didn't bother closing the slab of wood after Haldir threw it open and told me to rest while I could. I have nothing to hide from them. Nothing to prove, either. It isn't as if a door and a lock would keep them out anyway. Besides, after being locked in their cells again, I much prefer open doors to closed ones. Even if the unobstructed exit only provides the appearance of freedom.

I face Gelby. "If the shadows will carry my words to Keela, then yes, I'm telling them that no matter what, I am hers. Heart. Soul. Human or Fae. Whatever I am and with all that I have inside of me. I am hers."

He studies me. "I suppose that could be true. After all, you are just like her."

I step forward. "Hours ago, you insisted that I was Fae. Now you're saying I'm a vampire?"

His head shakes, the shaved sides catching the faintest sheen of light. "I am saying that you are one of a kind. The same way Keela is the only one of her kind. She has vampiric traits, but she isn't fully Vampir."

I swallow. "What is she?"

He looks away. "For the most part, she's Vampir, but she's...more than what the rest of them are. Different in ways no one is able to account for." His eyes slide back to mine. "Keela appears to be Vampir the way your fire appears to make you Dreki. Yet you are not a dragon, the same way she is not fully a vampire. Neither of you fit quite right with either kind. That makes you unique. A curiosity that makes you as vulnerable as it does valuable. You will be hunted the way Keela has been hunted. People will want you, either to destroy you or to control you, and all because different is dangerous."

I shake my head. "No. Different is simply different. You yourself have touted your magical skills as being different than other Álfar and that's something you made an active choice to work at so you could purposefully differentiate yourself from others. Keela and I didn't choose our differences. We can't help what we are."

He holds out a hand and a dark green backpack materializes out of thin air, dropping to the floor in front of me. "We do not yet know what you can or cannot help, Sean Winkle. So let us see what the Norns have to say about you, and then we will determine if you are on our side or against us." He lowers his hand. "For your sake, I hope your loyalty is rightfully placed."

11

Gelby

Rohan and Jofir are huddled together in one corner of the living room, the newly found mates unable to keep their hands and mouths to themselves no matter the direness of our situation, and no matter how much they disagree about every aspect of this journey to the land of the Norns. Not to mention the rising disagreements about their future together. Mate bonds are practically impossible to resist but accepting them does not remove the obstacles of life. Both individuals still have their own unique preferences and ideas, and Jofir's idea is to live among her own people. To raise her children in the same city where she was raised, on Álfar land, surrounded by her kind. Not humans. But Rohan is Bishop's heir. He has a duty to the Vasilis and to continuing Bishop's role in Midgard.

I do not envy my brother for the choices he must make where Jofir is concerned. If he chooses her idea of what their future should be, I will fill his role as heir, though I do not covet the position. It is one Keela often spoke of having before the time when Bishop officially named Rohan as heir. A wish I knew she would never be granted because not even Rohan, who would have given up his claim for her, could agree that the magic bestowed upon Midgard's protector should ever transfer into a body that is not Álfar. So while I am happy for my brother and am glad that in finding his true mate, Keela's unintentional hold over him is broken, Jofir's existence does not save me from the probability of becoming Bishop's replacement. But Álfar have very long lives and Bishop is nowhere close to the end of his.

Rohan, on the other hand, is in danger of being gutted by his mate. Her voice may be low and her mouth never far from his, but her harsh tone and the curl of her upper lip are enough to force me to have Sean Winkle remain on the stairs while I keep my own distance from the couple and stand on the opposite side of the room with Haldir. Jofir only warmed to Rohan enough to discuss their future *after* Keela left us. The superiority of the mate bond was not enough to quell Jofir's jealousy. Because of Rohan's affection for our sister, Jofir wanted Keela removed from his life, and I have not failed to note the timing of her appearance in Midgard or her insistence that she be allowed to go to the Völva compound with us. Concerns that I will keep to myself while Bishop investigates what happened. Mate bonds are sacred among our people and I will not dishonor my brother by bringing shame upon Jofir, but I do wonder at there being no sourness in his reaction to her considering her open hostility toward Keela.

"Is that what the *mia mel* thing is?" Sean asks from where he's sitting on the bottom of the stairs, an elbow propped on his knee and one hand cradling his face while the other flops in the direction of Rohan and Jofir. "If so, Keela is definitely my mia mel and I'd rather be kiss-arguing with her in a corner somewhere than going to see these Norn people, so can I just please go find her?"

Jofir growls at him over Rohan's shoulder. "Despite the destruction you've caused, not everything is about you, and it most certainly is not about Keela Vasilis." Rohan takes a step back and shakes his head at his mate. Jofir shoves out from between his arms, leveling her dark glare at each of us. "It's good that the rest of you aren't as single-minded as the human-fae trash, but I am appalled by your lack of haste." She sears a look into Rohan. "Especially *you*. If the journey you were ordered to take"—her eyes ones again meet all of ours—"was to fetch your beloved Keela, instead of sitting around here glum-faced, you would each be sizzling with energy. What message does that send to the Álfar you are supposed to represent? To protect and work for?"

None of us answer. She folds her arms over her chest. "May I remind each of you that Keela may very well be betraying all of us at this very moment?"

"Keela would never betray us," Rohan defends.

"Maybe not on purpose," Jofir barks. "But she is born of Loki, and it is *his* nature that she and her kind are ruled by. Without ever meaning to, she could be choosing actions that harm all of us because it is *Loki* and *his* kind who are destined to stand against us. Against Odin himself!"

A rumbling puff of black smoke erupts from Haldir's nose. "Keela would never—" His words break off, his head cranking toward the front door the same way mine and Rohan's are.

Magic coils in my fingertips. Sean races to my side, staring at the door the same way the rest of us are. "What is it? What can I do? How can I help?"

I ignore him, speaking only to my brothers as I douse my magic. "I'll take care of the witch and the wolf. The rest of you gather by the fireplace. I'll be back to open the portal in a minute."

Jofir's long legs overtake mine as we approach the door. "*I'll* take care of them," she nips. "After all, I'm the one who invited Monique and Leah, and I've already instructed them on what provisions to bring, so I'm sure they came prepared and can meet you and the other buffoons by the fireplace just as soon as my girls and I have a little chat."

I slam my magic against the door, not allowing Jofir to open it. "They are not going on this journey with us."

Her eyes narrow. "The problem with your statement is that *I* am going on this journey, and *I* intend to survive. To do that, *I* want people at my back who aren't preoccupied with their insufferable desires to *bed* Keela Vasilis."

Rohan steps around her, cupping his hand over the doorknob, his voice low as he glares at her. "It is no longer Keela I am preoccupied with bedding, and the sooner you finally give in to the full weight of our bond, the sooner you will have that proven to you." I release my magic and he slings the door open. "Uninvite them."

I wish Rohan's order held more weight than it does, but as Rohan's mate—one he isn't showing any indications of denying, Jofir holds special privileges. Even Sihoma, who humans would call my stepmother, is given deference because of her bond to Bishop. And theirs is only a chosen union, not a fated one like Jofir has with Rohan. The kind of bond I'll never have with Leah MacKenzie because the Norns are as shortsighted as everyone else when it comes to keeping bloodlines pure. When I meet them, maybe I'll ask them why they don't realize that hybrids could lead to peace because then the races would no longer be segregated by kinds. *If* I meet them. Few who set out on this journey ever do. And many never return.

My eyes immediately begin to soak up Leah, from where the tops of her solid leather boots scratch against her wide-legged cargo pants to the way she fills out that simple gray t-shirt. The hoodie tied around her waist is the only disappointment. It covers all of her rear-facing assets so watching her walk away, for what might be the final time, is going to be more frustrating than usual.

I move forward, casting a cursory glance at Monique, who is standing shoulder to shoulder with Leah. The witch smooths a hand down the length of her long braid, the tremble in her fingers so noticeable it piques my curiosity, but Monique's nervousness is low on my priority list right now. Leah is at the top, but even the overconfident Ulfr I've come to know is muted. Her anxious eyes dart between Rohan and Jofir, her bottom lip tucked tightly between her teeth. Jofir jabs an elbow into Rohan's ribs, waving the girls forward. "Come in. He isn't going to bother you."

Rohan blows out a frustrated sigh but does nothing else as Leah and Monique step over the threshold. I could easily keep them out but my arms itch to hold Leah one last time. To tuck her into a corner the way Rohan had Jofir earlier. "Welcome." I give her a comforting smile.

Leah walks forward and I begin to open my arms for her. "Sean!" she exclaims, running past me and throwing herself against him. My magic flares.

Haldir slaps a hand over my shoulder. "You okay?"

I shrug him off. "Will you be okay when Keela returns and crawls into his lap?"

Sean

Leah's body slams against mine and a fiery blaze of dragon spit turns to ash inches from both of our heads. I try to shove her to safety in case Haldir gets any more dragon-bright ideas, but she has a death grip on my neck. I attempt to unclasp her hands, but she digs her nails into me and presses her face against my shoulder. But it's the shudder that gets me. I curl my arms around her, shooting Haldir an *I dare you* glare while I go against my every instinct and hold Leah close to me. "Why are you crying? What happened?"

Her shoulders shake and her grip on me tightens. In all the years I've known Leah, I've never seen her like this. She's not one to get even a little misty-eyed, let alone full-out sob. My gut sinks. "Did something happen to Collin?"

She cranes her neck back and looks up at me, brows knitting, a sob on her lips. "No...I don't... They took you. By the time Dad and I... You were gone and Monique said Bishop..." Her lips quiver. "We had no idea if you were alive or dead. If they hurt you I swear—"

"I'm fine," I mutter, eyes connecting with those of the red-haired witch who's still standing by the door, eyes wide as she watches us.

Leah throws herself back against me. "I'm so sorry, Sean. Me, Dad, all of us...we're so sorry we let you down. We had no idea—"

"That I'm powerful?" I shove her off of me. "Yeah, neither did I. Kind of like I didn't know that shapeshifting wolves existed. Or witches, until I was forced into a circle of them and poof! My whole body was engulfed in flames." I pat my arms. "Without a single hair being singed. I don't even know how that's possible, and neither does anyone else, apparently.

So now I get to take a fun little trip to wherever these Norn people are and you get to go back to your daddy and tell him to kiss that protection money goodbye because no matter what the Norns say, the Vasilis are making it pretty clear that they're never going to leave me alone." I glare at Haldir. "Unless I'm dead."

The dragon clicks his tongue. "If you insist upon whining, make sure you state the facts correctly. I'm the only Vasilis who doesn't care what the Norns say. Unless you're dead when they say it."

Leah spins toward him, spitting whatever vicious words that make her feel better. I ignore both of them and head for Monique. Though the Völva using their magic on me has never been my choice, Monique has now been hurt twice because of me. Bonnie...*Beatrice*, the top witch who tricked me into giving her my first kiss when I was a teen, hurt the worst.

Monique's eyes widen as I approach, darting back and forth like some cornered animal. I hold up my hands. "I'm not mad at you, just them." I toss my head to the bickering behind me that's grown into a spat between everyone save for myself, Gelby, and Monique. "How's Beatrice? Is she...okay?"

Monique clutches her fingers together. "Despite what you did to her, Beatrice lives."

Great. That tone means she also blames me for things I have no control over. Things that are technically her fault and not mine. "I didn't mean to hurt her or any of you. I have no control over what your circle drew out of me."

Her face smooths over, slender freckled arms crossing over her chest. "Tell that to Beatrice. Despite you burning half of us to death, our coven still remains powerful. Yet even with that power, our high witch will have a long healing process. Because of the fire *you* shot into her." Her trembles subside as her anger rises. "You *cooked* her from the inside out. Who does that? *What* does that?"

I fight the images that want to come to mind. When Beatrice took my hands, she said she was going to be my conduit. That she would feel what I felt and see what I saw. In that moment, what I felt was my uncertainty hanging in stark contrast to the confidence of the Vasilis. By mixing their magic with the power of the Völva, Gelby and Rohan were *certain* they would finally get the answers they wanted. I didn't have a say in what happened, and I have no idea how I became a living torch. "I—"

"Are not to blame for what happened." Leah snakes her arm through mine, growling at Monique. "We were all there. The same way all of us are going to be there when Sean is presented to the Norns, since the Vasilis have once again decided to pull rank and make themselves the only ones who get a say in what actions should be taken to figure out all of this not-Sean's-fault stuff."

A surge of magic slams against my back and I stumble forward, toward Monique. She jumps out of the way with a screech. I get my feet under me and spin toward the source of the blow. Gelby. He's glaring at Leah. "We do outrank you, little wolf, so run on home to Daddy because another thing the Vasilis have decided is that you are not going with us."

I want to punch him, but I'll be shot down before I ever reach him. I shove my hands into my pockets to keep them from fisting up. "Agreed," I bite out. "Leah doesn't need to go anywhere but home."

Her mouth falls open and I see another true first in her eyes—sadness. Real, genuine, painful sadness. I try to think of what to say to her but thankfully, Rohan either doesn't see how upset she is, or he doesn't care. "Gelby is right. The realm of Urðarbrunnr is dangerous. We don't need extra bodies to protect."

"Who said she needs protection?" Jofir spits. "I watched her in battle, as I did Monique, and I feel as comfortable with them at my back as any of you."

Rohan points at Monique. "Exactly. We saw them in battle, and we saw how many witches they lost. The Völva need what remains of their coven to *remain* here with them."

"Actually"—Monique's voice is tender compared to the others—"we have lost many and our coven will take time to heal, but when Jofir called, it was the high witch herself who told me to come." Monique's eyes dart to me and back to Rohan. "Beatrice thinks the Norns will have information for each of us, because..." She swallows, a deep breath working through her chest as she looks down and back up. "She believes Sean Winkle is a message. Not an omen, exactly, but a message sent to bring us together."

"Why does she think this?" all three Vasilis males ask in unison.

Monique stops breathing, her eyes roaming between me and Haldir. "Out with it, we don't have all day." Rohan snaps, earning himself another elbow to the ribs from Jofir.

Monique's entire body goes still, her eyes now only on Haldir. "Beatrice said that Sean is not a dragon, but possesses a dragon's fire. One that is from a line older and more powerful than what anyone has seen in millennia. More powerful than..."

Haldir's fire singes the furniture before Gelby slams his hands through the air and the fire disappears. "Not in the house."

"Don't kill me," Monique whimpers. "I'm only the messenger."

I snort. "They don't care."

Leah takes a fighting stance in front of me and I roll my eyes at the back of her infuriating head, walking away to go back to my perch on the stairs. All of this arguing is getting us nowhere and I'd rather process the shock of what Monique just said while sitting down.

Rohan begins to glow like the pure blue flame of a camp stove. "No one is killing anyone unless I say so." He looks around the room, asserting his dominance. Jofir lifts her chin at his side, that power trip short-lived as Rohan finishes his little pep talk. "We don't have time to fight any more than we have time to coddle one another. We must consult the Norns, and then we must reunite with Keela."

Jofir storms away from him and Gelby throws a dozen glowing crystals into the air. "There are no phones where we're going so everyone except Sean Winkle, grab a crystal. If we get separated, these will be our only way to communicate with each other while we are inside Urðarbrunnr. But they only have so much energy, so use them sparingly. One call to anyone outside of the Norn territory and the crystal will be finished. Three calls within, and the crystal is finished."

Everyone, including Gelby, takes two crystals. Monique pulls two backpacks out of thin air for herself and Leah and as everyone stows their crystals away, I watch Haldir. I'm not a dragon but he still looks ready to challenge me to a death match. His slitted eyes narrow on me. My mouth goes dry. "You heard her. I'm not a dragon."

He tightens the straps on his pack, nearly ripping them off. "Which means you have something that does not belong to you."

I bang on the spot where Aether's fist plunged into my chest. "It has to be—"

"The Norns will tell us what it is," Rohan cuts in. "The Ulfr and Völva are coming, and we leave now."

He tugs on a backpack, as does everyone else, only Rohan's has swords hanging from the sides and crossed along the back. Gelby's has two crossed swords, Haldir has one thick-handled sword with a gleaming blade, and Jofir has two small daggers attached to either side of her hips. I look at Leah. She spreads her fingers, the nails growing into razor-sharp blades. She grins up at me, her red-rimmed eyes still catching me off guard. "Don't worry, I've got us covered."

I meet Monique's gaze on the other side of where Gelby and Rohan are locking arms. She looks away, fiddling with the straps of her backpack. My heart sinks. I'm leaving the only world I've ever known—what I thought was the only world that even existed—and I'm doing this surrounded by people who hate me. I look down at Leah. "Where's Collin?"

12

Collin

Lance shouts, the sound nearly cut off by the sharp crack of splintering ice. I sling out my arms, palms flat, signaling for the rest of my pack to halt. We're in the middle of a frozen river right now and all I can do is watch as veins spiderweb from beneath Lance's boots. He's fifty yards ahead of me and those tiny fractures are moving fast, rushing across the surface in every direction. I knew coming here was a bad idea, and crossing this river an even worse one.

Anger rises, forcing me to tamp down my wolf as I zero in on exactly who's to blame for this, turning my chin over my left shoulder and narrowing my gaze on Zara. The arrogant dragon is the one and only reason we're on this ice. She insisted the Seidr's words directed us to this place, but it was *Zara* who led us to the Seidr to begin with. And the longer we're stuck in this frozen wasteland, the more I'm beginning to wonder if the woman was even a Seidr at all. She could have been nothing more than an old crone with a bundle of weeds, and Zara nothing more than a grifter.

The dragon's head turns in my direction and I get a shot of eyes such a deep, vibrant shade of green that the spring grass must get jealous of her. But there's not a blade of grass anywhere around here and throughout this entire mission, we've had nothing but problems. Something the old bat, whom Zara was supposedly guarding, should have seen coming. And warned us about. Especially after how long it took for the woman to *divine* her sacred weeds. "Herbs of Vision my freezing foot," I growl, shifting my focus back to Lance. Out of all of us, he's closest to the opposite bank, but still too far away to make it if the ice breaks all the way through.

Tread lightly, Ulfr, over trails of giants, and find your destiny waiting across the shimmering dewdrops where no water flows, yet beasts swim. The *allegedly* ancient Seidr took her sweet time spitting those words out to me, staring down into her herbs for what felt like hours. Then she took me to Hel's domain and back again with the rest of her cryptic message, but it's these words about shimmering dewdrops that allowed Zara to insist we had to cross this river that's so wide, none of us could determine how thick the ice was all the way across. Zara also thought the part about giants referred to Jutenheim, and now we're here, on the outer dregs where we're all going to meet an icy death. I'll never be able to reach Lance in time and even if I could, my added weight would only serve to break the ice out from underneath us quicker. There's no way to stop what's happening. The splinters have already reached me and from the worried grunts of the others, the spiderweb of veins has now reached them too.

"Go slow, Lance. The rest of us will wait while you cross." I keep my voice calm, determined to get all of my pack across this river. If anyone is going to take a swim, it's Zara. She finishes crossing last.

Lance's head shakes, his eyes focused on the ice below him. I groan. His sudden display of cowardice shouldn't surprise me. Ever since the Seidr's cryptic message somehow led to Zara joining us, no one has been the same. According to the females, the dragon shifter was destined to travel alongside us until that time when her own quest would steer her to part ways with us. But having the pretty dragon tagging along has caused too much friction between my wolves. None of them are acting like themselves, and I'm about as tired of Zara as I am of guessing at the Seidr's words. If there's any truth to what the old woman told me, I have to complete our original mission and find the artifact the Fae are so desperate to get their hands on before I can save my father from some kind of terrible fate. A fate the Seidr couldn't possibly explain in any sort of helpful manner. *To abate fate, find what you seek within the shadows of time. But remember, young wolf, that one never knows what they believe they know.*

How that's supposed to help me is beyond me, but I do know that pretty faces are plentiful, and I don't care how rare female Dreki are, this one better hope my pack survives this river. "Move, Lance. You're the closest to the bank. Get there, and then I'll send Ethan over next."

"Uh, guys?" The tremble in Mark's voice has me craning my neck to see where he's made himself into a statue on the ice. He's looking down and to the right. "What are those?"

"On your left!" Nathan shouts, frantic hands pointing toward me. I spin and look down into the fracturing ice. Below me, a shadow spirals up from the river's depths, tunneling through the ice like a giant earthworm. Coarse gray fur erupts along my arms and spine, my canines elongate, and curved claws replace fingers as my hands morph into paws. My wolf is surging forward to complete the shift, but not fast enough. The head of a giant snake explodes from the river, sending shattering ice catapulting into the sky.

The beast buries its fangs in my leg. In return, I sink my teeth into its scaly neck, snout elongating and my teeth digging in farther as I complete the shift mid-bite. I toss my massive head and yank the snake's fangs from my leg, its scales crunching underneath my teeth. The sharp, acrid taste of its blood bursts into my mouth and I throw the overgrown serpent across the ice. Another one breaks up from below me to take its place. I clamp my jaws around it and sink my teeth into its sinewy body, my tongue slick with its blood. I toss it and meet the next one, snakes all around me now. Around all of us. Breaking up from the frozen depths, scales and ice bursting high into the overcast sky like a fireworks display. The river is frozen solid, right down to the ground beneath. There's not a drop of free-running water.

...where no water flows, yet beasts swim. I guess Zara was right. We were destined to cross this river. *Cross it.* Not die on it. I release a menacing growl, my wolves all shifted now answering me in kind. I tear into the snake weaving its body around me, claws raking over its scaly flesh and my jaws snapping tight around it, head tossing to throw the snake as far as I can away from my pack. A third charges while yet another flings its tail over my back. I spin, biting and gouging, fighting for space. Fighting to keep from being cut off from my pack. I catch sight of Nathan doing the same, inching his way toward an opening, and scan the rest of my pack. The snakes have Ethan and Lance completely surrounded and Mark is barely doing better than Lance and me, all of us taking on the

monstrous beasts while more break from the depths below us, cutting us off. Isolating us. But Zara...she's just standing there. Frozen. Looking wide-eyed at the slithering mass of snakes around her.

I counter to my left, swiping out with claws and teeth, moving toward her. Two snakes explode from the ice between us, both larger than all of the others, towering ten feet above the ice and bodies way too thick for my jaws to clamp around. One of them dives for me and I dig the claws of my back feet into the ice and rear up, gouging my front claws into its body. I bounce off the snake, as if the serpent's body is covered in some kind of rubbery armor. A kind of rubber reminiscent of the leathery armor dragons are covered in.

My eyes dart to Zara. She still hasn't shifted yet. If my wolves and I can't puncture the bodies of the largest snakes, then the dragon is our only hope. I pull my wolf back and crouch low on the ice. "Shift!" I shout at her. "Shift, Zara! Use your fire to burn them!"

Her wide, wild eyes meet mine and the head of the snake I just tried to gouge dives toward her, mouth open. It swallows her whole and keeps going, straight down into the ice, leaving nothing more than a tunnel behind. *...where no water flows, yet beasts swim.*

"Run!" The word breaks from my lips. We can't outrun them, not now, and not on this ice, but we have to try. *"Run!"* I shout louder, putting the full force of my alpha behind the order, as I shift back, paws scraping and clicking on the ice as I dodge the gaping hole left by Zara's snake. I leap as a snake comes up underneath me, coming down hard and sliding toward Nathan.

"Collin!" Ethan's voice is fraught with warning. I force my shift again, turning back into human form just as the head of a snake crashes into the ice beside me, my smaller human body making the snake's gaping maw slam into the ice instead of me. The others follow my lead, shifting, making themselves smaller targets and all of us racing for each other instead of the shore. My command wasn't clear and I don't know if my wolves would obey even if I tried for clarity now. Our nature is to protect each other. To fight. Until the very end.

I feel it before I see it. The tunneling snake. I zag. Zig. It makes no difference. This snake is the largest of them all. It lifts its head through the ice, jaws hinging open. I call my wolf forward, turning my hands into deadly claws, but the lethal precision of my wolf is useless against this repulsive snake. Its fangs dig into my stomach, jaws closing painfully around me. The edges of my vision go dark. I cast a glance out toward my wolves. Their bodies are writhing, all of them limp in the constricting coils of the snakes. The Seidr's final words spin through my pounding skull. *Fail in your quest, Collin MacKenzie, and casualty will have no guard. Bitterness will consume us all.*

Blood dribbles from the corner of my mouth. "I'm sorry." The words fall feeble and broken from my crushed body, ribs and bones crunching as the snake retreats, coiling back into its frozen tunnel, and taking me with it.

"Wake up." The sting of those demanding words isn't nearly as bad as the sting across the left side of my face. It hurts as much as the right side of my face, where the person owning that demanding voice keeps slapping me. My head is fuzzy and my eyelids refuse to cooperate, but the worst is my stomach. I'm about to puke.

I call my wolf forward. He's groggy but he senses the next blow coming. I reach up and snatch the hand out of midair, clutching the skinny wrist of my attacker in a fist. "Good, you're actually alive." Zara's voice cuts through the relentless buzz in my brain. *Zara*. I force one eye open. No small feat, and a battle I regret winning. The world is spinning above me, Zara's face blurring in and out of focus. I force my second eye to open but that only makes the dizzying effects worse. This must be how Sean felt that time when he got black-out drunk. I drank more than him, my wolf metabolism burning off the alcohol nearly as fast as I chugged it down. When Sean finally noticed that he was way more plastered than I was, I started pretending to be drunk, mimicking the way he'd slurred and stumbled throughout the night. The next morning when he could barely tolerate light and complained that his head was pounding, I lied and told him I felt the same way. But all I really felt was relieved that my best friend had something other than the death of his mother to think about.

"Karma," I mutter, a wave of nausea crashing over me.

"Zara," the annoying dragon corrects.

I let my wolf surface enough to growl at her properly and then roll over, puking up whatever I ate last. It left a sticky, sour taste in my mouth and vomiting it back up only coats that nasty taste in a bitter film. "I know your freaking name, Zara."

She lifts off her knees, straightening from where she was kneeling on the ground next to me. "It's the blood of the time serpents making you sick. It's poisonous, which is why you're not supposed to bite them."

I puke again, fisting my hands into earth and grass, choking it, while imagining the ground is Zara's neck and the grass is her eyes popping out of her head. "Time serpents? That's why you didn't lift a finger to help my pack escape. You could have cooked all of those snakes with your dragon fire, or, at the very least, held them back while we got off the ice. You could have flown us out of there!" My chest heaves and my stomach clenches. I fist the ground harder. "You dragged us there, put us on that ice, and then left us there to die." I turn my head and stare into her heartless eyes. "Not everyone wants a time serpent to drag them through the bowels of time. We can be dumped into our destinies in safer ways."

Her mouth pulls tight. "Unlike the graceful destiny moths, it's true that you are allowed to kill the serpents, but why would you? It's better to just let them take you to your fate. We're literally on a quest, and it isn't my fault that you didn't realize what the snakes were."

I press my eyes closed, forcing the fragmented memory show flickering in my brain to slow down so I can focus on what happened and where I am. There's grass here, so we're not in Jutenheim anymore. And the time serpents are creatures rumored to live in waters connected to the well of Urðarbrunnr. The Norns call on them to reset the balance of fate, ensuring their many streams of woven destinies tangle and untangle as those three fate-spinners intend. An unfair way to take the balance of choice and consequence away from the rest of us. "Destiny moths take you to challenges, the serpents can take you to challenges, but also straight to Hel. That's why you fight them."

Zara crouches, dipping her canteen into a small, clear stream on whose bank the Norns have now placed us. It's dusk, stars overhead already beginning to flicker in the water's reflection. As does the moon. It's full and low, and rimmed with a glow brighter than any harvest moon. I glance up through the thick canopy above us. This looks like any number of forests in Midgard, but the moon shouts to me that we are no longer in any realm I've ever been in before.

I bite my tongue against all of the things I want to yell at Zara, choosing instead to straighten into an upright crouch of my own. I examine my torso through the holes the giant snake's fangs left in my shirt. From what I understand, the poison blood of the time serpents doesn't usually kill anyone, it only makes them sick. Sometimes, sick enough they wish they were dead. Which is why Zara is right. I should have realized what the serpents were. They travel in packs, large or small, based on how big their body of water is, and it's only their young who can be penetrated with claws and teeth. The instant I bounced off the larger snake, I should have known.

She drops the canteen beside me. "You've been out for more than a day so the wounds are healed already. The vomiting should have purged the rest of the blood."

I grab the canteen and wash out my mouth. "Where are we? And where is my pack?"

She hoists her backpack onto her shoulders and I attempt to remember the moment when I lost mine, the pieces of what happened on the frozen river clinking into place as my shifter magic works feverishly to straighten out the tilt-a-whirl inside my brain. Zara still has her supplies because she didn't fight the snakes. She just stood there and let them swallow her whole. "The land of the Norns, and not here," she answers. "If the serpents took them, they didn't bring them here. And we need to move. It's dangerous to sit out in the open like this."

I glance around us, the scent of pine thick in the air. The land of the Norns is a dangerous one, the landscape ever changing, depending on what the Norns decide they want to draw out of you. It's their way of examining you so they can better direct your future. Supposedly. Personally, it feels like a power trip. It could be the alpha blood in my veins talking, but I don't like the feeling of being manipulated. "You planned for the time serpents to take us. You knew they were in that river so you led us there. How else would you know that this land belongs to the Norns?"

She snatches her canteen back and refills it in the stream. "You've been looking at me with accusation since we left the Seidr. It's about time you gave voice to your ridiculous ideas."

I slowly get to my feet, my throat is burning and my mouth is still sticky but the world has stopped spinning. I stick my fingers through the holes in my shirt. "Answer my questions, Zara. Where is my pack and why did you lead us into that ambush?"

She turns eyes on me that are so glacial they should be blue, not that crazy vibrant green. "The Seidr led you. I might have been the one to figure out where to go, but only because my own destiny is currently tied to yours. I don't know where the rest of your pack is and I'm not going to apologize for getting both of us to where we are supposed to be." A cruel smile works its way onto her lips. "And I know where we are because I've been here before. But this time, I didn't have to invite myself. It seems the Norns want to have a chat with me."

13

Keela

"Get dressed." Abhartack's mouth grazes along my chin. "I promised you a tour of Dökkbraek and if you continue to lounge naked in my bed, I will have no strength left in my legs to walk you through our beautiful land."

I slide away from him and slip off the edge of the bed, gliding toward the closet. Abhartack has finished honoring his fallen warriors in ceremonies I was not invited to. For obvious reasons. Many who fell in the battle at the Völva compound did so at my hand. Mowed down by blade and shadow alike. A battle that is beginning to feel as if it happened a lifetime ago.

Dökkbraek's time of mourning would have been a perfect time to escape, if I wished to attempt such a thing. But I don't. Not after last night. Their dinner only provided more questions, and so did my night with the king. We barely made it back to his room, our tour forgotten. All that mattered was us. And no matter how many times our bodies came together or for how long, it was never enough. I dined on him, and he fed from me. But it was how he held me afterward that unearthed a deeply buried desire that I've spent too many decades convincing myself I do not possess. I want to be loved. Truly. Deeply. Without compulsion or allure. I want to be seen and loved for exactly who and what I am.

Abhartack enters the closet behind me, pulling a gown of shimmering black fabric off a rack. "I can have the dresses removed. I just thought you wore only long pants because of some Vasilis rule. I didn't realize it was a preference."

I smile for him, because he noted last night how much he liked seeing it. "Dresses are inconvenient. I can't move as easily in them, but if you want to parade me through your land, the dress will go better with the necklace." I let my hand raise to the only thing he insisted I keep wearing last night, and ever since returning from honoring his warriors. "It isn't as if a dress hinders my ability to fight."

The king stares at my mouth. "Precisely why I thought it was Bishop who demanded you not show off how elegant you are. I could wrap you in heavy furs and you would still be deadly."

I take the dress from him and slip it on, turning so he can zip the scooped back closed. His fingers trail over my spine and my fangs begin to throb in that way they do when I'm about to beg him to take me again. I can practically hear his dark chuckle already vibrating against my ears, and yet my eyes are rabid for what the shadows are giving me the briefest glimpse of. Another whose body I crave. Whose embrace I have wanted since I first smelled him walk onto the campus of Merrymont College. If love had a scent, it would be Sean Winkle.

Abhartack leads me along a trail cut into the frosty ground along the bank of a stream. Its surface is covered in a layer of translucent ice, the water beneath pulsing with streaks of light that flow with a gentle moving current. I look away from the glassy surface, eyes roaming over the haunting beauty of this land. "The view from your tower hides the true loveliness of Dökkbraek."

Abhartack reaches up and touches the crystalline edge of a pale flower dangling from the end of a silvery vine. "I must keep it that way. No one outside of my nest knows what this land truly is. I do not grant tours to visiting *dignitaries*. Only those sworn to me are allowed beyond the forest edge."

I scan the patchwork of frozen moss below my feet. The bench nestled into the foliage along the far side of the trail. "Then why bring me here when I am not sworn to you?"

He looks down at me, longing unhidden. "I have no choice but to tell you things that I would not dare utter outside of Dökkbraek. To show you all of this land, because when our tour is finished, you will have answers to your questions about our food supply and so much more."

I turn my attention back to the stream. Its glow seems to pulse in time with the beat of my heart. "What's in the water?"

His fingers brush against the small of my back. "Those are your dreams, Keela."

I raise a disbelieving brow at him. "My dreams?"

He gives me a lopsided smile, his hand pointing to a runestone half buried in the earth on the far side of the stream. An ancient stone, not unlike the many others dotting this landscape. "You will find those across every space in Dökkbraek. They are etched with history and some of them tell stories of the Vampir. But the oldest ones, like that one, tell of the elemental forces that began *everything*. These most ancient of stones tell of creators. Destroyers. Of how the echoes of creation *still* reverberate within the Primordial Void. They are what gives us the power to navigate between life and death." He touches the gem at the base of my throat. "The void is the very nexus of Vampir power. This is why I have taken such risks, Keela. The Vampir are not simply predators. We are the keepers of ancient wisdom. The guardians of the threshold. Protectors of the void."

A laugh bubbles out of me. I don't mean to insult him and so far, I have caught him in no lies. Nonetheless, laughter still coats my voice. "You side with no one and fight no one else's war because you think you are special? Chosen to hold infinite wisdom? By a chasm?" I glance at the old stone. "The runestones here are ancient, but so are many other relics. Many of them useless. And anyone could have printed stories on your stones. I've studied runes and most of the ones carved here are like the ones inside Draugrkeep. I cannot read them."

Abhartack's jaw ticks. "The Vampir do not have the magic of the Álfar, and we most certainly do not have the blessing of Odin. But we are still destined to fight in Ragnarök, the same as they are. Only Ragnarök will not be the battle you and your beloved Álfar are expecting." His nostrils flare. "I know this because unlike you, I *can* read the runes."

I fold my arms across my chest. "And what do your stones tell you, *my king*?"

Fury slithers across his features. "They tell of a sacrificial feast. One not in celebration of the gods, but in honor of the spirits of the night. Those *things* whose bones are woven from the very darkness of the chasm that gave birth to them."

I huff. "You mean the Vampir?"

The edges of his lips turn up. "No, mi Dauði. The runes tell of offering the spirits' blood in place of mead, but the spirits are not Vampir. They are born of the chasm itself, not Loki or any other god. This is why many runes in Dökkbraek warn of the true meaning of Ragnarök. It will not be a war of the gods, as the gods themselves have proclaimed. No. The battle will be a catastrophic clash between the living and those of endless night." His eyes dart to my chest and then to the water. "Fate swims in the streams of Dökkbraek. Time serpents. Creatures trapped and placed here by Odin himself. But the Norns do not weave their tapestries for Odin so they do not call upon these serpents. They leave them in this form as a reminder that not even the All Father can change the fate he is destined for."

Abhartack turns away from the water and motions to the path in front of us. "We must continue on. Time is limited and I grow tired of your utter ignorance."

A pang of guilt traces through all of the hollow, empty places inside of me. Places that should be enraged at the king's insults. My feet move and I fall in line beside Abhartack, using the guilt to remind myself of where I am. *Who* I am. The king may not have me under his thrall but the longer I am with him, the more complacent I'm becoming. All too willing to lose myself in the luxury of his kingdom. The sensation of his blood. The comfort of his embrace. And then there's Caroline and her Vampir mother, who turned *me* into a hero for her human daughter.

"The boundaries of the human village are marked by bloodthorn." Abhartack nods to a twisted vine of crimson leaves spread across the path twenty yards ahead of us. "We call the village O'Dearg."

Complacent to a fault, I scan the twisted vines that crawl up the icy trunks of the sentinel trees on either side of the path, as if forming a poisonous fence around the perimeter. "You force the humans to live in a village named after a demon, surrounded by plants that are toxic to most supernatural beings?"

Abhartack's cutting glare shoves the knife edge of guilt deeper. "The plant causes no harm to the humans. Therefore, I have no reason to stop it from growing around their borders. They are not prisoners and if they choose to rise up against supernatural creatures, I assure you the Vampir of Dökkbraek will not be their target."

I turn away, plucking a bloodthorn leaf from a vine as we pass under an arch made by the vine twining itself along branches in the canopy overhead. To be toxic, one must ingest the vine's sap. I let a drop fall from the leaf stem before tossing it aside. I wish I could do the same with my guilt. I should not have spent so much time indulging in all that Abhartack has to offer. I have blurred boundaries that I've never crossed before. Not even with Sean Winkle. I kept myself from him, but Abhartack... "Humans are not without their cruelty, so it's surprising that you allow them to have such an abundant weapon. All it would take is for one of them to rise against you."

He shrugs. "What's surprising to me is that you've heard of the Dearg Dua. What do you know of her?"

I scan the forest around us. "There isn't much to know about the Red Blood Sucker. She was a human whose father sold her to a chieftain who abused the girl. She then hardened her heart against all men and in the moment before she took her own life, she begged Death for a chance at revenge. Death did not answer, but a demon heard the girl's plea and upon the girl's last breath, the demon entered her body, using the girl's skin to trick the living while the demon went on to slaughter hundreds of men, as was the demon's nature."

The king slips his hand onto the small of my back. "No, mi Dauði, the demon killed *thousands*."

My head whips toward him. He smiles. "Some say she is the original of our kind but those who say that are wrong. Indeed, the Dearg Dua was a demon in human flesh. A demon who lost itself to the plight of the human whose flesh she wore. They each...ceased to be. Fused together into something new. A terror that came to be known as the Red Blood Sucker. Their first kill was the chieftain the girl had been sold to, then they murdered the father who sold her, and the brother who also played a role in the girl's fate. By the time that rightful vengeance was meted out, the Dearg Dua was consumed with bloodlust. Her need for revenge only heightened with each kill because together, the demon and the girl had become scorn. Wrath. Hatred. They slaughtered thousands of men, and for this, Odin himself hunted the Dearg Dua. On the day he chained and destroyed her, all creatures large and small rejoiced. Well, almost all."

A knot forms in my gut. "You speak as if you knew her. As if you do not approve of Odin's actions."

Abhartack's fingers flex, hand steering me onto a wider path as we encounter an intersection of trails. "I did not know the Dearg Dua and I did not agree with Odin's actions. The girl deserved sympathy, not death."

I raise a brow at the softness of this king who is rumored to be as vicious as the Vampir under his rule. "How do you know so much about her story? And do not tell me you read it on a rock."

He chuckles, his palm remaining firm on my back. "How I know the story is not as important as why I have told my people of the Dearg Dua many times." The path widens, opening to a skyline dotted with houses and buildings. A metropolis hidden in the forest of Dökkbraek. "When people are oppressed…when they are not allowed to live freely, tragedy will always be near. For the oppressor and the oppressed."

I train my eyes on a house that is not unlike those in some parts of Midgard. It has stone walls and a tiled roof, with a chimney on the side that expels a white smoke thick with the scent of roasting meats. Abhartack waves at a group of kids playing kickball in the field beside the house. "Now do you understand why I surround the humans with plants that can be lethal to those kinds who would seek to harm them? Why I call this place by a name the ancient rulers of the worlds understand means death? Why I spread stories of savagery and shroud my family in these dark lands where I'm able to keep out those who threaten the peace we've built here?"

I tune my senses to the air around us. Hear the sounds of the street markets scattered through the town's center. The laughter. The weight of peace sprawling across a land ruled by those who have never been looked upon as omens of peace, but as harbingers of chaos and death. I walk forward, looking across a patio that is surrounded by a low rock wall. Lanterns mimic the sun atop poles adorned with baskets of flowers that drape down the pole and along the edges of the patio where three women are sitting at a table, sipping cups of tea as if they have no cares weighing down their shoulders.

Each of them looks up, smiling and waving at the king. He lifts his hand in greeting, earning himself a flurry of batting lashes and blushing cheeks. Until their gazes land upon me. The women wipe the smiles from their faces and duck their heads, pretending not to stare as they each cut glances at me from the corners of their eyes. Irritation lances through me. I walk past them. "I can see why the Vampir are loyal to you, but how have you managed the feat of getting the humans to feel the same way? If not for compulsion, then how do you even have so many of them here? O'Dearg is not the small village you've represented it to be. And there are *children* here."

Abhartack paces ahead, motioning toward a street with a sign indicating a school can be found in that direction. "Many decades ago, there was no village. Only trees and frost. My Vampir hunted on the shores of Midgard, returning to me often, and expending a great deal of energy in the process. It is much easier to get out of Dökkbraek than in." He takes a breath, capturing my eyes with his before continuing. "During one of my few excursions into Midgard, Bishop came to me with an offer. He said the human authorities in Midgard were in crisis because their prisons were overcrowded. A problem the Vampir could remedy. So I agreed that the worst of the worst could be sent to Dökkbraek. The deal meant that Midgard would be free of those they wanted protection from and the Vampir would no longer have to make the journey into the human world for food. Our meals would be delivered to the doors of Draugrkeep."

I look at him in disbelief. "Instead of killing them, you kept them as pets and let them breed?"

His eyes harden. "No. I turned them loose and let my Vampir hunt them. Every. Last. One. Each time a shipment arrived, we held a hunt, tapping into our most violent of primal instincts until every human had been slaughtered. Then I found out that the deal your beloved Bishop struck with the few humans in Midgard who are allowed to know about us was much darker than even the Vampir could conceive of."

I shake off his sudden rise of anger. "Darker how?"

A low growl vibrates in his throat. "By the time Bishop struck the deal, the war was over and all kinds were bound by new treaties. Some kinds were no longer allowed to step foot inside Midgard, but I found out that those who like the taste of human flesh were all promised to be fed a steady supply of humans."

I shake my head. His eyes blaze. "It is true, Keela. While Dökkbraek is the home of my nest and I myself rarely leave its borders, I never agreed to any treaty that would force my people out of Midgard altogether. Bishop tried but I refused. Vampir have too many ties in Midgard and I want them to be free to explore any world they choose, so when Bishop came back with his offer to empty the human jails into Dökkbraek, I once again negotiated on behalf of my people. I would not allow Bishop to ban us from Midgard. We retained the right to have a presence there, but I agreed that our numbers in Midgard would remain low." Abhartack scans the houses around us. "At first, I thought it was a fair deal, considering our food was going to be delivered, and I stupidly thought Bishop was truly attempting to bring peace to the worlds. Especially Midgard, for which he is overseer."

"Bishop *is* a harbinger of peace," I defend. "The Vasilis cover for all supernaturals in Midgard and enforce the laws when it is necessary. Fair laws. Those approved by Od—

"No!" Abhartack's teeth gnash. "The deal he made with me was clear. The prisoners we received were to be those who had committed heinous crimes. Those the humans had already sentenced to death. *That* is why we hunted them for sport. Toyed with them. Made a *game* of killing them." A growl rumbles low in his chest. "But Bishop is a *liar*. Not all of the humans sent to us were deserving of death and as time went on, fewer and fewer were deserving of the fate he sentenced them to." Abhartack stalks forward. "Some had done no more than steal food."

I back away, my heart beginning to race. Because the only things ringing in Abhartack's voice are rage and truth. I shake my head violently. "Bishop would not be involved in such a thing."

The king stops short of me, pity shining in his eyes. "Wouldn't he? Because many he sent to me were innocent, Keela. Harmless. They were being trafficked for no other reason than being human. I know this because not long after the influx began, a gaunt young man arrived. I could almost *smell* the innocence on him. I questioned him and every other human sent to us after him. I used compulsion so they could not lie to me and began to judge for myself whether or not the humans sent to us for slaughter were deserving of their death sentences." He glances back toward the three human women on the patio. "With increasing frequency, most were not." He brings his eyes back to meet mine. "I allowed the innocent to live. And their survival is why I needed you to come here, mi Dauði. For you to see. And know for yourself what is true."

He motions to the houses around us. "I could never send the convicted back to Midgard but I *could* allow them to establish a village here. It wasn't long before couples formed and those families started having children. On rare occasions, some of their children grow up and decide to return to Midgard. In those cases, their memories of Dökkbraek are replaced and we set them up with new identities before dropping them in Midgard."

My head continues to shake of its own volition. Sadness claws out of the king and rakes against me. "We sometimes still receive prisoners, but you see now why I have spent these past decades convincing Bishop and everyone else that my horde is dwindling. Why I've tolerated letting everyone come to believe we are nothing but mindless beasts. Bishop has no idea what I've built here. He just got a taste of it, though, and it won't be long before he finds out just how important the Vampir are to the very survival of his precious Midgard."

My thoughts swirl. "You're raising a human army. To attack Midgard?"

Abhartack's smile does not reach his eyes. "My immediate plans have little to do with anything other than you, mi Dauði."

"Yet you call me your death?"

"I do, mi Fagr Dauði."

I flinch. He's now adding to the old language and calling me his *beautiful* death. And accusing Bishop, the defender of Midgard, of crimes against humanity. I back into a wall. Abhartack continues forward, body settling over mine, his hands pressing against the wall on either side of me. "Many centuries have come and gone in my lifetime, and throughout them all, I've never wished to use any terms of affection on anyone else. My silent chest has always been waiting for you, mi Fagr Dauði."

My muscles constrict, throat tightening. "And yet you accuse my family of heinous crimes, call me pet names, and try to get me to play dress-up so I'll look more like these human women who paint themselves like dolls and throw blushing glances at you over their teacups. It is not me you want. It is power."

He makes a soft, purring noise, fingers rubbing strands of my hair between them. "On the contrary. I have enough power that I do not need to covet yours, and I accept you for exactly what you are." His lips brush mine. "That is why you fight me, Keela. I am giving you what you want but you do not know how to be truly loved. But I am devoted to you, mi Dauði. That is why I instructed my family to open their arms to you the way I have opened mine." His hand trails down the wall, curling behind my waist and pulling me off the wall until I'm pressed tightly against him. "You are to be their queen. *My* queen. And I will not wait any longer to give you what Bishop has so blatantly kept from you."

14

Sean

My gut is still upside down and tucked firmly into my feet. I'll never get used to the rolling darkness of the portal. It's like being adrift in a violent sea, your body stretching and bending with the rise and fall of the turbulent waters. But at least I got to walk through this last one of my own free will. Relatively speaking. And now I know that playing nice and obeying orders doesn't make the motion sickness any less severe.

I press the heels of my hands into my eyes. "Are you okay?" Leah's voice is as soft as her touch on my arm. Both of those things individually more annoying than the motion sickness. The syrupy kindness is so unlike her it's enough to make me queasy all on its own, no portal needed. If my knees weren't so wobbly I'd get as far away from her as I could. "No," I snap at her, dropping my hands from my face and looking again into the brightness of the fog-shielded dawn we've portaled into. There's little to see of the land itself. The fog is too thick and the light too dim. The others seem to know where they're going, though. Rohan and

Jofir are ahead of us, followed by Gelby and Monique. Only Haldir is left to march along behind Leah and me. "In the future, I'd prefer another means of transportation. Where are we anyway? What is this place?"

She hitches her backpack higher on her shoulders. "We are in the land that protects the weavers of fate."

I swallow against the layer of foamy bile coating the back of my throat and focus my gaze as far ahead as possible. "Protects them via fog?"

She points to the east. "Protects them in many different ways. We can't see the mountains from here in the valley, but ranges to rival the best of what you've ever heard of in Midgard are there." She points west. "And there."

I scrub a tired hand over my face. "Let me guess, we have to climb both of those mountain ranges in order to see these Norns who are going to do God only knows what to me, while *no one* is out helping Keela?"

Gelby tosses a sharp-edged crystal into the air. It's similar to the ones they all took as communication crystals, but different in the way it's cut. Despite the layered blankets of fog floating around us, the stone catches enough light to come to life, casting a dizzying kaleidoscope of colors over us. A dizzying effect I don't need. I press a hand against my stomach and Gelby snorts as if he has eyes in the back of his head. "Don't get yourself separated from the group and you won't have to find out what protections the Norns have, Sean Winkle."

I narrow my eyes on the back of his head and ignore the way Leah is looking up at me. *Adoringly.* "Don't worry, it's *my* family who is responsible for you and that's why I'm here. I'll keep you safe, Sean."

I channel the grating irritation of her words and put all of my effort into begging the lazy thing inside of me to burn a hole into the back of Gelby's head. "Your crystals can be used to call outside of this realm, right? So maybe I'll have Leah call her dad and he can start looking for Keela since none of the rest of you seem capable of doing anything other than wasting time while you think of new, *useless* ways to torture me."

Haldir manages to accomplish what I can't. He blasts a stream of dragon fire straight into the back of my head. It curls over my ears and down my nape. Leah shouts and jumps away, drawing the attention of everyone in front of us. Monique's eyes fly wide, fear leaking from her pores with such a heavy force that I can...*smell* it.

"Knock it off!" Rohan booms from where he and Jofir lead the group across the valley floor. "We must tread lightly on the land of the Norns. If we wish for those who shape destiny to gift us an audience, we must prove ourselves worthy. Starting with being *respectful*."

At his side, Jofir straightens. "There will be enough to fight. We need not fight each other."

"Enough to fight?" I ask, but Rohan and Jofir turn away, continuing on. Gelby's eyes narrow on me before he marches after them. Monique races to Leah and tugs the still stunned she-wolf forward, hurrying after Gelby. Leah looks over her shoulder at me and I fall back, coming into step beside Haldir. I don't know which one of us she's scared of but the two of side by side should keep Leah away from me. Besides, Haldir's arms might be larger than my torso but the only way to stop a bully is to stand up to him. "You already know your fire won't singe a hair on my head, so instead of wasting your snot on me, how about you prove that you're not as much of a prisoner of the Vasilis as I am? If you're *equal* to them, leave. Go after the Keela on your own." I glare at his stone-chiseled profile. "We both know that's what you'd be doing if you really had a choice."

A muscle ticks in his jaw. "That would require me to give up my chance at being the one to scalp you, and judging from the look on Gelby's face, I'm already going to have to fight him for the honor."

The Dreki stomps forward and I let him go. Sometimes I think Hal and I are bonding, but I also thought Gelby was the nice Vasilis. However, the look he's had on his face today is the same one that's been carved on him since the Völva compound *incident*. He wants to kill me. They all do.

I stop walking, watching as Haldir disappears into a thickening fog. I could run, let myself purposefully get lost out here, but then what? If I could figure out how to use the power inside of me at will, I'd stand a chance against...whatever Jofir was talking about fighting. Maybe. And maybe it would even be possible to use my power to open portals on my own, but how would I even begin to learn something like that? I hurry forward. "You guys are terrible prison guards."

"Moths!" Rohan shouts from somewhere up ahead.

I look around me. Look up. There's nothing here but fog. And screams. Loud horrible screeching screams ripping through the air from all directions. "Sean!" Leah's voice is frantic. "Sean! Where are you?"

I spin in a circle. "I'm right here. Where are yo—" A sudden rush of air takes my breath away, giant brown wings painted with gold and pink bands swiping down through the fog with powerful beats. Claws dig into my shoulders. I yank away but the claws dig in deeper and there's a horrible tug, my body flinging backward, arms popping as the pack is ripped off my back. My feet leave the ground and another shock of air rushes down, stealing my breath as dusty wings beat down on both sides of me. My body goes weightless. I reach for the claws on my shoulders, looking up at the underside of a massive body that looks a heck of a lot like a moth. A giant one.

"Leah?" I shout, warm blood trickling over my arms from where the moth's claws are digging into me, down through muscle and tendons. The abomination is carrying me away. "Gelby! Hal!" I shout into the air, the thick fog lifting, swept away with each beat of the bug's wings. From each wingbeat of the other moths fluttering in the sky around me. There are dozens of them.

Shouting erupts below me. I jerk my head, whipping it to the left where a flash of blue magic forms a dome. Underneath it, Rohan and Gelby stand with their hands and arms covered in crackling blue vines. They're creating a shield. But the moths aren't attacking them. They're swarming around me. I swing my legs back and forth, trying to kick them. Trying to wrench myself from the grip of the one flying off with me. "Help me!" I shout at the Vasilis. Rohan's eyes narrow and Gelby's jaw clenches tight, but neither of them do anything. They only care about protecting themselves. And Jofir, who stands behind Rohan, hand on her longsword and face pinched, making no effort to actually use that weapon. I whip my head to Monique. She's standing away from them but still underneath their sizzling blue shield, watching in horrified shock as I get carried higher and higher. Too high to survive should I fall now.

I reach for the moth's feathery leg but a growl breaks open underneath me and I swing back in time to catch sight of a fur-covered dart shooting up through the swarm of screeching moths. Pain slices through my calf, skin and muscle ripping as Leah's teeth sink into my leg. The moth swoops back toward the earth, the weight of the dangling wolf now anchored in my leg dragging it down. A cacophony of shrill, high-pitched sirens split the air. I throw my hands over my ears and Leah's wolf whimpers and whines. Below us, the Álfar and Monique fall to their knees, covering their ears against the splitting sirens of the swarming moths. Ahead of me, a shattered dragon falls from the sky. Air sweeps by me in another suffocating rush as the moth carrying me flaps its massive wings. Once. Twice. Rising again with every breathtaking beat until the fog closes underneath us, hiding away everything save for those mountains Leah said were here. Above the fog, I can see their peaks. And below me, I can see Leah, covered in blood. Mine, from where her teeth are clamped down against the bone in my leg, and her own, from where her canine ears are ruptured. I reach for her but she's too low on my leg. I can't get to her and even if I could, she's a wolf ten times the size of what a wolf should be. If she shifts back to human form, I could hold her weight against me...but I'd have to be able to reach her, and we'd have to time the shift just right. Too right to risk.

The moths fall silent, picking up speed. I wince, Leah's weight tugging her teeth down through what's left of my calf muscle, her paws dangling and twirling. Her watery eyes blink. Slow and final, an apology in their depths as her grip eases. "No!" I shout, chest tight. We're too far up. If she lets go... "No, Leah! Hold on. Whatever you do, do *not* let go of me."

I suck in a gulp of air, reaching for the thin, feathery legs of the moth but in my split second of shock, the giant creature lifted too far away, my fingers clutching nothing but air. The moth let go. Is soaring higher, letting me fall. *Us* fall. Leah's jaws unlocked from my leg the instant the moth let go of me. I look down, fresh blood spurting from my leg as I plummet, my body chasing her heavier form as we plunge toward a field of tall grass. She disappears into it, a thick wet splat rising up to meet me. A girlish scream rips from my lungs, my own body breaking through the sharp blades. It's death by a thousand cuts, slices blooming bright red across every exposed inch of skin while thick reedy shafts gouge and pierce.

I slam into marshy ground, head plowing through muck. Mud rushes into my mouth and I drag a lungful of it into my chest, spewing it right back up, sputtering and coughing as I push myself away from the muck, only to sink farther into the glob of mushy, watery ground. My hands sink, arms disappearing up to my elbows. My knees bury and my feet suction into ground that is trying to swallow me whole. I fight it, cranking my neck side to side, spitting muck from my clogged throat. "Leah?"

She doesn't answer. I work my fingers through the mud, moving up and toward a clump of grass, trying to force my heart rate to calm. Thrashing would only make me sink deeper but Leah's wolf form is heavier than me. If she didn't shift before she hit the marsh, she's already deeper. Already drowning. I don't have to like her to want to keep her from dying.

My fingers bump against the ball of grass roots and I dig into them, using the firmer soil around the plants to pull myself forward, dragging my body toward the firmer earth, straining with the effort of plucking each limb from the thick slush of muddy earth. I breathe in through my mouth and flare my clogged nostrils wide, forcefully exhaling as I scan the reedy, watery marsh. I don't see anything but mud and grass. And something dark, splotched with light brown fur, covered in mud and draped over a decimated clump of reeds.

"Leah." I spit her name out with a glob of muddy mucus, trying to clear my airways as I pull myself closer to the mound of mud and fur. I plant my feet as close to the nearest grass clump as possible, rising from the marsh like a creature made of the very sludge that clings to every inch of me. It's thick and heavy but I force my feet forward, shoving them into the base of the next clump and lurching forward, clinging to reeds, grass, roots, tugging and sinking, and forcing stuck limbs to break free. "Hold on, Leah. I'm coming."

Exhausted, I clear everything that's between us and reach where her limp tail flops against her haunch. This one little part of her is all that's above ground. "I'm here, Leah." I run my hand up her leg and down into the mud, clutching around the top of it where her hip meets her torso. I pull but the mud is too slick and suctioned around her. Tears blur my vision and for once, the beast within me answers my plea, rising up. Pacing. *Waiting*. I dig my muddy fingers back into the marsh and lean over Leah, wrapping my arm around her body. I grit my teeth. *Help me.*

I pull again and that *thing* inside of me bleeds into my veins, lending me its strength. With a sucking pop, Leah's wolf breaks free, her body beginning to rise from the marsh. I lean back and tug until her hips are behind me, one front paw peeking from the muddy depths. I reach forward and grab it, sliding my other arm down into the muck along her neck. "Come on, Leah." I tug her toward me, the thick mud sucking and clinging, but releasing her body to me. Her head slips above the muck and I drag her backward, draping her neck over my thigh. I tilt her snout down and try to pry her jaws open, slapping her back. I'm not sure what the protocol is here, or if anyone has ever tried to give mouth-to-mouth to a giant wolf, but I can feel the faint beat of her heart against my thigh so I'll do whatever it takes. "Come on, Leah. You can survive this."

Anger courses through me. If Leah dies, her death is on the Vasilis. They locked me up, tortured me, took away all my rights and freedoms, and crushed every dream I ever had. If I'd died today, it would have served them right. But other than Collin, no one would have cared. Leah… Despite her arrogance, her death will leave a trail of heartache in its wake.

My teeth grind. They don't get to do this. The Vasilis don't get to hurt anyone else. A sizzling streak of yellow-white light breaks from my hand, slamming against the center of Leah's fur-covered chest. Her body convulses, jaws hinging open and her tongue lolling out, gray and dull with mud. I freeze. Leah shimmers, features melting from wolf to woman, the heaviness of her body across my thigh lightening until there's nothing but the weight of female against me. Her eyes flutter open. Meet mine. I don't dare move, let alone breathe. Leah pitches to the side, vomiting, a slurry of muddy water erupting from her mouth. I stare at my hand. The beast inside of me grumbles. I can't hear it but I can feel its…discontent. It tenses, coiling itself into a tight ball, and disappears into my depths.

Leah turns back to me, resting her head in my lap. Mud clings to her thick lashes. "You saved me."

I stop myself from wiping the mud off her face. After what just happened, I probably shouldn't touch her again. "Barely, so let's not do this again."

She jerks upright, nearly crashing into my head. "Your leg!"

She slides down into the mud I just pulled her out of, trying to get to where she can look at my leg. I grab her shirt and pull her back, trying not to have any skin contact. "I'm fine. It doesn't hurt. We just need to figure out how to get to dry ground."

Underneath the mud, her face contorts. "Your leg doesn't hurt?"

I look away from her. I'm weirded out by what's happening more than anyone else, and I don't want to explain all of this to yet another person. "Since you seem to be moving around just fine, do you think you can climb onto my shoulders?" She has pants on, so I won't have to touch her skin. If that matters at all. Maybe I only...shock her when she has fur. "I'll raise you up so you can see over the grass and figure out which way we need to go."

She lunges and trails a hand over my muddy leg, slipping her way around me and pulling handfuls of mud from the marsh. "You're not bleeding, Sean. You should—"

I grab her wrists. "We need to get out of this mud. After seeing those giant moths, I don't want to stay here and figure out what hungry things are in this marsh. Understand?"

Her mouth opens and then closes, eyes scanning as if she's just now noticing what we're trapped in. She makes a worthless attempt at cleaning the mud from her face and motions for me to turn so she can climb onto my shoulders. "Legend says there's a great bog where the Norns send those who are unworthy. Where the unworthy don't decay. They *melt*, slowly becoming part of the bog itself."

My stomach rolls and the mud still clinging to my lips suddenly feels heavier. Thicker. More disgusting. "This isn't a bog. It's a marsh."

Her legs stretch over my shoulders. "Same thing."

I reach back and cup my palms over her muddy thighs to stabilize her. "No, it isn't. Marshes have grass and soil, bogs have clay and a lot of dead and dying things."

She curls her fingers into my hair as I get my feet, sending mud sliding down my face. "Like I said, Sean, it's the same thing."

I tuck against the reeds, trying to be as stable as possible for her as I reach my full height. "Like *I* said, they're entirely different. Can you see anything?"

Her breath hitches. "Yeah. Way over there." One of her hands lifts from my hair and points at a six o'clock angle. "Sean?"

"Yeah?"

"Run!"

15

Keela

Abhartack's throne is carved from the darkest obsidian. Sleek and elegantly sculpted, just like the man himself. I've explored all of his sophisticated angles, unwilling to push him away. Unwilling to leave. Forasmuch as I feel lost in this world, I feel at home in Dökkbraek. Content with my king. He takes my hand, lifting it to his mouth as we leisurely stroll toward the dais where Kythos, one of Abhartack's most trusted advisors, is finishing the last polishing strokes on the new matching throne now sitting beside the king's. I cannot stand the thought of sitting upon it, yet I raise no objection as Abhartack leads me toward what he intends to be mine. I'm too overwhelmed by the unexpected pang of loss tearing through me. Staying in Dökkbraek is madness.

My heart begins to pound, sharp and wild. I am no queen. I am death. *Dauði.* Abhartack's beautiful death. The amulet cushioned in the hollow of my throat grows warm. I lift a hand to stroke it, the king's lips brushing my cheek as we ascend the dais stairs. "You must learn to control yourself, Keela. Else you will force me to show you what little control *I* have when hearing your remarkable heart do remarkable things."

I turn with him, facing the endless rows of Vampir. There are no humans in attendance tonight. Only the horde, gathered together, inside the windowless heart of Draugrkeep. The dining hall is underneath us and it is there that many of the humans wait. I can only wonder if their heads are bowed as their Vampir brethren's are now. "What can you expect of Death's heart when she is surrounded by so many choice delicacies?" My voice purrs, unfamiliar to my own ears, and...right. As if the sound itself is the only true part of me to be found. "You have firsthand experience with my insatiable appetite."

Abhartack's hand crushes mine and my heart thuds to a stop. We are rarely gentle with one another and I *like* it. The force. The taking. The claiming of what we want without the need to compel the other into submission as we bite and claw, writhe and heal, tongues lapping and fangs piercing as the other bleeds underneath us. "Patience, mi Dauði. This is a rare day. One in which I am allowing you to feed on another."

I meet his penetrating stare but he turns away, greeting his horde. "Gott kvöld."

As one, the Vampir lift their heads and slam their closed fists against their chests. "Hraesvelgr."

The king reclines against his throne, pulling me down to sit on mine as he does, his hand still dutifully and firmly wrapped around mine. I slide onto the smooth, polished stone of my throne, raking my eyes over the Vampir who stand before us like statues. Silent and fierce. I meet their eyes, soaking up the blanket of excitement overlaying their every other emotion. Their king begins to speak, and I seek out a space devoid of light. One where the shadows might form the silhouette of the one person I desire more than Abhartack. The one person who might draw me out of this appeasing, appealing stupor.

"As all of you know"—the king's voice drones over the crowd—"when I give my word, it is a true word. I told you that Keela would be everything we hoped for. And more." He lifts our joined hands and I turn to him. He smiles. "Therefore, it is time for me to keep other promises. Ones I have made directly to her." He looks away, nodding to Kythos. "Bring him in."

The doors to the throne room open and my nostrils flare. Abhartack's chuckle reverberates through the room. "That is right, mi Fagr Dauði, Arsenious is here. And as I promised, the Fae bounty will now be permanently removed from your head."

I slide to the edge of my throne. Abhartack's hand clenches tight. "Not yet. I will give you the honor of being the one to kill him, but before you use his head as your own personal goblet, you will do me the honor of allowing me to be kingly. I wish to make a speech, and to savor the warmth of his shock before you end the miserable life of the Unseelie scum."

Now I understand the excited anticipation of the Vampir. Arsenious is here, and because of that, they will finally get to see for themselves exactly what Keela Vasilis is capable of. I train my eyes on the double doors at the back of the room. I do not care if Abhartack has designed this killing to be a spectacle. If it is a show the king wants, I will give him one.

The doors open and Arsenious struts in, trailed by a convoy of Fae. Not all of them Unseelie. I recognize Zyra, a Seelie Fae who was friendly with Aether, but it is not the fear in her eyes at the sight of me on this throne that holds my attention, it is the arrogance in the soon-to-be-sightless eyes of Arsenious.

The Fae king storms up the center of the room, his powerful posse behind him as the Vampir stand as if they are nothing more than statues carved from the mountain to adorn Draugrkeep. Arsenious comes to a stop at the base of the dais, sleeves of his gold tunic riding up his forearms as he thrusts a hand toward me, hatred searing from his eyes to meet that which is emitting from my own. He scowls at the king. "It took you long enough to contain her. Now remove your wards and allow me to portal us from here. It will be easier and more rewarding to take the abomination straight from the throne where it sits as if it is something special." A cruel laugh bites out of him. "By the time I am done with you, Keela Vasilis, not even the heart in your chest will be recognizable."

Abhartack makes a show of bringing my hand to his mouth again. "Those are harsh words. For a dead man."

Arsenios whips his focus to the king, a pale glow building around his hands. Fae magic. "You dare betray me?"

Abhartack lifts one finger from my hand. Then another. On the third, his horde attacks, descending upon the Fae convoy in a blur of motion that leaves the Fae dead before I even rise from my throne. All of them save for one.

Abhartack rises to stand beside me as his horde feasts on the powerful blood of Fae who never stood a chance against the fast strike of the Vampir. Arsenious's hands shake, his pale glow wobbling and dimming as he realizes his fate will be the same as theirs. In Abhartack's dark court, there is no mercy. The king's voice rises above the din of lapping tongues and ripping flesh, his Vampir continuing their feast as he passes final judgment. "Arsenious, king of the Fae, it is without a single burden of conscience that I break the alliance we forged. I only agreed to it because we both wanted this amazing, remarkable creature." Abhartack wraps an arm around my waist. "For different reasons, obviously. But not to worry, your death will serve a great many purposes. Chief among them, sustenance for my *very* hungry queen."

"Queen?" Arsenious spits, reclaiming his cowardly magic.

I snuff out his glow, calling the shadows to me. They gather from every corner of the room. From every space in between, blotting out every trace of light. Abhartack's hand tightens on my hip, a mocking laugh on his lips. "Yes, queen. Though you may prefer to call her Death."

Arsenious stumbles away from the dais, not bothering with magic he already knows will do him no good. "You won't get away with this!"

I stand as still as the other Vampir were earlier, the king's dark chuckle reverberating through the room. "Betrayal has consequences, Arsenious. I am fully prepared to face mine. The question is, *are you*?" The king's hand drops away from me. "Mi Dauði, be sure that we can send his body back to Faerie in the same condition in which those acting on his orders delivered his son's, because you have been right all along. Arsenious killed Aether."

A roar more demonic than Vampir retches from my throat, carried through the room by shadows given form. Sound. They screech, slinging themselves forward like beasts of ink, sucking and slapping as they draw their feet off the floor and stomp them back down again, rattling the stone, nothing less than the sounds of Hel's darkest pits screaming from their melting mouths to fill the whole of Draugrkeep.

Arsenious spins. Runs. Bounces off chests of Vampir who shove him back to the center of the room, their own jaws tense and hands trembling as my shadows march between them, under them, *over* them.

My shadows own the walls. The ceilings. The floors. There is no escape. Not after my king confirmed what I knew to be true from the moment I heard of Aether's demise. I stalk from the dais, shadows forming a living wall around a terrified Arsenious. He summons a feeble thread of his magic but I flick my wrist, turning the shadows into blades. They stab into him, jutting out of the Fae king in every direction. His eyes fly wide, blood dripping from his chin, mouth choked open by the sharp edge of a shadow piercing through him from smile to nape. I stare into those terrified eyes, pulling my shadows away so his body can begin to heal as I move closer. "Don't hold still, Arsenious. I intend to enjoy this."

I strike, reveling in the crunch of his bones and the taste of his blood in my throat. The shadows descend, swallowing me whole as I feed and shred, losing myself to the bloodlust and rage until there is nothing left of Arsenious but ribbons of skin flayed over bits of bone. It was fast. Too fast. And all-consuming.

The shadows dissipate. I stare at what I've done. Vampir do not eat flesh. We rend and tear, but it is only the blood we drink. But…I…I consumed *all* of Arsenious. Every morsel of the Fae king's body save for his skin and those fragments of bone. There's still bits of his flesh on my hands and his blood is soaked into my clothes. Abhartack approaches me, circling, his finger swiping through the blood covering my face. He places the bloody appendage in his mouth, wiping it over his tongue in a way that has my body wanting to crawl onto his. Shadows swim in his eyes and under his skin, a wide smile crossing his face as he looks down upon the pile of bones, seeing what his Vampir are seeing. Where there should be a husk, there is only skin.

"Bow to your queen!" His voice booms through the silent room. The Vampir hit their knees, fists pounding against their chests. Abhartack mimics their motion, getting on his knees before me. "Today, Faerie lost a king, and Dökkbraek gained a sovereign goddess of death." His fist pounds against his chest, the Vampir matching his tone, chanting, "Queen! Queen! Queen!" in time with the continuous beat of their fists. I shudder. Abhartack regains his feet, the sound of the horde continuing to rise, drumming against my ears as their chant becomes faster, their pounding harder. The king's hand fists into my matted hair, fangs extending, his beaten chest heaving with excitement. Desire. "Tell me, my remarkable queen, are you familiar with the human concept of a honeymoon?"

"For you," I whisper into the haze of blood-red twilight dancing outside my tower window, the hinged glass open so my words may be carried to Valhǫll, where Aether's soul must be resting. The Unseelie have a reputation of ill-repute, but I know Aether's true nature as well as I know my own. If Valhǫll is truly a place for valiant-hearted slain warriors, then that great hall is where Aether now resides.

I trace a line across my palm, my nail leaving a smooth cut. I flex, pooling the blood in my palm and reaching it out the open window, beyond the stone walls of Draugrkeep's highest tower. I turn my palm over, letting my blood spill to the ground far below. An offering. An apology. Traces of Aether's murderer now forever bound within me—the judge, jury, and executioner. "I will never forget." I bow my head and will my shadows to carry these words and the scent of Arsenious's death all the way to Valhǫll. To Aether. Letting my friend know that I have avenged him.

I pull my already healed palm back inside the tower and stare at the rapidly fading scar. *Friend.* While Aether lived, I never acknowledged how deeply I appreciated him. How glad I was that he was not under my thrall yet still enjoyed the fruits of our friendship without hesitation. Without strings. I was closer to him than I ever admitted to myself and now I have slaughtered his father. Brutally. I do not know if Aether will see the blood on my hands as what I meant for the killing to be. A way to honor a friend. Even if he doesn't, I do not regret killing Arsenious. I *enjoyed* killing him, and I fear that enjoyment will keep me from entering Valhǫll. If not the enjoyment, then the manner.

I look back up to the sky. Me getting into Valhǫll with the other Vasilis was only ever wishful thinking. Silly ramblings of the young. Back when my brothers still tried to convince me that I was not so different from other Vampir. They were wrong. As Abhartack is wrong now. I am not a queen. I climb onto the window ledge and jump down to the ground where my blood is still smeared atop the frost. A breeze kicks up, whipping my hair against my face, a frenzy of a scent that is not my own beating against my cheeks and into my lungs. I inhale deeply, dragging Sean Winkle down into my lungs. Letting his mouthwatering aroma fill every crevice inside of me. What a perfect day to escape Dökkbraek. Sean Winkle is here, and from the thick smell of him in the air, he is close.

16

Abhartack

Despite my unnatural stillness, Keela could still see me standing here in the shade of my forest if she wanted to. If she wasn't so distracted. I watch my unmated queen crouch on the ground outside my tower, second-guessing my decision to delay telling her the truth about what she is. I needed more time. *We* needed more time. I could not put off the Fae reckoning any longer, though, and that has led to her manifesting power I still am not fully prepared to divulge the truth of. It may be selfish of me, but no worse than the treachery of the gem planted into the collar I placed around her glorious throat.

My fangs extend, throbbing with the memory of how it feels to feed from that throat. But it's my lips, tingling with the memory of how it felt to kiss that throat centuries ago, when we were both human, that is most captivating. For me, those memories are as fresh as those from this morning, when Keela sat atop me, unaware of how many times we found ourselves in that same position underneath a star-bright sky in one of Midgard's most distant countrysides.

I close my eyes to savor the memories I have of her, both new and old. With that gem at her throat, she will remain in Dökkbraek, where I am strongest, and where the blasted void I've been sworn to protect is finally delivering on its promise to give me my mate. All that remains is to win Keela's heart, so I can drain every last drop of blood from her body.

The air shifts and I snap my eyes open. My queen is on the move. Heading straight for the chasm beyond the castle. Wind lifts from its depths and I begin to run. "Keela!" I shout after her. She doesn't break her stride. "No!" I force my voice to boom over the landscape that is tied to my soul. For Keela's sake, and to rebuke the void. It cannot have her. "Do not believe them! Whatever the void is telling you, it's a lie!"

Her speed increases, the void's edge growing closer. My queen does not even realize how fast she's moving. How being so close to the void amplifies her innate power. Her mind is no doubt clouded with thoughts of the Fae she sought retribution for today. His father whose death happened in a way unnatural to the Vampir, but wholly natural to Keela's nature. She just doesn't know that yet. And might never know, all because of my stupid decision to place that gem around her neck.

I push my legs as hard as they can go, drawing on the power of the almighty chasm that is encased upon my own throat. My voice morphs into the thunder of a thousand storms as I throw all the force of my compulsion into this one final command. "Stop!" If she doesn't, she will die. Whatever Keela is hearing or thinking, that chasm is no ordinary hole in the ground. It is *the* Primordial Void, hidden in plain sight, and guarded by the master of Draugrkeep.

Her foot hits the edge and she leaps. I do the same, one hand skimming her shoulder. I dig in with everything I have, extending further, stretching my fingers over the curve of her shoulder and clamping down as I throw my body against the rocky side of the chasm. The jagged stone slices my palm but I dig my nails into the craggy surface, slamming to a jolting halt, the weight of Keela's dangling body threatening to rip my nails from their beds. I grind my teeth, clinging harder as I set my feet against the face of the cliff. Keela looks up at me, wide-eyed and wild. My chest heaves. "Climb!"

Her head jerks, threads of her shirt ripping, setting my already strained muscles on fire. "Climb, Keela! You cannot survive this fall. It is the void. The *Primordial Void*."

Relief settles on my shoulders as she scrabbles for purchase along the jagged edges of the sharp rock, each of her movements causing the unforgiving face of the cliff to slice through my clothing and into my skin. Still, I do not let go. *Will* not let go. "CLIMB!" I order her again, using every bit of magic gifted to me by the void. The void that *created* Keela's kind. Retaliation against the gods. But she no longer belongs to the whims of gods and voids. She belongs to *me*.

"Keep moving," I order as she tucks her feet against the wall and reaches high overhead, angling for the lip of a protruding knife edge of stone. She pushes herself up, bloody and scraped, some of her weight transferring to the will of the stone instead of my strained muscles. Still, I do not let go.

She finds her next grip on the wall and pulls herself up, legs following, and feet tucking against the last handholds. Inch by inch, my queen moves up the side of the chasm. "Good, mi Dauði. Keep climbing. Come to your king."

She hesitates, the desperation in her eyes matching my own. "Please," I whisper, still clinging one-handed to the frayed fabric of her shirt. "You live, or we both die." She looks down into the endless depths of the abyss, a shudder moving through her before she pushes up once more, reaching and tugging, pulling and pushing, until she's at my side. I release my grip on her shirt. "Keep climbing."

She does as instructed and I follow her up the cliff face until we both throw ourselves back onto the patch of frozen, solid ground that stretches around the rim. I flop onto my back, looking up at the sky turned crimson by the void, a reminder of my pledge to look over this land. To bring my Vampir here and groom them into a force beholden only to the protection of the void itself. I promised that I would not bow to anyone, even the gods themselves. And that I would be the disrupter of balanced power whenever the void demanded it.

I turn my attention to Keela. She's kneeling, looking down into the chasm. "I wondered how long it would take you to hear them."

She reclines back on her heels, staring between me and the void. "Hear who?"

I lift onto my elbows. Without the gem I placed on her throat, I wonder if she would have been susceptible to them. She is a part of the void, after all. "Those things that live within the void do not bother the others, but they relentlessly call out to me." I glance at her necklace. "I had a hunch they would begin to speak to you also."

Her brows furrow. "The Primordial Void is a yawning chasm that gave birth to the cosmos itself. No one knows its location. Or if the old stories about its existence are even true."

I sit up and toss a loose stone into the chasm. "There are few who know the truth. About the void, and about how it created this place,

Dökkbraek, specifically to be the balance between life and death." I glance at her. "Most of the Vampir do not know that the great chasm running alongside Draugrkeep is the very same void where fire and ice first met, giving birth to the gods themselves, among other things. All anyone knows is that I forbid them to come near this mighty ditch."

The rock I just threw in shoots up from the darkness like a bullet, digging a chunk out of the frozen ground where it collides with soil and root. She scoots back another foot from the edge, voice thin and low. "What does it say to you?"

I frown at the rock. I'm restricted from saying too much, but Keela now wears the void around her neck, the same as me. "Mostly, the void likes to constantly remind me that it is powerful. That along its edge, being and nothingness first danced."

She looks over her shoulder, toward where Draugrkeep rises high overhead. "Did you build the castle?"

My hand floats to the warm gem at my throat. "No. I have always been powerful, but when I arrived here, inside the boundaries of the land sworn to keep watch over the birthplace of us all, I became more so. The castle was cold and empty back then, but I found that I liked the way I felt here so I claimed Draugrkeep for myself. Not long after that, I realized the influx of power was ultimately coming from this void, not the castle."

Her face pinches. "How could you determine that?"

I drop my hand and slide closer to her. "As I said, I felt the power of the void almost immediately. Once I figured out that my...*changes* were because of it, I spent my unlimited immortal time studying its very essence. I found that it is an unending veil of darkness. A place to commune for ancient spirits who are stitched from chaos itself. Between them, they are the darkest of voids and brightest of lights. The vilest of evil and purest of virtue. The wisest and most foolish. Unorganized and organized. They are compliments and opposites, selfless and selfish, and they only told me their secrets because they did not expect me to live long enough to share them with anyone else." I cup her jaw. "But when I jumped into the void, they made the mistake of showing me *you*. So I found a way to traverse the depths. To bargain and plead. And that is where I learned to read the runestones, mi Dauði. In the pit of the cosmos, where visions of a dark queen undid me."

She leans into my kiss, her mouth covering mine with the unbridled desire I've come to love. A groan escapes my throat and I pull her close, hunger rising as she trails a finger along my throat, her sharp nail pressing into my jugular. I smile against her lips as she climbs onto my lap and pushes me back against the hard ground, my body responding with matching desire. I tighten my hands on her grinding hips. She rips them off and pins them above my head. I growl. "My heart may be still as death, mi Dauði, but every time you surprise me, my chest is a swirling vortex. Full of shadows and darkness, all howling for their queen."

She leans forward. "Good. Because I am familiar with the human concept of a honeymoon, and I won't be doing anything close to that with you." She strikes a sharp nail across my throat, slicing me open. Not deep enough to kill me, but close. I close my hands over my gaping neck, drowning on blood and unable to get to my feet as Keela stands over me. She presses her fist to her chest. "Be well, my king."

I yell, the sound buried in blood. My dark queen jumps into the void.

Chaos. No matter how many centuries I live, I will never understand that *thing* which binds the cosmos. How it drew me to it. *Deceived* me. Then gave me leave to survive my desperate leap into its very center. The last time I was inside the Primordial Void, it popped and hissed, echoing and clanging from every direction as I fell, my body contorting into unnatural angles as I plunged deeper into its raw energy. It meant to kill me. To *absorb* me. Taunting me with images of what my life could have been, flashing them in bloody, broken pieces as I dissolved into the nothingness around me.

I could not fight back then any more than I can now. My Vampir body and strength are no match for these things that create and destroy, and the magic I possess was given to me by them. The void whispered to me across oceans, telling me where I could find the gem at my throat. Once it was around my neck, I belonged to the void. Chosen not because I would be its best defender, but because I had destroyed that which it created. The void laid the trap, gave me jewels and a castle, and then drove me mad enough to think I could rip it apart. But the void cannot be destroyed.

The symphony of guttural murmurs and high-pitched squeals gets louder as I fall through the emptiness inside the chasm. A pit of nothing filled to the brim with *everything*. It pulls, tugs, scratches, and breaks...tossing me to and fro—the same as it did all those many centuries ago when it first painted Keela's face against my eyes. *She was to be yours,* the noises had seemed to say, their cacophony coming together in a blend of screeching whispers. They showed me who she was. Who she had been. And I begged them for her. They laughed. Then they plied me with sights and sounds. Secrets. Knowledge so ancient even the oldest supernaturals have forgotten it. They deciphered the runestones placed around the void. As warnings. Histories of the histories, and the truth of what will come to pass when we all fail to stave off Ragnarök.

Back then, I *begged* the void for life. Told Chaos that I would do anything. *Give* anything. Save for the soul of the one who was supposed to be mine. Keela was my reason to survive, and I begged them to give me the chance to feel her mortal heart beating within the chest of the demon who now wore her skin. The demon who changed me. The Lilitu who created the first Vampir. Until the void, I had not known that the two were united. By the time I recovered from my change and dealt with the shame of my bloodlust, Odin had already destroyed the Dearg Dua. Or so everyone thought.

I endure the familiar pain of the void and look beyond those visions it wants me to see. Will myself to hear beyond what it wishes me to hear. "Where is she?" I shout. "You said she was mine, so give her to me!"

The hums and clicks fall silent, echoes retreating until I'm free falling through an empty drum. "Please," I beg. "Do not take her. I have kept my promises to you, so you must keep yours. She did not know...I did not... Please. I built you an army so now give me my queen!"

A distant howl begins to reverberate in the darkness around me, growing louder. Closer. Building like the roar of a devastating tornado ripping apart the chasm itself. I brace for the impact, but none comes. The void only shows me our bargain. Their amulet gave me the power to control the shadows within myself. To use them as the Dearg Dua commands all other shadows. And my promises inside the void gave me the freedom to keep all of what Chaos had shown me, and to use that knowledge to shape the future, even when that future demanded that I wait to be united with Keela. For that is the one thing the void would not reveal. Her location. I searched, but could not find her. When Bishop took her to Midgard, I suddenly felt her. But by then, it was too late. I told myself our lost years were only drops in the bucket of the eternity we would spend together, but I did not plan on the Dearg Dua jumping into the void.

A tear streaks down my broken cheek, the bones in my body already beginning to crush under the pressure of the void. "Please," I whimper. "Do not destroy her. Take me, but save the girl."

My words disappear into nothing, the void's onslaught of visions ripping out my soul. From the first moment I saw her on the shore of that golden Isle, Keela has been my queen. *United in life and death.* Wind carried on the tip of a million little shadow-stiff daggers slams into me, howling, roaring, *screeching* as it pierces through me. I slam into the rough-hewn side of the chasm, mouth gasping open. The slicing wind rushes down my throat and up my nose. Visions paint against the inside of my bulging eyes, images flipping faster than I can comprehend, my body swelling, ready to explode. Chaos may have given life to the cosmos, but it is cruel. It only gives so it can have the satisfaction of taking away.

17

"Keela." I place my palm as gently as possible against her bloody chest, scanning the unnatural twist to her arm and the splintered leg. My queen's clothing and face are shredded, and her hands... I look away from the exposed bone. The chasm flayed skin from her bones but Keela's heart still beats. Barely. Yet another deceitful answer to my pleas, the void's way of reminding me that *it* is what gives and takes away. Not the gods it spat out. They may take credit for creation but the void created *them*.

I scan the desolate terrain of the rugged mountainside the great and powerful chasm has decided to toss us out upon. We're not in Dökkbraek anymore. Another cruel twist to my answered plea. Away from my home and castle, my power will wane, ebbing until it vanishes altogether. This is why the void destroyed my queen so thoroughly. In her current condition, she cannot be moved, let alone pulled through the veils between worlds. If I place her inside of a portal, she will die.

My fangs extend. No matter her condition or what is destined to become of me in the end, I am grateful her life was spared. She will heal, and afterward, I will not spend a single moment of my cursed eternity forgetting what the Primordial Void did to her. To *us*. I will never forget how she looks now, and how this mutilation is only because the void decided to call her to it. Otherwise, she would not have jumped, and I would not now be forced to once again take away her choices. I rip into my wrist. Without my blood, Keela will die. I pry her mouth open and press my wound to her lips. "Drink, mi Fagr Dauði. *Drink*."

My blood pools in her mouth, the cut on my wrist healing too quickly. I gnash it open again, deeper this time, fisting my hand to pump the blood from my veins into her. It spills over her lips. Her throat doesn't work, not even to gag. Her pulse dulls to a stop and I gently press a kiss to her bloody cheek. "Forgive me, mi Dauði." Without another thought, I shove my fingers into her throat and work it open, reclining her forward as I force my blood into her body. The pooling liquid begins to gurgle down into the hollows and I call upon my shadows. They spill from my hand and create a funnel in her throat, bracing it open as I rip through my own flesh, draining myself into her mouth. This isn't how I wanted to bond her to me, but she cannot die, and this is the only way in which I can save her. The cruel, vicious void has shown me our fate. In sorrow, life, and death, all we have ever had is the hope of each other. Of love.

Tears burn my eyes, words I have longed to say spilling over my lips. "Since we first danced under the moon on the summer solstice, I have loved you. I loved you when we were both human and weak. And I love you in the strength of our death. I take you, Keela, my human love and my Lilitu, to be my mate, bonded by our blood, for *all* eternity." I freshen the gash on my wrist and press a kiss to her neck, eyes slipping shut as my fangs sink into her neck. By the time the thunder of the distant storm reaches us, she will be mine, and I will be hers.

———

Sean

Leah's body convulses with shivers that have nothing to do with the temperature. The chest-deep water we're soaking in is warm and the blanket of muggy, humid air hanging over the swamp has sweat coming out of places I didn't even know I had pores. I stretch a comforting arm around Leah, barely moving my lips and keeping my voice low. "Try to be still."

Her wide eyes dart over the reeds and gently swaying grasses that surround this pool of hell we've found ourselves stuck in. "Where is it?"

"Shh." I pull her closer into my side. When she first told me to run, I had no idea why. Then a massive, greenish-gray snout poked through a patch of tall grass, a bright yellow slash of puckered skin cutting across it as if something raked a claw across the crocodile's face. Something bigger than the car-sized crocodile. Like a Dreki. An attack the oversized crocodile lived through. So we ran, that jagged, tooth-lined snout pushing through reeds and grass, snapping at us from all angles. Over and over again. So many times I started to think the scar was a species mark. That we were being hunted by a pack of crocodiles, not just this one. Then we cleared that last clump of grass and fell into this pit of water, the relentless beast falling silent behind us, and I knew it had herded us. Snapping from different angles only to force us onto the course of its choosing. Driving us deeper into the swamp where the quicksand-like mud gave way to dark, soupy water. A pit for its prey.

Something slimy brushes across my leg but I don't dare react. It's too small to be any part of the crocodile, and I'd rather not know what else might be hiding in the murky depths of the swamp. A tinkling breeze cuts through the landscape, setting the grasses swaying and reeds rattling. The perfect amount of movement to keep us from being able to detect which way the croc will attack from. It's most likely going to slip into the water and take us both out at the same time. Clamping us between its massive jaws and dragging us to the bottom. Drowning us.

I swallow, spine stiff as I slowly remove my arm from around Leah and let my hand stretch ever so gently down into the water, tracing her arm down to her hand. I lock my fingers with hers. Leah is faster than I am, and she's nimble. She has the best chance of escaping through the swamp's maze of tangled roots and mud. We stumbled our way here. Pulling. Tugging. Shoving. Fighting for each step and knowing each one might be our last. If I can get her far enough ahead of me, figure out where the croc is and make sure it decides to eat me first, she might be able to find solid ground and shift. Her wolf will be better whether she needs to run or fight, but it's too heavy for the swamp.

"On three," I whisper. "We run straight ahead." Her chin dips in a tight, small nod, signaling she's ready. I begin to count. "One…"

She screams, jumping away. I go under, our hands still locked together and my foot sliding underneath what I really hope is only a root. I splash back up through the surface, spitting out chunky bits of swamp. Leah grabs my shoulders, helping me regain my balance as I unwedge my foot. "I'm sorry," she breathes, swiping at my face as if that's helpful. "Something touched my leg. I freaked a little bit. You know, because of the crocodile hunting us."

My teeth grind. "Something slimy? Yeah, I—" Every cell of my body freezes, eyes fixed on a green-gray lump sitting just inside the line of grass behind Leah.

Her body trembles. "No. Gods, Sean, please tell me you're just mad and not seeing what I think you're seeing…"

I keep my eyes fixed on the beast. "Come closer to me, Leah. Slowly."

She takes an uneven step, the terrain not allowing for any smooth movements. Unless you're a fifty-foot-long crocodile. It pushes off the grassy edge of the swamp and glides underneath the water without so much as making a ripple. I clutch Leah's waist and sling her behind me as hard as I can. "Go!"

Momentum takes her closer to the far side of the pit and she screams. "Not without you!"

I push toward the center of the pit, feet kicking off the muddy bottom as fast I can get them to go. "Run, Leah. Hurry!"

Shorter than I am, she struggles to find enough momentum on the bottom and begins to swim. Her hands hit the bank just as teeth sink into my thigh. Unlike when Leah bit me, there's decisive pain. I can feel my bone cracking. A shout tears out of me, and I turn and punch down onto the monster's snout. It plunges into the water, keeping me in its vice grip. Leah's scream ripples through the water above me and I slam my fist into the beast again. And again. Silent prayers going up that I can keep this monster occupied long enough for her to escape.

The crocodile spins into a death roll. I try to curl forward and wrap around its snout but it slings its head, splintering the bone in my leg. A yelp of pain coughs up my throat, stealing my little remaining air. One more head shake and I won't have a leg anymore either.

I rear up and put all my might into one last pounding punch, straight into the tip of the beast's nose. It rolls across the bottom of the pit. My head bangs into the thick mud, my lips breaking open. I throw an elbow, missing as my body flails and water fills my lungs. The beast thrashes, spitting me out as another set of raging jaws come out of the murky darkness by its head and clamp down. Straight through the beast's eye.

The croc rolls, trying to knock Leah's wolf off. My heart pounds, vision darkening. I kick up off the bottom and push down with my one good leg, shoving my head above the surface. The water in the pit is no longer still. It's a tempest born of two beasts who shouldn't exist battling each other to the death. I spit out the debris-filled water and suck a lungful of choking air into my burning lungs. Leah drives forward, coming at the crocodile from the side but her wolf can't find purchase on the muddy bottom. Her heavy paws are sinking and her thick coat is soaking up the water, weighing her down even more. The croc disappears under the surface, into water that's even more murky now that so much fresh mud has been kicked up. I lunge in Leah's direction. "Run! Go! Now! Get out of the water!"

She disappears with a yelp. I dive under the water, clamping my stinging eyes shut as I move forward, arms waving in all directions. Something big and furry slams into me, knocking me on my butt. Claws clip the top of my head and I reach out for her but Leah is gone again, her wolf being tossed around like a rag doll. I can feel the brutality of the thrashing.

I dig myself out of the mud and stand up, gulping air and pushing myself toward the pulsing water where claws frantically scratch, disappearing and reappearing as the crocodile death rolls Leah's wolf. "Let her go!" I shout, my broken leg dragging. It tangles in a mass of roots and I trip back down into the water. I double over and rip at the slick shafts of the root, tearing at them and pulling on my foot until it slips free of the hovel of godforsaken plants that have grown in this godforsaken swamp. A growl vibrates the filthy water and I push myself back up to standing, slipping and falling forward again. I land on a knee and spring back up. Leah is on the grassy edge of the pit, the crocodile in front of her, a chunk of meat hanging from its throat as it snaps and hisses, backing her into the reeds. "Run, Leah!" I shout.

Her eyes flick to mine. So does the single remaining eye of the crocodile. Its hissing intensifies, wide body swinging around, tail colliding with Leah and batting her away like she's nothing more than a fly. I swing in the opposite direction and stroke as hard as I can for the nearest spot of higher ground. I can't escape the beast, but I can draw it away from Leah. "Run!" I shout again, knowing without looking that the crocodile is closing in on me. I clamber onto a mound of grass sprouting up from the side of the pit, fingers desperately digging into the earth, my body sliding and slipping across the muddy blades. The crocodile's bone-crushing jaws snap shut behind me and relief floods through me. Leah's aim was good. The crocodile isn't so accurate with only one eye. That doesn't level the playing field, but it buys more time to draw it away from her.

Its powerful jaws snap again, grazing the bottom of my foot. I kick forward, turning at the waist and raising a hand, hoping for that light magic to spill out of me again. It doesn't. And that *beast* inside of me might as well be dead. *I die, you die!* I scream my thoughts at it. It…laughs. The crocodile snaps, shredding through the grass inches from my head. Fire races up my spine, erupting along my body. The ground beneath me sizzles and snaps. The crocodile hesitates, turning its massive head to watch me with that one demonic eye. *Thank you*, I tell the half-awake beast. *Now let's cook this overgrown dinosaur.*

I lunge forward but it's Leah, crashing up from the water underneath the distracted crocodile, who strikes first. Her mouth clamps onto the crocodile's underbelly and they both go airborne, Leah attacking like a great white from the ocean's depths. Her head shakes violently. The croc arches and then both wolf and reptile crash back into the water. My flames douse as I jump back down into the swampy water that's turning a sickly shade of crimson. "Leah!"

A dark object launches out of the water and bites down on the back of my neck. It's Leah, her wolf dragging me out of the water and away from the edge. She drops to her knees beside me, her shift taking place faster than I can blink the mud from my eyes. "Can you walk? I don't know if it's dead, we have to move."

I wrap my hands around her face. "I told you to leave fifteen minutes ago."

She shoves my arms away and tucks her body into my side, using her shifter strength to lift me. "And I told you I wasn't going *anywhere* without you, so get your lazy butt up and *walk*."

18

Keela

My fingers tingle, the sensation climbing higher, crawling over my wrist and up my arms. A dull throb follows in its wake. Pain. An agonizingly slow trail of pain splintering through me. I lie still. My body was just weightless, wind rushing up to beat against my face as I fell through a chaotic jumble of disoriented noises. Voices. Powerful ones. Those belonging not just to destroyers, but *conquerors*. Ones angry with me for bringing scorn to their creation without ever answering my anguished pleas of how, what, or why. My eyes fling open. There is stone above me. Beside me. Underneath where I'm flat on my back against the cold, hard surface of…a cave. Is it possible that this could be the bottom of the Primordial Void?

I turn my head. There is a soft cushion underneath it, cradling my skull. My senses sharpen. There's a distant groan. The scrape of flesh on rock. I scan the faint trickle of light illuminating the thin slit of the cave's mouth, clenching my fists as the noise comes closer to the opening. Sharp pain has my fingers flying open, agony screaming out of me. "Keela!" Abhartack ducks through the opening, mouth dripping with blood. "No, mi Dauði. You mustn't move." He rushes to my side, cupping a hand over my shoulder as his eyes scan my body. He meets my stare, his blood-smeared smile spreading wide across his face. "She lives."

I swallow, my throat dry and swollen. "Did whoever belongs to that blood survive meeting you? Because I am hungry."

He runs a thumb across his lips, licking at the sustenance. "Skarthorn. I've never thought to eat one before but I, too, am hungry, and there are not many options around us." His gaze drops to my throat. "Not since *you* were removed from my menu."

"Skarthorn?" I breathe.

He nods. "I believe this cave must have been a place it was accustomed to using as a den. When it arrived this morning, I could hardly believe my luck."

I try to sit up, crying out once again as pain rips me in two. The king slowly lowers me back to the earth-scented pillow, hands lingering and eyes brimming with sorrow. I bite down against the pain, not yet wanting to know the full details of why and how I am here. The void's cruelty still echoes in my ears, forever to remain inside of me. But Abhartack, he is...my salvation. "Not many people would call an encounter with a Skarthorn lucky."

He smooths his hand across my middle, gently caressing my ribs as if he knows the exact spot causing me pain. "Most people are not me, and in order to continue feeding you, I needed to find a food source of my own." He places his wrist to my mouth. "Drink, mi Dauði. You must heal, and I will kill every creature great and small to ensure you do."

My fangs descend, the muscle around them as sore as the rest of me. "How long have I been…"

He sighs. "On Hel's doorstep? Too long. Those forces which live within the void were not kind to you, mi Dauði. But while you did not emerge unscathed, death was never to be your fate." He lifts his wrist to his own mouth and rips his pale skin open, returning the bleeding wound to my lips. "The destiny of the Vampir queen is one to be remembered for generations to come. So drink and rest, my queen."

I latch onto his wrist. Currents of warmth shoot from my head to my toes. My heart thuds and the king smiles. I tug his blood into me and close my eyes. Before I jumped, he had asked what the void whispered to me, but it never told me anything until after I was inside those inky depths. Lured there not by whispers, but with the scent of my deepest desire.

Abhartack warned that the void would kill me, and it tried to. But he did not let it. I don't know how, but it is from my savior's wrist that I now drink. *My mate.* The words fling my eyes back open and my lips part. The king leans over me. "You are safe, mi Dauði. I have done everything within my power to be reunited with you, and I have sworn even to the void itself that I will protect you." His lips press against my forehead. "Sleep now. I will be right here beside you."

•

Sean

We've been walking for days. Even when Leah shifts into her wolf form, hoping time after time that she'll find solid ground to dig her claws into, her fur is soggy and matted. Never dry. Never clean. Never anything but exhausted from her efforts to get us out of the marsh. We've left the higher swampy water behind but the humidity is worse here, those thick blankets of fog that descended before the moths attacked spread over us, trapping the sticky air and causing even the dryest parts of this already moist environment to be soaked through. At night, the insects are so loud that Leah and I can barely hear each other. That first night, I was glad for it. She kept trying to fuss over my leg and while it hurt, I knew the pain wasn't nearly what it should be. Something I don't want to discuss with her. I'm just glad she has the same quick healing ability because in this environment, if we weren't supernaturally gifted, we'd be dead.

Leah moves closer to me, the two of us huddled together on what we've been calling islands. They're nothing more than tightly growing mounds of grass, and they're barely large enough for the two of us to curl up on, but when we need to rest, these islands are better than nothing. The best part is that Leah has been shifting into her wolf. Its thick fur hinders the bugs and it's much less awkward for me to curl up against her when she's an oversized dog rather than herself. But tonight, she's still human.

I break more blades from the clumps of grass, busying myself with a makeshift pillow to keep from speaking to her. In part because she's Leah, but mostly because it feels wrong to have the kind of abilities I have. *I* feel wrong. Like some fraud with powers I'm not entitled to. Something given to me, not something I was born with the way Leah was. Or even something I earned. My abilities just popped up out of nowhere, handed to me for no reason. Some by Aether but the beast was there before, and I can't even use it when I need to. I couldn't save Keela. I couldn't free myself from the Vasilis. And Leah almost died trying to save me. *Twice.* I should have been able to free myself from the moths, and I should have been able to kill that crocodile.

She swats at her arm. "I never knew how much I hated bugs before being stuck here, but at least these mosquitos aren't the size of eagles."

She's right. Since our run-in with the crocodile, everything else we've encountered has been normal sized. Normal to find in a marsh environment. Bugs, frogs, snakes, and even a turtle. We've tried to catch snakes and frogs for food but we're too slow moving in the mud. Leah says we're not dead yet because our magic is keeping us alive. Until it doesn't. "The bugs aren't as bad for you when you shift."

She scratches a spot on her shoulder. "Do you think..." She lowers her hand and I catch the tremble. "Sean, I'm really cold."

I bite down on the inside of my jaw and tuck my arm around her shoulders. I've been so busy avoiding talking to her that I've let myself become selfish. I look to where her pants legs are ripped. She told me her outfit is spelled to come and go from her body with her shift, but between trudging through this muck for days on end and battling giant creatures, we're both wearing nothing but tatters. The moths took my supply pack and Leah lost hers when she shifted and tagged along for the ride. We'd both give anything for the comfort of dry clothes right now. But even more than that, we'd both like to finally stop being too afraid to rest at night. During the haze of the daylight hours, we barely allow ourselves to catch our breath. Leah hurt the crocodile but we're not sure if her final attack was a fatal one or if the crocodile is off healing somewhere. Or maybe it's already out there stalking us again. "Go ahead and shift and get some sleep. We have to be nearing the edge of this place, maybe we'll finally get out of the mud tomorrow."

She stretches her legs out in front of her. "I just hope we get there before our feet rot off."

Her toes are painted in mud, same as mine. Each time we stop, we take our shoes off and clean the gunk out of them. Our feet are never dry though, and neither are the shoes when we put them back on. "Tomorrow we'll find dry land and food."

She rests her head on my shoulder, her muddy, tangled hair squishing as she does. "That's what you said yesterday. But I'm pretty sure you could dry us off right now."

Her words startle me. "No, I can't."

She tilts her chin up toward me. "You could summon your fire."

"And kill you in the process," I snap.

She lifts off my shoulder. "You don't need to go nuclear. Just summon a ball of fire into your hand or whatever, dry out this grass and start us a fire. I can gather sticks—"

"I *can't*."

Her brows furrow. "You're serious? You can't control the fire?"

I look away. "Bingo, genius."

She shoves me. "You don't have to be a prick about it. We're out here starving, and I'm *freezing*. Even in my wolf form, I can't get warm. My skin is too waterlogged. Everything is so wet I can't get my body temperature back up." She crosses her arms with a huff. "You seem to be doing a lot better and I'm guessing that's because you have freaking *dragon* fire. But instead of using it, you keep telling *me* to shift. And don't think I don't know that's because you don't want to talk to me."

I shake my head. "You're right, I don't want to talk to you. But I'm not *purposefully* keeping us filthy and wet. I'd give anything to be dry again but I'm not a dragon, I can't start a fire, and I sure as heck can't fly. I'm as useless in this situation as you are." She drops her hands and I immediately feel ashamed. "I didn't mean *useless*. I meant...stuck. We're both just stuck, and it sucks. Believe me, if I could get you out of here I would." I meet her eyes. "Even over myself. If I had the choice, I'd stay here indefinitely if it meant you could go home, Leah."

She sighs. "I know. You've always been loyal like that, Sean. Noble. The way *dragons* are. And I saw you burning at the witch compound and then Haldir's fire didn't bother you. That can only mean you're a Dreki. One more powerful than Haldir, like Monique said."

I smash a mosquito that's biting my leg through a hole in my pants. "Monique said I *wasn't* a dragon, just some weirdo who has the fire of a dragon. And Haldir said the same thing, that I'm not Dreki. But he also said my fire isn't exactly dragon fire, or not like his...I don't know. He says that I stink now, different than I smelled before Monique and her witch friends got their hands on me."

Leah rests her muddy hand on my equally muddy shoulder. "You do smell different, but it's not a bad smell and you're not a weirdo."

I snort. "Then why are we in this godforsaken place? Why did everybody have to come on this big journey to bring me to these Norn people? Why are you wet, cold, and starving right now? It's because of me, Leah. And because the Vasilis won't leave me alone. I didn't have fire randomly leaking out of my pores before I met them."

Her eyes trail over my shoulder, going distant. "We have to be here because my family let you down, and now Monique says you have some kind of dark spell on you that's hiding your true nature..." She refocuses on me. "You were what you are before you met the Vasilis, we just didn't know because of the spell. My dad tried, though. It's just that Beatrice alone couldn't detect the spell and he didn't think there was any reason to go to more extreme measures, the way the Vasilis are." She frowns. "I bet the witches and Haldir are all wrong and you *are* some kind of dragon. The last of an ancient line." Her lips twitch up. "A prince."

Fresh waves of irritation lace my voice with an icy bite. "This isn't a fairy tale, Leah. This is real. You saw me grow up. There was nothing abnormal about me until the Vasilis came into my life. And then they all just stood there while that moth carried me away. They could have killed it, but they chose not to. And you chose to bite me, and now we're both stuck here when all I ever wanted was to go to college and finally start living a life that wasn't completely screwed up. But you, your dad, Collin...all of you lied to me my whole life, and now I'll never get to accomplish the one thing my mom was always so sure I would. I'll never graduate from Merrymont because we're both probably going to die in this swamp. Compliments of the Vasilis and giant moths, and because I can't freaking use the fire! It comes and goes whenever it wants, and we almost got eaten by a giant crocodile because it wasn't in the mood to help us!"

She stares at me. Silent and still. I turn away and curl up on my side. I shouldn't raise my voice at her but it's already so noisy out here we practically have to yell, and her stupid little grin over her stupid little idea of me being some kind of special dragon was absurd. Plus, I'm tired, hungry, and so unbelievably sick of being drenched in sweat and mud. The last thing I want to do is hear Leah fantasizing like we're teenagers at summer camp. We're not even friends.

Her body curls against my back, still not in wolf form. "I'm sorry," she whispers against my ear. "The secrets that my family kept from you...that *I* kept from you...Sean, I'm so sorry we hurt you. I can understand why you hate all of the supernaturals around you, but all of us, even the

Vasilis, really are trying to help you. Well, I guess I should only speak for myself and Monique, but...the Vasilis didn't attack the moths because they *can't*. No one is allowed to kill them. They are servants of the Norns, tasked with carrying people to whatever destined obstacles the Norns see fit. Hence the name *Destiny* Moth."

I close my eyes. "Whatever. It doesn't matter. I'm stuck here in a destiny of hell and it's just too bad for you that you realized too late that I'm not the fairy-tale prince you were hoping for. I'm a supernatural fraud destined to rot in this armpit of a swamp. I guess that means you should have stuck with Gelby after all."

She tugs my arm from my side and fits herself underneath it. "The Norns need to find you worthy, Sean. They don't grant an audience to just anyone. And don't ask me what they're trying to prove by dumping you here because I have no idea. No one knows what the Norns value. All I know is that if you want answers from them, you have to pass some kind of test, and no one ever has the same stories about visiting this land." She nuzzles in close to me. "So stop being cranky. I'll help you figure out how to use whatever magic you have. Even if we don't get out of this swamp tomorrow, like you've been saying we will for the last three days. I'm also not shifting tonight. It's your turn to keep *me* warm."

19

Leah was right about me being wrong again. Yesterday, I could have sworn that we were gradually trudging onto higher ground. The mud didn't seem as deep. As thick. But today, it's as if the marsh is conspiring against us, making every step we take deeper and muddier than the last. We've been sunk up to our thighs in the noxious-smelling mud for what feels like an eternity now, struggling to free ourselves. Each other. Sinking deeper and then starting the process all over again. We're both tired. Thirsty. Hungry. *Desperate.* And yet the marsh is unrelenting. We tried to turn back once we realized how soft the bottom was becoming but even when we stepped into our old tracks, they were deeper than they had been. Then we lost them altogether, the fog creeping in so thick we can now barely see three feet ahead.

I reach back and slide my fingers through Leah's, her hand clutching tight around mine as I use what little strength I have left to be an anchor while she wrenches herself from the spot of her last step. Her movements are slow. Methodical. We've been doing this for so long that we both know there's not a single reason to hurry. No reason at all to burn more fuel than necessary. She'll eventually pull herself to my side. I'll then use her as my anchor and move forward, bit by painstaking bit. And then I'll anchor for her again.

"It's getting dark," she mutters.

I don't answer her. I'm not sure how far we've moved through this sea of endless mud. The vegetation died off not long after we set out this morning and we haven't stumbled across one of our little islands of grassy refuge since. The fog is too disorienting for us to do anything other than try to keep a straight line. Once we realized there was no turning back, we picked a direction and decided to stay the course until the visibility came back and we could see what was ahead of us. But that never happened, so we're staying our course.

Mud suctions around Leah's upper thigh and she grits her teeth, letting out a furious growl. I lean backward, trying to add leverage to her plight. "Pretend an oversized crocodile is behind you."

She lets out a harsh laugh. "The only thing keeping me going is knowing it's not dumb enough to follow us into this mess."

The mud relents and I pull her forward, no longer caring how close our bodies are twined together. We tried putting her on my back but that only made me sink so deep that I couldn't free myself without her climbing down to help me out. Then we both got stuck in the same little plot of mud. We've writhed and crawled all over each other to the point that I don't think there's a spot on either of us that hasn't been groped by the other.

She settles in at my side. I clasp our hands back together and begin the slow, methodical process of taking a single step. Leah is strong, and I'm thankful for her shifter genes. Without her, I don't think I'd be able to get through this. If tunneling through mud is some kind of test from the Norns where I was supposed to survive the marsh and make it out alone, I've failed.

I get my foot up far enough to push it forward. The tip of my foot scrapes against something hard. I freeze. Leah's fingers tighten on mine. "Do *not* tell me there's something down there."

I swallow. "Well, there is, but it isn't alive. I don't think."

"You don't think?" she snaps.

I glare at her. "Now who's cranky?"

She rolls her eyes and then fixes them on the spot where my leg disappears underneath the mud. I slowly grind my foot forward. It skims over the hard surface. I flex my toes, dragging my shoe up the side of whatever it is. Finally, I break over the top of it. I press my toes back down, shimmying my foot over the top. It's smooth. Like a step. So I use it like one.

Between Leah and the solid platform underneath me, taking this step was easier than the last fifty have been. I get both feet planted atop the smooth surface and reach back for her. She follows my actions, methodically moving forward until she feels the solid object. Once she's up beside me, we begin again.

"What in the..." I skim my foot over yet another solid object, this one taller than the last. "Leah, come here." I go ahead and anchor for her. With the flat, hard surface underneath us, and the few inches of reprieve from the weighty mud, we both move forward, bit by bit.

We make it onto the next, taller surface and Leah shuffles forward, her foot hitting the next platform seconds before mine does. Like the last two, this one is a few inches taller than the level before it. "Steps," she shrieks.

I glance ahead. For as far as I can see, the only thing ahead of us is mud. But between the fog and the ever-darkening sky, that isn't saying much. "Keep going. As soon as we lose the height of whatever this is, we stop."

She nods her agreement. "Let's hope these go up high enough that we won't drown in the mud if we doze off tonight."

I move forward with a little more urgency. A little more ease. Leah does the same. We find the next step and a giggle escapes her lips. I can't help but smile as well, both of us hurrying forward, finding yet another step. And another. Rising higher out of the mud with each glorious step. Night seems to be falling faster than it should and the buzz of insects intensifies, almost sounding like they're being projected through some hollow tunnel ahead of us, but I don't care. At this point, I'd much rather sleep in a tunnel full of every biting insect known to man than stay trapped in this mud. Leah would, too, but I move ahead of her, just in case these are giant insects instead of normal ones.

Do you think you could wake up and spare a flame, buddy? I ask the beast who hasn't bothered to even blink open an eye since lighting me up too late to kill the super-croc. Or maybe it lit up just in time to distract the crocodile because it somehow sensed that Leah was coming up for the kill. She hasn't mentioned seeing me on fire and we haven't discussed the specifics of what happened that day because I've been avoiding talking to her. Something that will probably continue.

I move ahead of her, climbing onto the next step. Then the next. And the next. Going up and up until my legs and feet no longer fight to break free from the grip of the mud. I step up again but this time, nothing is there. No mud. No more steps. Only a solid surface that looks a whole lot like a floor. A clean one, but there's so little light it's hard to tell.

Leah steps up to my side, her breathy inhale a mirror of how I feel. She laces her fingers back through mine. "Let's move slow. It would be just like this stupid bog to bring us up out of the mud only to make us fall off a cliff."

"Marsh," I correct her, even though what we just went through can't really be called a marsh either.

She moves forward, tugging me with her. "My mistake. Now I see that the boggy marsh brought us up here so that *I* could throw *you* off a cliff."

My mouth ticks up but I look away, over my shoulder and into the darkness around us so she doesn't see. We move forward, slow and steady, feeling out with our feet before committing to the step. So far, the ground beneath us is solid and sure. We take another step forward. And another. "Wait." Leah stops, her voice echoing back to us. She tilts her head. "It's hard to make out with the fog, but I think we're in some kind of building."

I squint into the darkness. "One that's cavernous enough for an echo? Which means it's plenty big enough to house oversized lizards?"

She dips down and runs her hand over the floor. "At least it's dry. We'll stay here at the entrance and take turns sleeping."

"Sounds good to me." I plop down beside her and begin to scrape the mud from my feet and legs. "I'll take first watch. If something tries to eat us, you're our best shot at survival so get some rest. In your wolf form, so I can use you as a backrest."

I dozed off a few times last night but I knew I wouldn't be able to fall into a deep sleep, so I left Leah alone and let her rest. Now that the light of dawn is beginning to peek through the arched openings of the domed rotunda, I climb to my feet and look around. The floor is white marble, the domed ceiling held up by smooth, towering columns carved from the same kind of marble. Even the arched doorways are perfectly smooth. Pristine. Clean. Save for the mud we've tracked in. And there's no fog. Only bright rays of a dawning sun stroking over the marble. It crawls across the floor, lifting up the walls as it rises, illuminating the single archway that's not open to the outside the way the rest of them are.

I walk to the center of the rotunda and stare into the cavernous room that swallowed our noise and echoed it back to us last night. The sun isn't illuminating much beyond the archway. Everything behind it is dark. Except...I take another step. Maybe I've been staring too long, imagining the worst, but I swear there are tiny glowing specks of light coming from deep within that room.

I hurry back to Leah and kneel down beside her, keeping one eye on the room as I clamp my fingers over her furry shoulder and give her a gentle shake. "Wake up." *Before some monstrosity runs out of the back room and kills us.* I knew this rotunda was too good to be true.

Leah's furry legs stretch, the hind ones going straight and then curling back up against her body. I shake her again. "Dry doesn't mean safe. Get up."

I pull away from her and straighten back up, watching the dark room for any sign of movement. There's shuffling behind me, then a very human-looking woman is standing beside me. Leah gasps. "This is like being in the Rome! Oh my gosh, it's beautiful." She walks across the marble floor. "Plain, but still *really* beautiful. And clean!" She smiles at me. "Sean, we're dry. In Rome!"

I raise a brow at her. She shrugs. "Fine, not Rome. But we're still dry, there's no fog, and it's *warm*." She looks up at the ceiling. "Dad always lets me tag along when he goes to the Ulfr conventions, and my favorite was the year it was held in Rome."

I groan. "Of course there are wolf conventions. Why wouldn't there be? Humans don't know shifters exist but you're still out there having conventions right in plain sight."

She steps into a ray of sun and holds her arms out wide. "Some humans know we exist."

"All except the ones you befriend," I snap, walking toward the darkened archway. "We need to see what's in here. Be ready, I thought I saw some kind of tiny lights, like maybe giant bug eyes or something."

She falls in step beside me. "Wasn't it you who was just bellyaching about how much better your life was before you learned about supernaturals? I'm pretty sure that means you should be thanking us for all those years you got to live in blissful ignorance."

I cast her a weary glance. "Keep going, Leah. Tell me how I'm not entitled to any of my feelings." She stops walking and I snort. "You've never had a problem telling me exactly how *you* feel so go ahead, let me have it. Tell me I'm bellyaching and ruining your vibe."

"Sean." My name floats off her lips on a breath of air. I turn back to where she's three paces behind me. Her eyes are wide and staring far off to the left. She lifts an arm, finger pointing, a smile cracking across her face. "I think we made it."

I follow the trail of her eyes and finger, my gaze passing through an open archway and landing on a red-tiled roof. To the right of it there's another roof, this one rectangular and steeply sloped. To the left of that one is another, and another, roofs of different heights and sizes dotting the landscape in every direction. And beyond them, a forest. An honest to goodness forest with trees, not reeds. We've made it to the end of the marsh.

We both break into a run, crossing the marble floor at a dead sprint. Leah beats me to edge of the rotunda, slamming to a screaming halt, her feet teetering on the rim of the floor and her arms flinging wide. I throw myself to the ground to stop my momentum but my body slides halfway over the edge that's more of a ledge. The marsh really did spit us out onto a cliff edge. From here, it's a sheer drop of a hundred feet down to the coral-hued water pooled between the flooded buildings. They rise up out of the water, hiding the water's true depth the way the water hides their true heights and shapes.

Leah regains her footing and steps away from the edge. I push myself back onto the solid floor. For all we know, this place could be one giant, sprawling building, flooded by a storm whose water is trapped by the wall of mud we traveled through to get here. Maybe even this rotunda was once flooded, the water draining out of it to form the chaos we just traveled through. But it's too clean to have been flooded.

"Do you think there's fish in that water?" Leah asks.

I get to my feet and walk around the perimeter, checking all of the other outer edges of the rotunda. An enormous wall of mud is on the side where we came in, and all the rest is the sheer cliff face we just about went over. "How would we get down there even if there are? The only stairs leading down from here are the muddy ones we came up on."

She shrugs. "I can survive this jump. And so can you. You're a supernatural, whether we know what kind or not. And you have crazy fast healing capabilities. Faster than mine."

I consider her logic. "You think we should risk jumping? The forest is still pretty far away. It looks like a two-day journey at best, and that's if we don't drown before we can reach it."

She hooks her hands on her hips and stares down at the water. "At this point, I'm willing to risk just about anything. We need food. But my fur is barely dry as it is and I *really* don't want to be sopping wet again."

I move to the archway she's looking out of and nod in agreement. "It would be hard to scale any of those buildings to get to a roof, and who knows what's even down there. Let's just explore this rotunda and see if there's any food or clothing. Maybe we'll get lucky and find a fishing pole with a big spool of line."

She spins around. "And a nice king-size bed."

"Or stairs," I add to our list of hopes and dreams. "There could be lower levels."

She claps her hands together with a happy grin and hurries toward the dark archway. I follow her, excited about the possibilities. If we find food, dry clothes, and a decent bed to sleep in, we might not leave this place for a while. Not after what we just went through. And the view from up here is nice. It's not every day you see a city that seems to rise out of the water like this one does. But we're not in Rome. We're not even in Midgard. I tug on Leah's arm to slow her down. "I know we're both imagining a steak dinner waiting for us in here, and you're a big bad wolf who can probably see in the dark, but I can't. We need to be careful. After I kill Collin for not telling me *anything*, he'll kill me if I let you get hurt."

I can feel the smart retort forming on her lips but instead, she purses them, sadness flicking across her features. I give her hand a squeeze. "You miss him, too."

She nods. "Dad should have heard from him by now, but before I left, no one from his group had reached out. I'm actually really worried. About all of them."

"Where did they go?"

Her eyes meet mine, a tiny smile curling the ends of her lips. "Wolf business. And I bet you can see in the dark if you'd just try."

She rips out of my grip and races into the cavernous room. I run after her, following the sound of her slapping footfalls until the echoes begin to bounce them around. "Leah," I whisper, slowing my steps.

"This way!" she shouts, no regard for the following echo. "The room makes a turn. Go right. It's like a big giant hallway and there's another room back here. It—"

Her words cut off with a sharp squeak. "Leah!" I race to the right, banging against the smooth curve of the wall. I follow it around until... "What are those?"

A giggle bubbles out of her. "I have no idea."

I watch the tiny arcs of warm light float around her, brushing her hair, tickling her face. She holds up a hand and a flock of them land on her palm, running up her arms and taking flight again from off her shoulder. She looks like she's standing in a shower of golden light. Even with her still covered in mud and her hair matted in thick chunks, the sight is still a beautiful one. But outer beauty has never been Leah's problem.

I step inside the now dimly lit room. "Let's hope they're as harmless as they look."

They scatter, light going out as if my voice spooked them. "Great job, Sean," Leah huffs.

"Not like I did it on purpose," I snip back, walking farther into the room. "What else can you see in here?"

"Nothing," she mutters. "It's empty. Except for that table over there. And the sword. Well, now that I think about it, that's probably an altar and the sword is what those tiny fairies use to behead dragons who refuse to use their power."

A growl that sounds a lot like those that come out of Haldir rumbles through my chest. "I already told you, even the dragon says I'm not a dragon."

"Dreki are stupid," she shoots back. "Which is why they're practically extinct. All brawn, no brains."

I think back to the way Haldir was thrashing in that net, trying to use his brute strength when clearly that wasn't working. After I pointed that out to him, he calmed down and started helping me dig, freeing himself from the net in no time. Had I not been there, though... "If one good night of sleep puts you in the mood to be yourself, I'm going to insist you stay awake until we're out of this place and away from each other."

I find the table and slide my hand over the top of it. Those tiny wisps of light turn on, twinkling across the ceiling that's high above us. "Runes," Leah gasps, scanning the length of the illuminated carvings, eyes tracing the glistening gold streaks of the runes carved into the gray stone of the ceiling.

"Can you read them?" I ask.

She paces along the outer edge of the circular room. "Some of them. The Álfar and Fae are typically the ones obsessed with runes, but Ulfr learn the basics." She points to a group above her head. "These say something about divine rites. Those beside it are runes representing time and loss."

I stare at the bar-height stone table now visible in the glow of those tiny wisps of light dancing by the thousands along the ceiling. The base is the same gray stone the room is carved from, but the top is darker. Stained. My throat tightens. Leah was right, this is probably an altar, not a table. And those are probably blood stains, not wine. "Maybe there's a good reason this city was flooded."

"The moon and stars align..." Leah continues to circle the room, reading what she can of the runes.

I fix my eyes on the sword. It's housed in a scabbard of dark leather that's reinforced with bands of gold. Swirling designs of intricately detailed images are carved into the leather, runes nestled between other symbols, all of them dancing as if alive with the firelight of the tiny things glowing above us. I glance up at them, asking Leah, "So the divine rites are lost until the moon and stars align?"

She shakes her head. "More like the rites themselves are lost to time, referring to whatever rite it was that could only happen when the moon and stars were aligned. But...wait...no, not *the* stars. *A* star. Look at this." She waves to a patch of flat ceiling. "The same symbol for moon is used here, but it's with this one. See how the rune is basically a mirror image of itself?"

I let my eyes trace the center of the rune. If you cut the symbol in half, the slashing and curved lines of each half would be an exact mirror image of the other. "That names a star?"

Leah nods. "Anytime you see a mirror image rune, it's the name of something specific. Like a person or a place. In this case, the grouping of runes is giving the name of a specific star."

"Which one?"

Leah shrugs. "No clue. It could also be talking about an eye instead of a star."

I give her a sidelong glance. "The rune for eye and the one for star are that similar?"

She shakes her head. "No, I just can't remember which is which. But that one over there is definitely moon, and stars pair better with the moon, so process of elimination. It's probably star, not eye." I cross my arms over my chest. She groans. "Don't be mad at me. You don't know any of these, and maybe if you'd go catch me a fish I wouldn't be starving, then I could think better."

I drop my arms. "Catch your own breakfast."

She rolls her eyes. "Says the dragon who could catch *and* cook my meals for me."

"I'm not a dragon!"

The lights blink out. Leah sighs. "Would you stop yelling. You're scaring them."

I reach back and grab the sword. It's heavy, but the weight is...comforting. It's too heavy to swim away from here with, but while we're stuck in this building, I'd rather have some protection than none. I curl my palm around the rather bland hilt and let the sword dangle at my side. "You don't even know what these things are, Leah. For all we know, they could be getting ready to descend upon us like a group of piranhas. And if we can't read the runes, there's no reason for us to be back here. The walls are all solid and there aren't any stairs, so let's go."

She stomps along behind me until I bang into the wall. "He could just use his dragon sight," she mutters under her breath as she walks past me. "But no, he'd rather run into the wall."

I start to growl at her but then remember how much I sound like Haldir when I do. And how, devoid of the *super* part, growling isn't *natural*. Humans don't do that. I clamp my mouth shut and follow the sound of her footsteps, relieved that after so many days of muck and mud, water and fog, the sun finally seems to be emerging in full, filling the rotunda with sunlight. The humidity is gone from the air and it feels like a nice, warm summer day in July.

Leah strolls across the rotunda to the archway we looked out this morning. And jumps.

20

Leah's laughter rings out, buzzing all around me, echoing as she flips and rolls through the sky, putting on an aerial show like it's her job. Only, her body is a rocket on a collision course with water we don't know the depth of. Water that could be an illusion. Or lined with spikes. I begin to sweat, scorching beads of perspiration running down my arms to where my glowing hands are curled on the edge of the marble, my body hunched over my knees as I uselessly sit here kneeling on the ledge while Leah falls. My temperature is rising but the beast knows its fire won't help, and neither will whatever is seeping out of my fingers.

Leah's hands stretch over her head, arms and legs straightening out, toes pointing. Her body meets the colorful surface of the water and slips underneath it, almost as seamless as the crocodile. My parched mouth dries out even more, throat sore and hoarse as I yell her name, helplessly staring down at the epicenter of a faint circle of soft waves. I begin to pray. Leah's head breaches the surface three feet from the epicenter and that prayer turns into a curse. "Are you insane?"

She laughs, smoothing back her hair. "Getting down was never our problem, Sean!" she yells back, disappearing under the surface again, feet splashing over her head as she rolls and plays, reminding me of those early years when we were younger and all the kids would gather at her house to swim in the pool. We'd have contests to see who could do the most underwater flips. Fun that ended that summer when Leah made sure I was the most humiliated teenager in Richlands.

I run a hand down my face. She could be dead right now. Or thrust away from me and into some other part of this world. But maybe that would be better for her. Maybe she'll find food while she's down there and get herself the energy she needs to make the swim to the forest.

I sit back and scan the view. The tingling glow in my hands is gone and my temperature is falling, but the forest looks farther away now than it looked this morning. A three-day journey instead of two. Hopefully Leah will take time out of her play session to notice that, and she'll get started on the long swim ahead. She's a wolf so the forest should be the perfect place for her. Me, on the other hand... No one even knows what I am.

A wet glob of slime slaps across my face. I smack at it, a peal of laughter jarring me awake. I don't even remember falling asleep. I was sitting with my back against the arch, watching Leah, and—my eyes fling open. Leah is doubled over in front of me. Soaking wet, wearing nothing but her underwear, and laughing so hard she's crying. I look down at the water and back at her. "What did you do? How did you..." I look back at the water. The surface is smooth and flat. I'm not dreaming, Leah really made it back up here.

"There are handholds in the side of the cliff." She wipes the tears from her face but continues to laugh. "You should see the look on your face. No, you should see what's *on* your face."

I wipe at the gooey mess, tendrils of translucent snot clinging to my hands, stretching and smearing, and making it so much worse. "What is this?"

Her smile is bigger than any I've ever seen on her. She points beside me to a mucous-covered ball of tentacles and scales. The thing looks like an octopus mated with a trout...and a snail. "That thing is dead, right?"

"I don't know," she answers, toeing it gently. "It was floating in the water so I thought I'd bring it back with me and see what you thought about it."

I watch as one of the tentacles slides down from the top of the gooey mass. Instead of suckers, it's covered in eyes. "I think I'm not eating it, and I'd appreciate it if you wouldn't hit me in the face with it anymore."

She starts laughing again. "That was an accident, I swear." She tosses a scallop shell into my lap. "I tied these up in my shirt to bring back but I had to hold the fish-thing, so I really only had one free hand for the climb, and that last step is a doozy."

I scan her bare torso and set the scallop aside, turning onto my stomach and hanging down over the ledge to see what step she's talking about. "You climbed up here using those little grooves?"

She crouches beside me. "It took me a while to find them, but those grip-holds must be how the original inhabitants of this city used to get up here. *If* anyone ever lived here. This land is rumored to be home to those who protect the Norns, but I've only ever heard of those protectors being creatures like the moths or even the crocodile, things whose existence is tied to serving the Norns in some way. I've never heard of there being any sort of *civilized* creatures."

I squint at the handholds. They're nothing more than indentations but they do look as if they've been intentionally cut into the vertical walls of the mountain this rotunda is built atop. I look down into the reflective water that's hiding a whole city. "There are stairs on the side where we came up, remember? So maybe the grooves were made by whatever creature started climbing up here after the city got flooded and walled in by mud."

"Either way, we have a way to get up and down now," she replies. "And we have a bunch of anomalies to eat!"

I slide back up to sitting. "Anomalies?"

She gets up and crosses the floor to where her ragged shirt is holding a bundle of scallop shells. "Scallops don't live in fresh water, but Sean, the water down there is the purest fresh water I've ever tasted. And I've tasted a lot in forests all over the world, when I'm out letting my wolf run."

"You drank the water?"

"Duh." She winks at me. "You need to drink some, too. I obviously couldn't bring any back with me but now that we can climb up here, we can jump down whenever we need to. And there are tons of these scallops below us. *Tons.* I was diving as far as I could go to see how deep the water was and found these scallops living on almost all of the submerged roofs."

"How deep is the water?" I ask, watching her clean hands pick through the pile of scallops. It's been so long since either of us have been without dirt that I almost forgot what a clean person looks like. Even

Leah's ripped-up pants look better now that they're freshly washed and spread out on the marble to be dried by the sun.

Her head shakes. "Deep enough that I could never reach the bottom. Those buildings are skyscrapers, but there's no glass or anything in most of the windows. They're just openings, like the rotunda has."

I glance at the nearest roof. "That's odd."

She dumps the rest of the scallops on the marble and spreads out her shirt to dry. "Once we eat and you're finished pouting, we'll be able to explore them easier."

I look at my mud-crusted hands. While she was down there cleaning up and finding food, I was sleeping. "I'm not pouting. I'm thinking about how I would have jumped in after you but I didn't think it was a good idea for both of us to be so reckless."

She huffs. "What you call reckless, I call brave. And I know what it looks like when you pout. You've been pouting for days, so get over yourself already and let's eat."

My jaw clenches. "Yeah, I'm the one who's self-centered."

A claw snaps from the end of her finger. She gives me a devilish grin as she uses that claw to pop open a scallop. "Glad you agree. Now I'll open these and you can cook them. Just a little hit of your dragon fire is all we need."

My temper flares. "How long are you going to keep this up?"

She opens another scallop. "Until you stop being a baby. Pouting isn't going to help the situation and denying how powerful you are could very well get us killed. This isn't a simulation or one of the stupid video games you and Collin used to play. What happens in this land is permanent, Sean. The starvation is real, and the dying will be *permanent*. The Norns are giving us a gift right now so instead of complaining, we need to be brave enough to take it."

My temper explodes. Leah's pep talk isn't for my benefit. It's her way of letting me know that she isn't getting what she wants out of me. That I'm not easing her discomfort the way she wants me to. And I didn't miss the look in her eye when I first woke up and took in the shock of her stripped body. She was watching for my reaction and no doubt hoping I'd make a fool of myself by gawking at her. A mistake I'm all too glad I didn't make. I stand up, back to the open expanse of air behind me and face turned toward Leah. No matter what we're going through or what we've already been through, she will never change. Leah will always be self-serving. So important to herself that she doesn't care what she does or who she does it to, so long as she gets what she wants. "Do me a favor, Leah. If you make it out of here alive, tell the Vasilis that they should add you to their list of torture methods because anyone in their dungeon would prefer to be stuck with their man-eating warden than have to be trapped anywhere in this world with you." I fall backward, enraged eyes locked on hers until my ungraceful fall from the ledge takes her out of my view.

In my anger, I didn't notice the flames erupting along my arms. They fan out above me as crisp air rushes past my ears. I look up at the ledge. It seems so far away now, but standing there watching me fall is Leah. I hit the water, the flames dousing with a hiss as the cool water engulfs me. I close my eyes and sink deeper. Leah was right. I've been pouting. Denying. Fighting the changes that are happening to me instead of embracing them. And now I have to climb back up there and tell her so. Eventually.

I roll over and kick down deeper into the water, opening my eyes and sucking in a big, long drink of the refreshing water. Another thing Leah was right about. It's good. Really good, and I desperately needed it. I kick back toward the surface, scrubbing my hands through my hair as I go. Despite everything, Leah is the one person who has actually been willing to answer my questions, and I just flipped out on her. And for no good reason. Seeing her that happy... I dive back under the water. I'll clean up, find some more scallops or some other food that doesn't look like a giant glob of snail snot, and force myself to go apologize. Apologize to Leah freaking MacKenzie.

I throw myself over the top of the ledge, impressed by my own strength. During the climb back up the mountainside, I had my doubts about trying to scale the sheer drop. My hands and feet barely fit inside the little grooves, and I couldn't decide if falling would be good or bad. If I couldn't make it back up the way Leah did, I would be embarrassed, but I would have also deserved the humiliation.

I haul my body up onto the floor of the rotunda. Leah's back is to me. Her clothes are on and she's sitting watching out over the wall of mud that we fought our way through to get here. I drop my shirt full of scallops onto the floor beside the ones that she didn't bother to finish opening after I left. Well, after I ran away like a little boy throwing a tantrum.

"Leah, I'm sorry. I've been having a really hard time controlling my temper lately. Everything is just so out of control and..." I run a hand up through my wet hair. Reasons aren't excuses and I need to do better. For myself as much as for her. "I'm sorry. I've been horrible today. You don't deserve to be spoken to the way I've been talking to you. I'm really sorry. The way I went off on you wasn't about you—"

"It's fine," she responds, not turning around.

My shoulders slump. The Leah I know would be rubbing my face in how much I was wrong today. I walk toward her. "It isn't fine, and we both know it. I'll try to do better and if I don't, please deck me. You have my permission to bust my nose every time I'm being a jerk."

She shakes her head, her clean hair brushing against her shoulders. It's wavy and a little frizzy, so unlike the way it normally looks, all sleek and styled. "I was pushing you, and you were venting. We're even."

Natural hair or not, I don't believe her for one solitary second. She's upset, and I'll find out how much later. When I'm least expecting it. I glance to where the sword is still propped against the wall. I'll have to keep an eye on that or else she's going to stab me in my sleep. "I brought back some more scallops. Let's eat and figure out where we want to sleep tonight. I thought it might be more secure back there in the altar room, but we could also be more easily trapped back there. I'd like to hear your thoughts on it so we can make a decision and both get some sleep tonight."

She doesn't move. I walk closer to her. "Leah, I don't know what I am. I'm confused, and I'm *scared*. I don't know what's going on most of the time, and if anything happens to you because of me..." I take a breath. "I wish you would have stayed with the others, because then your chances of survival would have gone way up. But I also know I'd already be dead if you weren't here with me. So on top of everything else, I'm...mortified. Worried. Trapped. Helpless. You name it, I've got a bad case of it. But most of all, I'm sorry for letting my anger hurt you."

She climbs to her feet, facing me. "I chose to come with you and the Norns allowed it, so don't beat yourself up over my choices. I'm no more helpless than you are. It's just that I happen to know neither of us are helpless, but only because I was raised to know it." She looks away from me. "Your anger... Sometimes wolves, especially the males, are like powder kegs. Small things will set them off. There are many reasons why." Her eyes meet mine again. "One of them being a failure to shift."

I scrub a hand over my jaw, trying not to get mad again. My leg is completely healed now. There's not even that faint twinge of pain that I was feeling yesterday when tugging it through the wall of mud. That doesn't mean I'm a dragon, though. "Haldir's fire doesn't erupt from his body, it only shoots from his mouth. At least, I think that's all it does. I don't really know what abilities anyone has, including you. I just know I'm different than Haldir, and both he and Monique said I'm not a dragon."

Leah shrugs. "If an Ulfr doesn't tap into their power often enough, their wolf becomes antsy. Stir-crazy. Then aggressive. That magical part of us is unrelenting until we're forced to shift. I think that could be part of what's happening to you. I won't push the issue on you anymore but if you ever want to explore your abilities, I might be able to help." Her shoulders lift again. "I might not. But I'm willing to try if you are, because if I were you, I would want know exactly what I was capable of. And I vote for sleeping in the altar room. I'll take first watch, right after we eat our scallop sushi."

She walks past me, lifeless in a way I've never seen her before. Her chocolate eyes are dull, as if I snuffed out some part of her that glowed from within. A part I didn't even know was there until it was gone. I look at my arms. "Do dragons shoot fire from every pore on their bodies, or only their mouths?"

"Mouths," she answers. "And Ulfr have wolf abilities. We're strong and fast, compared to humans, and our senses are heightened. We also have the ability to heal, like you've seen, and our lifespan is longer than a human's. We age more slowly, but not by much. That's why we're able to live in towns and mingle with humans so freely. Vampir, Álfar, Fae…most supernatural kinds, live way longer. They barely age. To the point that many of them are considered immortal. Technically, not all of them are, though. They die eventually. Just hundreds or sometimes even thousands of years later."

I follow her to the pile of scallops. "Thousands?"

She sits on the floor and begins opening our dinner, a sleek claw prying them open like it's nothing more than opening a peanut butter jar. "Thousands."

I sit beside her and start separating the scallops from the shell. "I caught fire again, on my way down to the water."

She nods. "I saw."

I take a deep breath. It feels so strange to be talking about this, especially with her. "The fire was only on my forearms this time. I can try to get it to happen again so we can cook these, but don't get your hopes up because the only times I've ever caught fire is when there's something happening to threaten my life. Or…"

She tosses some of the empty shells over the ledge. "When you think Keela is in danger. Another reason I think you might be a shifter."

I study her solemn features. "Can you explain why?"

Leah goes back to opening scallops. "It isn't possible for Keela to be your mate. The Norns are the ones who chart the fates of us all, and they've never ordained different kinds to be mates. But she was there when your powers unlocked, so that dormant part of you could have fixated on her, and now it's driving you to protect her the way a wolf would be pushed to protect their mate. All kinds have that sort of drive but it's particularly aggressive and...obnoxious in shifter kinds."

I force a smile onto my face. "Are you saying I'm obnoxious?"

She looks around the rotunda. "I could attack you but you would know I'm not actually trying to kill you, so I don't think that would trigger you. Did your fire go out when you hit the water?"

I pluck another scallop from a shell. "It did, but that could have only been because I knew at that point that I wasn't going to die. I barely even felt the impact." I sink my teeth into my lip. I want to tell her that I also burst into flames when she was in danger, but I'm not so sure that wasn't only a self-preservation response. "If you attacked me, I'm not so sure I wouldn't believe you wanted to kill me. In the past, I thought that was the case plenty of times. That me dropping dead would have been cause for you to celebrate."

She gets up off the floor and crosses the room to where the sword is. She picks it up, unsheathing the sword and swinging it through the air like she's checking to see how it balances in her hand. I smile. At least she seems to have a little light back in her eyes now. "See? I knew it was just a matter of time before you stabbed me."

She studies the subtle markings along the hilt, muttering. "Fitting."

I narrow my eyes on her. "What's fitting?"

She raises the sword, its blade catching what little light remains of this day. The honed metal shimmers and I notice the tiny rubies running around the underside of the hilt. Instead of pointing the blade at me, Leah angles it toward her own heart.

I spring up from the floor and race across the room. "What do you think you're doing?"

She presses the tip of the blade against her chest. "The blade is pure silver. The only metal that will kill a wolf even without piercing the heart. Maybe this was put here for me. So my family can make amends for keeping our truth from you."

I yank the sword away from her. "Saying sorry is good enough. I don't need the apology in blood."

She motions to the room we're in. "The Norns led us here for a reason. This is a place of sacrifice and the blade they placed here is one of the few things that can kill me by poisoning my blood, so do the math, Sean. I'm supposed to stay here while you continue on. These flooded ruins are my fate."

I grab the scabbard and shove the blade back into the leather. "I don't care what the Norns did, said, or fated. And the Leah I've known my entire life wouldn't be letting anyone tell her what her fate is, either. She'd make her own destiny." Fire licks up my arms. "Screw the Norns, Leah. We leave here together, or we stay here together. That choice is *ours* to make. *Together.*"

A grin ghosts over her lips, falling short of her eyes. "You might not be a dragon, Sean, but you have the heart of one. I thought maybe anyone's life being in danger—even mine—would kickstart your magic, and I was right. You've always had a genuine goodness about you." She shoulders past me. "Don't let the fire go out. I'll bring you the scallops."

21

"Do you know what these markings mean?" I ask Leah, the two of us sitting on the edge of the archway overlooking the flooded city. When I woke up this morning, she was already down in the water. When I jumped in with her, she held up the shirt full of scallops she'd already collected and then swam back to the vertical climb and made her way up to the rotunda without a single word being spoken between us. When I returned, she was dressed and lying on her side, looking out over the wall of mud. She didn't move until I asked her if she was ready for breakfast. Last night, I only managed to cook about half of our scallops before my fire sputtered out. Half was better than nothing, but I had to keep thinking about things that made me angry in order to do even that much. This morning, I couldn't get there. I think because Leah looks so sad.

She tosses another one of this morning's discarded scallop shells down into the water. "The markings on the hilt of the sword represent the heart of a dragon."

Her plain affect bothers me as much as her words do. I look between her and the adorned underside of the hilt. The small rubies are surrounded by grooved lines that run between them and crisscross, extending out from there to wrap over the hilt and all along the grip. "Are you being serious right now or is this another attempt to provoke me? You going to start spouting nonsense about me being dragon-hearted and righteous again? Just to make sure your lunch isn't as cold as your breakfast was?"

She tosses another shell, this one going out farther than the last one. "You asked me a question and I answered it."

I sigh. The only thing worse than a perfectly happy, clean, and conceited Leah MacKenzie is a sad, quiet, and brooding Leah MacKenzie. "So the sword really is meant for a dragon, and you think that dragon is me because I'm supposed to be some kind of defender of innocence?"

She shrugs. "I don't know why the Norns brought us here, but not all dragons are noble. They're as complicated as the rest of us."

I rest my hand on her knee. "Leah, I—"

She readjusts, effectively removing my hand from her. She points at the sword. "That grouping of rubies represents the crown of nine dragons who supposedly ruled all the worlds of Yggdrasil in the beginning of time. The etchings running from each ruby represent the lives of the dragons. Their hearts. My guess is that the silver blade is supposed to represent their purity, and the runes on the leather scabbard are meant to represent the fragile threads of fate that the wielder will be choosing to align with whenever they draw the sword. Dragons are into stuff like that. Puffing themselves up on pride and honor, pretending they are these wise old creatures, when there are so few of them that they don't even have a realm of their own because they can't get along with each other long enough to even find mates." She shrugs. "Dragons are warriors. And hoarders. They like to claim things for themselves and not share with anyone. Especially other dragons. So no one believes their old stories. No proof of their ancient kings has ever been found."

"So I was right about Haldir being full of hot air?" I grin.

She throws another shell, sending this one soaring high into the air and watching as it curves back down to the water. "Like I said, dragons are as complicated as the rest of us, but kind of worse. They've been known to kill their mates because they're so territorial that if they feel threatened, they attack first and ask questions later. Female dragons are extremely rare but still, there are stories about males shredding apart a female who entered their territory before even taking the time to realize the dragon letting themselves be ripped to shreds was only there because they'd felt the call of the mate bond, and they didn't fight back because of it."

"Geez." I suck in a breath. "Is that why you don't like Haldir? Because dragons are hotheaded and violent?"

She looks down between her dangling feet. "Haldir is a typical dragon, but he's also Vasilis, so that makes him more bearable in some ways but worse in others. He basically claimed Keela, so as long as you don't break the rules or dare look at her, he's tolerable enough."

I growl and she gets up. "Don't shoot the messenger, Sean. You're asking me questions and I'm answering them. I don't know about their whole relationship because my family doesn't speak to the Vasilis much. We follow their rules and stay out of their way. That's pretty much what everyone in Midgard does."

I turn and look up at her. "You're chummy with Gelby, though."

She huffs out a joyless laugh. "Gelby is fun. He's not as stuffy as the other Vasilis, but I didn't know that until you started college." Her throat works. "In Collin's absence, I was sent to watch over you. I knew right away that something was wrong on campus. There was too much activity from supernaturals who weren't even supposed to be on campus. But...I didn't realize it was because of you until it was too late. And partly because I met Gelby and he distracted me. And...well, I needed the distraction so I took it."

I didn't realize she hadn't known Gelby until recently, same as me. "I didn't know anything was happening on campus either. Not until it was too late. I guess that means we both get to blame the Vasilis for ruining our lives."

I pat the spot on the ledge next to me, where she was just sitting. She looks away, breaking the first willing eye contact she's made with me all day. "The Vasilis didn't give you power, Sean. They might be the catalyst for the emergence, but they didn't make you what you are. And it's in everyone's best interest, most importantly yours, to find out exactly what you're capable of."

Since she won't sit back down, I get up. "Do you think that's why the Norns brought us here? So I could get off my high horse and let you help me figure this out?"

She stares out at the distant forest for so long that I'm worried she's deciding never to speak to me again. I deserve the silent treatment, based on how I've been treating her these past few days, but she also treated me poorly for years and I need answers. Before the Vasilis or anyone else gets their hands on me again.

I take a breath. "I think you might be right about me being a shifter, Leah. I feel something inside of me, like a separate being. It moves around and has its own thoughts and emotions. It's like having someone else's soul inside of me. Is that how you feel with your wolf?"

She nods. "My wolf is separate. Her own being. I can feel her moving around inside of me and I feel her emotions. Hear her thoughts. The same way she can hear and feel me. It's a symbiotic relationship. Separate souls bound together by magic."

I step closer to her, trying to force her to look at me without grabbing her and shaking her. "So that's what I am then? Some kind of shifter whose other half has a bad attitude? Like a dragon does?"

She paces away from me. "You have shifter traits, so it could be that you've just never bonded with the other half of you and that's why the spirit inside of you never takes over." She stops, her face scrunching. "When you begin to burn, do you ever feel like your bones are moving? Or breaking?"

"No," I answer with a sigh.

She finally looks at me. "I can try to help you connect with whatever is inside of you. Teach you how I connect with my wolf and see if that works for you. If you want me to."

All we have is the rags of clothing on our backs, this sword, and each other. "Leah, we're surrounded by mud and water, and we already know what's out there on the mud side. Our only option is forward, through the remains of the flooded city. If I'm some kind of supernatural being that can help us get someplace truly safe, then I need to set aside everything else, even my differences with you, and learn. I'm ready. And I really appreciate you setting aside your differences with me, and how you've been so willing to help me even when I was being too self-centered to care. Thank you for helping me, Leah. Maybe this is the start of something new for us."

Leah

Sean's brows pinch and smooth as he sleeps, whatever his dreams are showing him not something his face seems particularly happy to see. He isn't moving around, though, as he's done before. He's perfectly still, flat on his back with his hands crossed over his stomach like some stoic god. A portrayal of him my brain has insisted upon conjuring too many times over the years. I'd see him standing on the sidelines while Collin wrestled with one of our cousins, and think to myself that Sean could beat all of them. Then I'd wage a mental war against such an outlandish idea. A human could never best an Ulfr, and back then, I was sure Sean was human. It's what everyone thought he was.

I sit up, still watching him sleep. He describes the thing inside of him as a *beast*, yet whatever he feels is not fighting him for dominance the way a wolf or even a dragon would if either of those parts of a shifter were tamped down and not allowed to express themselves. Especially to the extent that Sean is suppressing that which lives within him.

My wolf purrs her agreement. She would never stand for a life of being trapped within my human body. Never to be released. Never allowed to run free and commune with her own wild nature. So why would Sean's beast? We spent the better part of the night working on their connection but they still haven't bonded. Sean was able to summon his flame at will, though. Without being in danger. Without being angry and irritated with me. At least, I tried my best not to bug him. Not to be...me.

I scan his face one more time and then silently climb to my feet, thankful for the stealth of my wolf. I suppose it's possible that Sean isn't a shifter, but that would make the fact that Haldir's fire didn't burn him even more strange. And I don't even want to get stuck in the loop of considering how both of them are obsessed with Keela. A lot of people are infatuated with her, and not by their own choosing. *Dragons are stupid.* My wolf growls and I smile at her attempt to cheer me up. I've never believed all of the outrageously *noble* stories about dragons, but I have believed a lot of the stories I told myself about Sean. Stupid childhood fantasies.

Across the room and along the ceiling, those tiny wisps of light reappear. I bypass the altar and position myself underneath them, whispering, "Hello, my friends." They twinkle in response, coiling themselves into a tight rope that bends and circles until a patch of runes is lit up. I study the markings. "You want me to read these?" The lights grow brighter. I smile. "Runewisps, then. That's what I'll call you from now on." I trace my eyes along the lines of the runes. "Bonds of the past and present?" I ask them. They grow dim, scurrying across the ceiling to a new set of runes. I sigh and move across the room to see what they'd like me to interpret incorrectly this time. With today's modern technology, I've always thought learning to read these old runes was a waste of time.

I move underneath the wisps. This time, they float into the lines of the runes themselves, lighting up the symbols as their flickering becomes a steady glow. I mentally stroke my wolf. She's agitated. These wisps are trying to tell us something and it's frustrating that they're using the runes to do it. But I know these symbols. I tilt my head, whispering to them. "These are a warning. To prepare one's heart." The wisps dance off the ceiling and circle around me, darting under my arms and through my hair. I hold in a burst of laughter. No need to wake up Sean. He'd probably only yell at me for interacting with these miniscule orbs of energy, anyway.

"Does this mean I got it right?" I ask them quietly. They tickle across my ribs and then dart back to the ceiling, disappearing into a darkness that even my wolf eyes can't penetrate. "Whose heart needs to be prepared? Mine or Sean's?" I take a few breaths, waiting to see if they come back to answer me, but it appears they've had enough of me. The same as Sean. So I leave the room behind, carefully and quietly exiting until I'm standing on the edge of the rotunda. It's still early but I don't need much light to traverse the waters below. I've been studying the ruins of the city each time I go for a swim, and this morning I'd like to go out a little farther, beyond what can be viewed from here, to see what's behind the largest rooflines to the south. I strip off my shirt and pants, tossing them into a heap by the wall, and dive.

I twirl and spin, my wolf yipping with glee. Just before we connect with the water, I close my eyes, extend my legs underneath me and point my toes. We shoot down into the depths like a torpedo, the cool water rushing over us in a refreshing wave. If the moths hadn't shot down Haldir but instead let him follow us, we would have escaped this test of the Norns long before we ever reached this place. In this very moment, that seems like it would have been a shame.

I kick upward, breaking above the water's surface and begin to paddle toward the peak of a roof that juts out of the water at an angle that hides the lower roof of the building behind it. I trail my fingers across the tile shingles as I flutter past, diving under the water once more to follow the line of the lower roof beyond it, to where the shape of an angular building darkens the water. I can tell this spot is deeper than the rest because of how cold the water is. The lower I travel in the water column, the icier it gets. I'm curious to know exactly how deep it is and if the effect is because of a valley, but I've gone as far as I can when it comes to exploring the depths of this water. It isn't in my destiny to walk upon whatever watery terrain spans the landscape beneath me.

I break for the surface once more, gathering a lungful of air before pushing on to the next building. This one is wider than the others. Taller. It's the building that blocks a portion of the view from the rotunda. I dive down along the side of it, feeling my way over the rim of a glassless window. My fingers trace over the smoothness of the inside walls. There's no slime or growth of any kind. I blink, pushing my wolf to the forefront to use her better eyesight. Other than smooth walls, there's nothing here.

I paddle back out through the window and surface, gulping down air as I swim around the building, finding another unobstructed window on a different floor. I dip inside and use my wolf's enhanced vision to scan the room. In the very center, there's a staircase winding down to the floor below. I use the handrail to pull myself down the stairs. Everything I see is utterly pristine. It's like looking through a globe of water at a picture of an empty building. There's not a stitch of furniture or signs of any living thing. Not even algae.

I swim across the room and exit through a window on the far side of the building, kicking back up to the surface for yet another lungful of air. These buildings not having glass in their windows makes the exploration a lot easier. I don't have to swim all the way around them. I can take a peek inside and then use the shortcut they provide to dart across to the next one. When we're ready to journey to the forest that seems to be getting farther away each day, the shortcuts through the buildings will save us a significant amount of time.

I extend my arm and begin to stroke for the next closest building. This is the farthest I've been from the rotunda. I duck through a window, do a quick sweep of the inside, and then swim out a far side window and continue on to the next building. I reach the side of it and come up for air. Music catches my attention, coming from behind me. I spin around. "Sean?"

The music shifts. Moves. It's off to my right now, and growing distant. I pull my wolf forward again, using her strength to propel me. The richness of the music is incredible. I've never heard anything like it before. Each stroke I make brings me closer to the divine sound and I press my wolf for more speed, eyes scanning the ruins of the flooded city, looking for the source of the music.

The sound is growing closer. So close. I kick around the corner of a building and there, perched on the flooded corner of a low roof, is a man to make even my unrestrained nature blush. He's shirtless. Glistening muscles on full display as he caresses his fiddle, the music tumbling away from it, only to crash against me like tumbleweeds in a windstorm.

His head tilts, his long dark hair shifting over his shoulders. Our eyes meet and for an instant, I forget what it feels like to breathe. He is... My mouth waters, pulse picking up as my mind swirls and stutters over the many unworthy words that I could use to describe this man. His body... My own can't get to him fast enough. I throw myself into my strokes, swimming straight for him. The speed of his playing picks up, his music matching the racing rhythm of my beating heart, the sound a symphony of fireflies swarming through open fields inside of me. I dive, drowning the roar of the wolf in my chest. She can't have him. He's mine.

I break up through the surface at the man's side, gripping the edge of the roof he's perched upon with enough force that a crack splinters through the tile. His eyes dance, long fingers guiding the bow across the fiddle strings in powerful, delicate strokes. My watery mouth goes dry. "I've never heard anything so beautiful."

His music dips and rises, each stroke against the strings a step into a landscape of emotions. Joy. Loss. Love. Sorrow. I move closer to him, his music a firm hand against my back, leading me deeper into a dream. A memory. A yearning desire for more. *More.* "Please," I beg. Asking with that one word for him to take me. Ravish me. Eat me alive and spin me back out through his fingers, where I'll live forever within the breathless, yearning energy of his beautiful music.

He smiles, the knifepoints of his teeth glistening in the early light of dawn. The sun's brushstrokes of color have never been so vibrant as they are right now, alive with the melody of his music. "Please." I tremble, reaching a hand up to rest on his thigh. My chest heaves in ecstasy, his music wrapping around me in an endless touch. Everywhere all at once.

"Come closer, wolf." His voice is a song my body is desperate to sing. "My fiddle is yours."

"Yes," I breathe, my wolf nothing but a distant howl. I lift my hand and reach for his fiddle.

22

Sean

The sky is extraordinary this morning, the rays of the dawn slashing across a pale blue backdrop in strokes of emeralds and violets. I've never seen anything like it before. Wherever Leah is, I hope she's taking the time to look up. Not even Rome stands a chance of having a sky like this one.

I scrub a handful of cool water over my face. I don't like that Leah was already gone when I woke up this morning, or that she's out here in this watery world all alone. She's strong-minded and brave, but we need to find a way to form ourselves into a team that works together, not separately. We've had glimmers of being teammates but then we start acting like independent survivors again. Mainly because of me. But Leah was right about my anger issues having to do with me not tapping into whatever power is inside of me. Last night, she helped me figure out how to summon my fire. Not much, but the beast inside of me gave a little and I could feel myself relaxing every time I managed to call up a flame at will. Today we're supposed to work on getting that flame to only sprout out of my hand instead of all over my body.

I swim toward a building that's blocking my view. I didn't see Leah from the rotunda so she must have swum out pretty far today. I don't want to rock the boat of our newfound truce but now that my mind is calming down and my agitation levels are bottoming out, other feelings are creeping up. Leah is basically family. I should be keeping a better eye on her, even if she'll probably black *my* eye for trying to be protective of her. Still, she shouldn't be out here alone. Neither of us should.

I roll underneath the water's surface, scrubbing at my hair as I propel myself forward, looking for scallops or anything else not resembling snot that might be edible as I go. I tied the sleeves of my shirt together and made a little pouch that I could tuck at my waist and bring back some breakfast for us. Leah is better at finding us food but her shirt was piled on top of her pants this morning so I'm hoping I'll be able to gather our food and be the provider today. She's done enough to help us survive. Including putting up with me snipping at her. Over everything. A few months ago, if anyone so much as suggested that I would one day have even a fraction of a reason to offer Leah MacKenzie so much as the barest thought of gratitude, I would have died in a fit of laughter.

I come up for air and dive back under the water. My eyes focus on a grouping of scallops growing along the edge of a submerged roof. I swim toward them, realizing that my eyes have been open this whole time. There's no stinging, burning, or blurred vision. I can see as well under here as up on the surface. And *farther*. I blink. *Is this because of you?* I ask the beast inside of me. It doesn't answer. The same way it remained silent this morning when I decided to drop down into the water like a bull busting through a china shop window. The slap of the water should have at least stung, but it didn't.

Ever since my injuries started healing unnaturally fast, it's like my skin is toughening. Thickening. It still moves and looks the way it always has, but there's a heavier quality to my body now, And I'm noticing fewer and fewer sensations of pain. I was going to ask Leah about it last night, but though she was helping me, she was only speaking when necessary. Holding back and barely even making eye contact. The old non-magical me would have been happy to have her avoiding me. But in this new world, we can't afford to have those old wedges between us.

I kick back up to the surface and swallow a gulp of air, wishing Haldir was around so I could ask *him* about the confusing changes in my body. At least what's happening now isn't the embarrassing sort of body-wide changes that my dad had to help me navigate as a teenager, so I think I'm safe to ask Leah about them. If I can find her. She could be swimming on the other side of one of these buildings and I'd never see her.

I tread water and listen for splashing. Any sound that can help me figure out which way to go. My ears catch on something melodic. Like music. "Leah?" I call out to her. There's no answer. Only an increasing tempo. I swim toward the sound, curling around the edge of the closest building. In front of me and to my right, there's another building. The music sounds like it's right on the other side of it. "Leah?" I call out for her again. There's no answer. Only music. Unease settles in my gut. I slip under the water and swim toward where I think the music is coming from, scanning all around me as I go. Not sure if finding Leah in this direction will now be a good thing or not.

In addition to my enhanced vision, my lung capacity is increasing. The old me, the *human* Sean, would have had to surface for air by now. But this new, might-be-a-dragon version of me is pretty awesome. I'm nowhere near being starved for oxygen. And I can sense...a shift in the water. It's getting colder, but I can also feel something...moving...swimming in the water up ahead. I reach the building I was swimming for and stick close to the side, hoping to stay concealed while I scope out whatever is moving and playing music around the corner. If it's something that looks like it wants to eat us, I hope Leah is already back at the rotunda.

I stay under the surface and peek around the side of the building, narrowing my gaze on the spot where two lean, feminine legs are swaying gently back and forth. To the left of those two legs hangs another pair. They're wide and thick with muscle. And covered in scales. My heart pounds. I follow the scaly legs down into the darker water, beyond where Leah's feet end, to where fins, not feet, flip against the water.

Fear pushes me out of the water like a shooting star. I break above the surface and swim for her. "Leah!" She doesn't turn in my direction. She's focused solely on the fish-legged man perched on the roof next to her. His dark eyes skip to mine, the music he's playing picking up speed, each note a warning. A threat. Leah's mouth falls open, her hand clutching the fiddler's thigh. He looks at her. Her hand rides higher. I swim harder, screaming. "Get away from it! Get away from *her*!"

That *thing* smiles. Showing me its full mouth of flesh-shredding teeth. They're almost as bad as the ones in the face of the man-eating dwarf the Vasilis use as their prison warden. "Leah! Move!" I try to get her attention again. The fish-man pounces, latching onto her neck and diving down into the water. Leah doesn't put up a fight. Her body is limp. She's letting it take her.

I pull in a lungful of air and dive, hurtling straight for where the merman is dragging Leah deep into the icy water, blood streaming from where the creature's claws and teeth are dug into her skin. It narrows its eyes on me, flicking its wrist. A wave of water crashes into me, sending me flipping head over heels away from them. I toss myself to the side but my body gets rolled again. It's like I'm stuck in a raging surf, the creature's magic shoving me back. Away from it. Away from Leah.

Not today. I growl in my head and the beast in my chest roars. I shoot straight down in the water, aiming to get underneath the creature's magic. My hands begin to tingle and my whole body glows bright. But not with fire. It's the light that shocked Leah back to life. A light that's shocking the fish-man in a whole different way. He hesitates, my unexpected glow-up giving me the window I need. Instead of trying to surface, I go deeper, getting underneath the creature to cut it off at the pass. *What's the light do?* I ask my beast, angling for an attack that won't get Leah hurt further. *You seem to reserve this light for her, so tell me how to use it.*

Fossegrim. The word appears in my head, like a name being recalled from memory. *Kill it.* Two more words. These like an instinct. A knowing sowed directly into my brain rather than words spoken from the throat of my beast.

You've got it. I grit my teeth and steel my nerves. *Now tell me how?* My beast throws itself against the walls of my body. I try to allow it to take over, the way Leah instructed me to last night, but nothing happens. The Fossegrim changes course, diving deeper and away from me. I shoot through the water and barrel into its side. It rakes its claws across my back, whipping around and throwing Leah behind it. Her limp body hangs suspended in the water, then begins to sink. I lunge for her but the creature blocks, nails and teeth slashing and biting. I lift a foot and kick it straight in the gut. The Fossegrim flings backward, bumping into Leah.

I rush for Leah. The creature catches my throat in its clawed hand. I slam the palm of my hand into its face. It arcs backward, releasing my throat and wrapping its long legs around my torso. My beast roars and my body grows hot, spikes of fire shooting out of me like spears. They fizzle and die in the water but not before burning the Fossegrim. It leaps away from me with a hiss that vibrates the water. Leah's eyes pop open. Wide. Like she's coming out of a trance and finally seeing what's happening. I dive for her. The Fossegrim slams into my back, setting us both on a collision course with her body.

I flip over the head of the creature and shove my forearm under its chin, cranking back on its neck. I'm not a fighter, but I've learned a thing or two wrestling with Collin, and fish-man is human enough. I wrap my legs around its waist and lock my feet at its side, leaning back, focusing on the tingling sensation in my body. I channel all of that energy into my arms. Whatever happens, this thing isn't getting its claws into Leah again.

My grip tightens and I hug the thrashing creature against my body, controlling him while imagining my hands turning into roaring balls of flame. Instead, they explode with light. The Fossegrim lets out a shriek. And dissolves in my arms.

I press my hand over the wound in Leah's neck. "Why hasn't the blood stopped yet?"

She clamps down harder on the wound she's trying to staunch in her side. "That..." Her voice quivers, eyes not entirely focused. "Fossegrim. That was a Fossegrim. Their bite is poisonous."

My head empties of all thought. "Poison?"

Her haunted eyes meet mine. "I need to shift. The poison won't kill me, but the blood loss will."

I look at the water around us. I managed to haul her onto the low corner of the roof where I first saw her with that...Fossegrim. The roof is slanted and the tiles slippery. "Okay, shift. I'm strong enough to hold your wolf now. I can keep your head above water."

Her smile is weak. "You were always strong."

My stomach turns. There's defeat in her eyes. Her breath rattles and she closes her eyes. I lean over her. "Shift, Leah. You are not dying on me. You hear me? *Shift*. Right now! Shift!"

"Sean," she breathes, words barely able to form. "You're Fae."

Leah's been asleep for two days. I moved her wolf onto a better, flatter roof, and her wounds are slowly closing up. But each time I clean them, there's still more blood leaking out. At night, I curl my body around her wolf, trying to keep her warm. Letting her know I'm here. That she isn't alone. During the day, I drip water into her mouth and talk to her. About everything. Except the fear I have that she's going to die. I run my fingers through her soft fur, scratching gently behind her ear. I don't know if wolves like that sort of thing but every dog person I know swears their animals love to be scratched behind the ears. "You're doing great, Leah. I'm proud of you."

The animal fades away, leaving a bruised woman in its place. "That's a first."

I bite back tears. I should have known she would fight through this. The way she should have fought that creature. "The first time you've been bitten by a Fossegrim, or the first time you've heard me swallow my pride?"

"Both," she answers, her breathing shallowing out.

I remove my hand from where it's tangled in her hair and pull off my shirt. It's worse for wear, and I wish I had something better to offer her. Even her own shirt. But I haven't chanced leaving her long enough to go back to the rotunda. I tuck the fabric I have around her shoulders. "You *are* doing great, Leah, and I *am* proud of you." Her chest rises and falls in the steady rhythm of sleep. I curl up next to her, a pit smoothing over in my stomach. "Keep fighting. So you can hear me say that again and again."

<hr>

"Eat a little more." I hold up another plump bite of scallop to Leah's lips.

She turns her head aside. "I can't right now. My stomach isn't ready for more."

I chuck the lightly seared mollusk through the archway and down into the water below us. I didn't think she was ready to make the climb back up to the rotunda but she insisted. I stayed glued to her, practically cocooning her body underneath mine. I imagine she would have been complaining if she weren't so exhausted. "You're sure the poison has passed out of your system?"

She sighs. "After three days, yeah, probably."

I eye her. The bruising on her neck is heartbreaking and the teeth marks are still there. Still weeping. "Probably?"

She stares at the pile of scallops I cooked up for her. "You should eat these. Especially after all the effort you put in to getting your hand to catch fire."

I slide across the wall. A little closer to her. "I'm lighting up easier now, thanks to you. The beast thing is finally listening to me." It grumbles in my chest and I smile. Whatever it is, it does *not* like being trapped inside of me. "There are plenty of scallops out there. I can find more whenever I get hungry. I cooked these up for you so you can get your strength back."

She falls silent. The uneasiness between us is growing thicker each time she wakes up. Building to something I'm afraid of. She doesn't have much to say and I don't know what to say. Leah was assaulted. Physically by that creature, and before that, verbally by me.

Her eyes lift to where the sun is setting, its glow low on the horizon. I watch it with her. She shifts, suppressing a grunt as she moves. I reach for her. "What do you need?"

"To move on my own," she answers, freeing her arm from my hand. "We can't stay here."

I swallow. "I know. As soon as you're better, we'll head for the forest.

She shakes her head, teeth gritting and hand lifting to cover the jagged marks on her neck. "The Fossegrim is a water spirit, and water spirits aren't evil by nature. Sometimes they're even helpful. But that one lured me to it and would have killed me had you not...intervened."

I grunt. "Who knew a dragon could breathe fire underwater."

She steadies her shoulder against the wall and climbs to her feet, eyes wary. "They can't. What you did..."

I jump to my feet. "I shot fire. Before the glowing thing, fire came out of me. So I can't be Fae, right? I'm a dragon? Maybe even that prince you talked about."

I give her a teasing smile but she looks away. "You're definitely not a dragon but we can talk about that later." Her voice lowers. "It's still out there, Sean. I can hear its fiddle."

I strain my ears to hear, walking to the edge of the rotunda. "Now? You hear the music now?" I look at her over my shoulder. She looks...broken. I walk back to her. "I killed it, Leah. I'm sure it's dead."

Her jaw works and she lowers her head. "In this land... It's still out there. Playing for me. I hear it even when I'm asleep. I think the Norns...they allowed me to come so I could show you how to use your power. Now that you can control it...they want me gone. But I don't want to die. I want to go home."

I cup her face in my hands, thumbs stroking over her cheeks as I force her to look at me. "Leah, I don't give a damn what the Norns want. They're not separating us. And I'm nowhere near in control. You still have a lot to teach me, and I have a lot to tell you about how I'm changing. So we stay together, we look out for one another, and if these Norns decide to send another bare-chested fiddle-playing spirit to lure you away, then we'll show him to a violent death. *Together*." I rest my forehead against hers. "If the Norns try to take you anywhere but home, I swear to every god they worship that I will play them a tune none of them will survive." My beast roars in violent agreement. "I'll burn their whole world down if they touch you again."

23

I glance at the silvery glow of moonlight casting down through the fog hanging over the distant forest. Leah isn't one hundred percent but we've both agreed that today is the day. As soon as the sun comes up and there's enough light for us to see, we're heading for the forest. If there's a water spirit out there, it dies. Over the last week, I haven't let Leah leave the rotunda without me at her side, and even then, I've insisted that she only go down for a quick wash or a drink, sticking beside the cliff where she can easily race back up if anything pops out of the water. Surprisingly, she hasn't fought me on that.

I reach over and curl my fingers through hers. We're sitting side by side, shoulders touching as we wait for the faintest trace of light to streak across the water below. "Together," I remind her. "You hold on to me, and I hold on to you." We've gone over this plan a hundred times but I can't keep myself from repeating it one more time. "We swim holding hands until one of us needs a break. Then we stop, find a roof to rest on if we can, or just float on our backs, one at a time, so one of us is always able to watch below us."

"If we see something, we say something," she finishes. "Then we formulate a plan on how to deal with it. Together."

I give her fingers a squeeze. "Together. We don't let go unless I have to burn...or glow."

"Or I have to shift," she adds. "But before we leave, I need to tell you something. Just in case."

My jaw clenches. No matter what I say or do, she still talks as if her days are numbered. "I need to tell you something, too. I haven't been entirely honest with you about my power. I've told you everything that I can do and about how the beast inside of me feels."

She sighs. "Which sounds like a shifter, but it doesn't speak to you the way I can actually hear another voice inside of me. So not a shifter."

My beast seems to nod its head as if she's right, I'm not a shifter. But I don't feel or look like the Fae. "You said the glowing thing is Fae magic, but you've never heard of a Fae having a separate being inside of them, so your theory is that Aether put the beast inside of me. But, well, that's not what happened." She turns and looks up at me. Waiting. Still a woman of few words these days. I swallow. "I don't know why your family was paid to watch over me from birth, but the day I arrived at Merrymont, I saw Keela."

Leah's hand goes limp in mine. "And you fell for her."

I blow out a tired breath. "Fell is an understatement. I know about the vampire allure stuff, Gelby explained it to me, but...that's not...I think I actually *belong* to Keela. Like that fated mate stuff everyone keeps talking about. I know you think that's impossible but that day when I saw her, even from a distance, I just had this...knowing feeling. Like I had to be near her. Long story short, I followed her and caught her making out with her Fae boyfriend. That's the first time I felt my beast. When Aether was alive and kissing Keela. Before he ever punched his fist into my chest." I meet Leah's eyes. "I was supernatural before he touched me. That's why someone hired your family to keep an eye on me."

Leah closes the distance between our mouths and kisses me. I yank away from her, pulling back my hand a fraction before my mouth leaves her lips. "What are you doing?"

She studies every inch of my face. "Seeing if it's possible to make you forget about Keela. Seeing if...if it's possible for you to find someone else."

I stand up and pace along the edge of the rotunda. "Leah, I...we're... I don't look at you like that."

"You used to," she mutters.

"And you made me regret it," I snap. "You wanted nothing to do with me. *No Shot Sean*. Remember the summer when that catchy tune was all the rage? Compliments of you?"

Her head drops. "I was ashamed."

"You should be," I grumble.

"No." She looks back up at me. "I was ashamed...that I liked you."

I snort, the ridiculousness of her claim too much to bear. "I think you're mistaking shame for arrogance. I might have gotten the worst of your wrath but all the other guys you flirted with and teased over the years felt just as rejected as I did when you decided you were done with them."

She climbs to her feet. "Did you just imply that I'm a tramp? Or is it only that I'm a tease? Which is somehow more offensive to guys than me being easy to bed."

I fold my arms over my chest and stare her down. "I'm saying that you didn't make it easy for Collin. He did everything he could to protect you, but you were hell-bent on getting the attention of every warm-blooded male in sight. And once you got it, you moved on to the next." I drop my arms and walk toward her. "Nobody cares about your sex life, Leah. It's the way you treat people that matters."

Tears form in her eyes and for more times than I can count now, they're real. "I was a kid when I hired that band and—"

"So was I," I cut her off, turning to look at the view instead of her. "This is stupid. We don't need to have this conversation. Ever. And definitely not today, of all days."

"You got to say what you wanted and now it's my turn." Her voice cracks. "You think I'm a horrible person because that's the person I had to be. I wasn't flirting and getting attention for the fun of it. I was doing it for the very same reason I just kissed you. Only, it was to get *my* mind off of you instead of your mind off of someone else."

I look at her. Tears are trickling over her cheeks. "Leah—"

She holds up a trembling hand. "Stop. I know you don't believe me but I need to tell you the truth anyway. I want to get this off my chest while I have the chance." She lowers her hand, resting it on her stomach. "Before I knew that I'd caught your eye, I'd started getting these funny feelings in my stomach whenever you were around. I'm Ulfr, though, and we're raised to believe that we're superior to every other kind. Raised to believe that power and strength are to be coveted. Sought. Honored."

I run a hand through my hair. "And I was nothing but a weak human."

She wipes her face. "You weren't weak. Not by human standards. But I'm the daughter of an alpha. I'm expected to make a powerful match." Her watery eyes meet mine. "I knew if I let myself feel what I felt for you, it wouldn't be a simple fling. Not for me. I knew I'd want my childhood crush to turn into a sappy love story, and that my wolf and I would fight to never let it fade." She looks down. "I had already fallen for you so hard that I knew if I allowed myself to be with you, I would never be able to accept another. Even if the other was my mate."

My brows furrow and I turn to look back out on the darkness still coating the sky. "Rohan's love for Keela was broken by his mate bond with Jofir. It doesn't really seem like anyone has a choice once these Norns get involved with their love life."

Leah sniffs. "Most supernaturals don't have a reason to fight fate. But all of my instincts, and even my wolf, told me that I would turn down my mate for you. That doesn't mean much to you because you weren't raised as a supernatural, but in the world I grew up in, being soul mated is an honor. Turning your back on such a bond is looked down upon, and the denial is painful for both parties. Physically as well as mentally." She steps away from where I'm standing. "With my position in the pack, I couldn't run the risk of hurting a fellow wolf like that. My mate was...*is* sure to be powerful. My rejection would weaken him and put pressure on the always fragile bonds of pack alliances."

I resist the urge to gain back the distance she just put between us. "Back then, I was just a human. Not important to your pack or any others."

"Mostly," she admits. "You meant something to my pack, but because I thought you were human, I also believed that in addition to everything else, if I let myself love you, I would be loyal the way we wolves are. And you would be lukewarm, the way so many humans seem to be." She sighs. "I thought I'd choose you over all others and then one day, after I completely blew up my world for you, you'd just...walk away. Tell me you fell out of love with me, and that would be it. I'd be out of my pack and left alone, knowing the pain I caused my family, my mate, myself...it would all have been for nothing. It was a risk I couldn't let myself take."

I glare at her. "So you tormented me? That was *your* solution to *your* problems? Torment the innocent guy who didn't have a single clue what you even were, let alone how you felt?"

She swipes at her tears again. "It was stupid, but I was young when all of that started. I thought making you not like me would somehow make me stop wanting to be with you. It didn't, but at least you never acted on any feelings you had toward me and that was better than nothing because..." A sob breaks from her throat. She covers her mouth. "If you had ever pursued me, I wouldn't have stopped you."

I scrub my hands over my face to keep them from holding her the way they're itching to do. Only because she's a crying female. Not because I like her. "You know, Leah, maybe you should have considered that I could have fallen for you and never looked at anyone else. That I'm a stand-up guy who would never cheat or leave. That if I commit to someone, I'm as loyal as you are."

Her laugh is harsh, her tears only falling harder now. "That sounds good, but you forget that I knew people like Keela existed. Without a true mate bond, you are a lamb waiting to be slaughtered. Especially when it comes to Vampir like her. Even now, when you're not around her, you're so infected by her allure that I know exactly when you're thinking about her. Because I can smell your desire, Sean, and I know it isn't seeping out of you over me. It hasn't been over me since that horrible summer, when I had to break my own heart."

She turns and dives down into the water. I go after her. "We had a plan! Stick to the plan!"

She dives under the water and comes up farther away from me, giving me an answer that doesn't require words. I trail after her. "We're not kids anymore, Leah. Getting yourself killed out here isn't only going to break your heart *and mine*, it'll devastate your family. So give me your hand and for once in your life, trust me not to leave you the way you're always so hell-bent on leaving me."

Leah and I are barely speaking. Our mutual desire to forget the things she confessed spurring both of us to focus solely on those primal instincts that drive us to survive. To protect ourselves. Unless the conversation has to do with food, shelter, or danger, words are no longer welcome between us. The growing divide has its perks. Our journey through the flooded city was faster. We didn't point out the marvels of the architecture we saw or waste breath wondering aloud about what the city is, why it exists, or why it's underwater. We swam. Against all odds and at any costs, we pushed forward with all our strength, each overtaking the other as we moved through the water without stopping. Without touching. We slowed when we needed to, aware enough of each other to at least follow the physical cues, but we never, *ever* stopped.

"This is a good place to camp for the night," I mutter, crouching down and cupping my hand in the trickling water of the stream we stumbled upon our second day in the forest. Leah is up ahead, getting her own drink. I can see the silhouette of her wolf behind the towering ferns that grow along the water's edge. We swam for two days and one night. The instant we touched land, she shifted. That was three days ago. Since then, she's been in her wolf form the majority of the time.

When we found the stream, we never had a conversation about the benefits of following it. Leah's wolf just started walking near it and I fell in line behind her, both of us driven by our instincts. We have to have water, and the stream has been a good source of food. There are fish in the deep pockets and Leah is good at catching them. Better than me, but I'm not a wolf who grew up running through the woods honing my predatory instincts. I have hands, not claws. But I also have fire.

I move away from the stream and begin to collect small sticks and other bits of dry wood. Our first night in the forest, we were wet and cold, and neither of us wanted to be near the other so sharing body heat was out of the question. I gathered wood and lit a fire. The tension in Leah's body amped up and I understood why, but even not knowing what kinds of creatures lurk in this forest, I couldn't let us freeze to death. After nothing came to eat us that first night, I went ahead and started a fire the second evening and we roasted the three fish Leah caught, plus the one lonely trout that I managed to snag from the stream. From the sound of Leah splashing in the water, we'll have a similar meal tonight.

I walk deeper into the forest, filling my arms with kindling and looking for a good place for us to sleep tonight. It's hard to know how far from the ruined city we've traveled. It disappeared behind a wall of fog the instant we pulled ourselves from the water. Since then, we've walked. Slept a little. And walked some more. Falling into a pattern that requires little talking. I'm on fire-starting duty and Leah usually shifts back to human as I roast our fish, choosing to eat her meals in her human form. At night, I take first watch, waking up her sleeping wolf when I get too tired to keep my eyes open. When she's ready to leave camp in the morning, she shifts back, puts out the fire, and returns to her wolf form before nudging me. I'm usually awake but choose to remain as silent as she is while she works to put out what remains of my flames.

I move around a moss-covered boulder. This could be a good place for us to camp for the night. I duck under a low branch to get a better look at what's on the far side of the rock. Dirt slides over the edge of the boulder and I look up a second too late. A padded paw covered in thick gray fur slams into my face, the wolf's teeth sinking into my shoulder as the animal collides with my back and drives me to the ground. Fire erupts along my body. The attacking animal yelps. Retreats. And comes at me again.

"Collin!" Leah screeches. "Collin, stop!"

I spit the dirt out of my mouth and roll onto my back, blood dripping into my eyes from the mouth of the wolf standing over me. I wield my still burning arm like a torch. "Are you freaking kidding me? Collin? Is that you?"

The animal morphs into a man. "Sean?"

I kick him between the legs. "You just BIT me!"

He falls to his knees, cupping himself and gaping at his sister. "Leah? How in the..."

She drops down and throws her arms around his neck. He wraps his arms around her and holds her tight, lifting to his feet with her in his arms. "I missed you, brat. I really, really missed you."

For the briefest of moments, her eyes meet mine, tears streaming down her dirt-stained face. She tucks her chin into Collin's shoulder, sobbing. His grip on her tightens. "I'm going to kill Dad for sending you after me."

I sit up. "He didn't send us. And it's you who's getting ready to die because *I'm* going to kill *you*." I stand up and wipe the blood off my shoulder. The bite wound is already healed and I ditched my shirt after Leah was back in the rotunda and wearing her own. It was nothing but a rag and her bloodstains wouldn't wash out. Not enough for me not to continually see her bleeding for days on end every time I looked at it. "Take care of your sister and make her happy, and then you're dead."

His wary eyes look over his opposite shoulder, hand tucking against his sister's head as he holds her close and studies me. "You burned me."

"And you spent twenty years lying to me," I clap back.

His jaw sets. "I didn't have a choice. Why do you not smell like you?"

I fold my arms over my chest. "Why do you not know how to warn your best friend about evil fairies, giant elves, dragons, or *vampires*? Huh? What about zombies? Witches? Portals to different worlds? How about telling me there are pockets of worlds within all these other worlds that I've never heard of, where those giant elves take people to be tortured? Huh? Did any of that ever cross your mind in the last twenty years!"

My voice rises with each word, and Leah lifts her face from Collin's shoulder. "There's a lot we need to tell you, brother. But I was catching fish when I smelled you, because *you* still smell like *you*." She smiles. "Let's go get some fish for dinner. Sean will cook them. With his *dragon* fire."

The blood drains from Collin's face. "You're a dragon?"

A female voice rises behind him. "No, he is not Dreki."

We all turn to the woman standing twenty feet away. She's tall, with long brown curls cascading over her shoulders. Her green eyes are fixed on me, leaving me speechless. Leah peels herself out of Collin's arms and squares off with the green-eyed beauty. "No one said he was Dreki.

Just like no one invited you to this conversation, *dragon*." Leah flicks her hands, sprouting claws. "I suggest you see yourself out."

Collin chuckles and throws his arm around Leah's shoulders. "Zara, meet my sister. A wolf with an attitude about as bright at yours. We're all going to get along just fine."

Her eyes haven't left mine, Leah's threat having no impact on Zara at all. I swallow, repeating her name, as if that will take away the threat I see deep within her irises. "Zara."

Leah's head cocks, I see her glare from the corner of my eye but I can't take mine off Zara. "It looks like you're right about the fire wielders hitting it off. Let's go, Collin. The lovebirds can have their privacy while we catch up. Where are Ethan and the others?"

Her voice fades as they walk away. Zara raises a brow. I summon fire to my palm. "It's complicated."

She walks toward me, eyes dropping to my flames. "With the wolf? Or the fact that you stole that fire from my ancestors?"

24

Zara

If the death of Collin's friend would release the spirit of the dragon held captive inside of the boy, Sean would be dead. But the might of my ancestor is tied to the boy's soul. Stolen by Odin and bound to a lesser soul by magic leeched from the Norns themselves. *The dragon with no body.* The Seidr warned me what would happen if I killed the body. *Death claims one and both princes die.*

I lean back on my elbows, studying Sean from across the fire. He and Collin are deep in conversation. Collin's sister is also deep in conversation with her brother, but not the dragon thief. She barely looks at him, but he watches her, averting his eyes every time they stop on her pretty face. It's curious. But not as interesting as finding out who this boy is. *Brother betrays brother. By blood not by birth.* The Seidr's words click into place as I listen to their years of betrayal. But if the wolves thought the boy to be human, his dragon's ability only manifesting when he came into contact with the Álfar, then what prince is he? A human one is of no value to me, and my prince being trapped inside of his body even more of an affront. I drop my eyes to the center of his bare and highly muscled chest, directing my thoughts to the Dreki inside of him. *I will free you, and you will save our kind. You will restore our crown and return our kingdom to its rightful glory.*

The sky above us is bright with the glow of a full moon. I lift my eyes and wonder if the prince inside of the boy can feel that I am near. His warrior, lying in wait. As a changeling, I was never given a chance to fight for my kingdom. The Seidr visited my home long ago. Long before the last war. She took me and left another in my place, while I was too young to grow up with any memory of what my mother looked like. From that time, all I have known is a life of servitude. One dedicated to the Seidr. Filled with books and learning. Cryptic words and brutal trainings. The Seidr sharpened me to be her sword and once her visions for me began, I finally understood why. As the original of her kind, my Seidr has always been at war. She swapped me with another child, giving my mother someone else to raise, so that I could survive fate. So that I could alter the destiny of all Dreki. Me. A dragon with no fire. A magicless dragon who can't even shift.

"Then we got separated." Collin reaches the point in his timeline that brought us here, to this land not bound by physical laws. The land where my magic was stolen. A punishment from the Norns. The consequence of me stealing a vial of their sacred water. A smile breaks over my face at the memory and I bite my lip to rein it in. The Seidr spent a very long time collecting the right offerings from seekers, compiling them and sending me to trade them for other goods over the course of many years, until she finally had what she needed to convince the head of the

Völva coven to create portal stones powerful enough to break through the enchantments covering Urðarbrunnr.

Beatrice delivered two stones. One to get me into the well, and one to get me out. I'll never quite forget the look on the faces of the three Norns when I appeared in the middle of their precious well. I only wish my arrival, and not the timing of it, was what shocked them. From what I could tell, the Norns were readying themselves to greet seekers of their own. Me popping in to fill a vial wasn't part of that preparation, and not something they cared to let their seekers see happening. Word getting out that it was possible to bypass their wards would be bad for their business.

"You two are the first people I've seen since Zara let the time serpents drag us here," Collin complains.

I drop my eyes to his. "Let's just hope the Norns find you more worthy than I have."

He rolls his eyes, no less suspicious of me now than he was before. His sister seems to share his distrust. "If the two of you have been lost in this forest for weeks, going in circles, and yet you claim that you've been here before, maybe it's *you* the Norns aren't finding worthy. I've been in this forest for days now and haven't once walked in a circle."

I smile at her. Only because it infuriates the little wolf. "The stream you were following is the same one we've been following. The same one I followed the last time I was here, and *met* the Norns." I don't bother telling them I cheated. The witch's stones were only strong enough to get me inside the well if I was already in this land. The Seidr used stones gifted to her by a different coven to get me to this forest, and I splashed into the well from here.

Collin shoves a hand in my direction. "I've tried to ditch her fifty times but even when we both walk in opposite directions, we still end up coming right back together. And while I like my women hot, I'd rather this one be a giant lizard, but she refuses to shift."

"Sounds like the opposite of my problem," Sean mutters, cutting off any further scrutiny over my lack of shifting. I can still feel my dragon inside of me, but I can't hear her. Can't access her through the wall of the hex the Völva coven placed on me. A double-cross the Seidr didn't see coming.

Collin looks between Sean and Leah. "What is going on? I know you two don't get along but—"

"But you ditched me and I got stuck in this situation," Sean interjects, eyes cutting to Leah before landing back on Collin. "*We* got stuck in this situation. But why did you even leave to begin with? That last day I saw you at Merrymont, where did you go?"

Collin looks at his sister. She nods and he sighs, rubbing his face before answering. "It sounds like you know almost everything else, so long story short, my pack was hired for a job. By the Fae. But not only one faction of them. We were approached by both the Seelie *and* Unseelie. They're each looking for the same artifact. Normally we're pretty good at finding things, but they didn't give us much to go on." He nods in my direction. "That's why we went to see the Seidr, and how all of the rest happened, and I ended up here. The thing is, both Fae factions claim the artifact is theirs. That it was created by the gods and has this power that only the Fae can use. But they don't know what it looks like because they said it can change forms. Like be a necklace or a sword...anything. So they want us to just sniff out powerful items and bring them the right one."

My hackles rise. "Sounds like the Fae are working together to collect a whole bunch of powerful artifacts. How many has your pack turned over to them?"

Collin groans. "We're not stupid. Unless we're hired for a specific job for a specific item, one with a unique identifying feature, anything we find, we keep. We're pretty good at tracking down histories and figuring out who or *what* the artifact originally belonged to. Until then, we keep the stuff in our safe, and no one gets in our safe. It's warded with a thousand different spells. Only three pack members can even open it. My parents and me." He nudges his sister. "This squirt doesn't even have access."

Sean leans around Collin and attempts to meet Leah's averted eyes. "Do you think it could be that sword we left behind? It looked old and it was in that room with all those runes."

Leah shrugs. "Why don't you swim back out to the city and fetch it?"

His gaze narrows. "You're the dog, why don't *you* go fetch it."

"Hey!" Collin shouts, so loud the birds nesting in the canopy take flight. "Low freaking blow, dude. And that's my *sister* you're talking to like that!"

Sean straightens and levels his angry glare on me. "Maybe you should go fetch it, Zara. Leah said it was some kind of dragon sword. Silver blade for how pure of heart you are, and rubies under the hilt to represent your kings. Yours, not mine, since I'm not a dragon. Or a wolf. Or a pointy-eared fairy!"

The three of them descend into an argument and I dig my fingers into the ground, holding still, trying not to draw attention as my screams echo inside my too-hollow chest. *Firebrand.* The sword he speaks of is Firebrand, a weapon that symbolizes Dreki power. One forged by the ancient kings and imbued with eternal flame. It was meant for the highest-ranking prince but as the Dreki were slaughtered and the bloodlines ran dry, the sword was lost. "Flames?" The word slips from my mouth. Three sets of angry eyes turn to me. I swallow. "When you held the sword, did it ignite?" *Like it should, if you have the soul of the last remaining prince inside of you.*

Sean's head shakes. "No. Why?"

A screech pierces the night sky and we all jump to our feet. My heart seizes up in my chest. Defying one's fate is considered heresy. An act against the natural order. As pointless as rowing a boat against a fierce wind because once you are tired and worn, and the Norns have punished you for attempting to circumvent that which they have woven, the Norns are relentless in their quest to mend what you have sought to change—their shaping of the cosmic order an inescapable force that even the gods themselves are subject to. Only Urd, Verdandi, and Skuld, the weavers we call the Norns, are not bound by that which they alone mold. Which doesn't seem fair at all. Because I happen to know they are not the impartial arbiters they hold themselves to be. The sisters do much more than maintain structure and order within the cosmos. They play favorites, hold grudges, and spend so much time arguing with one another that they only have themselves to blame when their power is manipulated and misused. So if they brought me here hoping I would beg for their forgiveness, I will not. If they brought me here to die, they can try.

I hoist my pack onto my shoulders and finger the side pocket where my two remaining portal stones are hidden. Now that I know where Firebrand is hidden, I'll make the Norns pay for their arrogance. "Run for the stream!" I call out to the others, only a drop of remorse plunging into my stomach. "Those are oracle vultures. They hate water."

I take off running in the direction of the stream, the white feathers of the bird-like creatures filling the sky above us. They gleam like bones, their screeching said to rattle even the deepest roots of Yggdrasil, sending shockwaves through the cosmos each time the Norns send their killers for their prey. And unfortunately for Collin and his friends, the vultures don't mind getting wet.

I let the three of them overtake me and once they're far enough ahead, I veer off into the cover of the forest. If I can find the water Leah and Sean described, I'll swim to the rotunda. If not, I'll portal away from these birds. But I'm not leaving here without Firebrand.

Gelby

The wind outside my tent howls. Shivers trace down Monique's arms and I once again wonder how I got stuck with the witch. Only Rohan, Haldir, and I had tents in our packs, magically spelled to be condensed. When Leah and Monique showed up at our door, I didn't even consider the sleeping arrangements. Jofir was always going to stay cozied up with Rohan and Sean Winkle was supposed to remain with me, trapped inside this tent by my magic. Haldir would be the only one to sleep alone. According to Monique, Leah had their tent, carrying more of their supplies because of the shifter's strength. Now, because Monique is terrified of Haldir, Rohan ordered me to give shelter to the witch. If Leah hadn't run off like a puppy chasing a new toy, Monique would be the one with her own tent because Leah would be with me. Haldir would be the one babysitting Sean Winkle. I would have made sure those were our permanent sleeping arrangements. We should have killed the moths and sought forgiveness afterward. It isn't like honoring the Norns and showing respect for their divine wishes has gained us anything.

"Here." I offer Monique a bite of my bread. "It might help you to heal faster." Out of all of us, she is the one who doesn't have the benefit of rapid healing, and even I'm battered and bruised. But not like Monique. Her lip is split and the gash on her eyebrow looks infected. Her fingers are scraped raw, hands flecked with cuts, and her sunken, hollow eyes are rimmed in shades of black and blue. She shivers again, pulling the blanket tighter as she takes the bread, silently chewing as we both listen intently to the brewing storm. The last one turned into a cyclone, and we barely kept our supplies from being stripped away from us. Barely kept each other from being stripped away.

I stretch out along my side of the tent and curl an arm under my head. Between the relentless storms and the attacks from creatures as unique to this land as they are in their purposes of serving the Norns, we are all exhausted. Monique's magic is long depleted and even I have spent too much in my efforts to defend us. To find Sean Winkle and his traitorous wolf. "If you can, try to sleep, Monique. I'll watch over you, and Haldir is right outside."

She turns her head toward the door, as if she can see Haldir standing guard. He's been on the verge of shifting ever since the moths shot him from the sky, but every time even a single scale appears on his body, he falls into agony. The Norns have cursed the dragon. They've cursed us all.

"Do we…" Monique's voice is frail. "Do you… I didn't bring an offering for the Norns. Do you think they know?"

I consider whether or not I should tell her about the gifts we carry. Rohan holds a vial of water from the frozen lakes created by the ice giants. I possess a tapestry woven by the hands of sprites. And Haldir holds a seed from the mighty Ash—a tree that represents Yggdrasil all throughout Midgard. Each offering is symbolic of the forces of fate. Meant to show our reverence for the interconnectedness of life. Gifts to symbolize our respect for the sacred duties of the Norns. "Did you not intend to seek your own audience with the Norns? It's a long way to come with no ambition of earning something for yourself."

She smooths back one of the many stray hairs that are loose from her braid. "Each Norn represents a different thread of fate. Skuld is the holder of prophecy. She sees the outcomes of all possibilities. Verdandi reigns over the ever-changing present, always aware of events unfolding in the here and now. But Urd...she knows the past. Every decision. Every mistake. Every right choice." Monique's hollow eyes meet mine. "Urd draws from history, knowing every single thing that has transpired. She is the one who knows us best because she doesn't have to guess at what we'll do. She doesn't have to contemplate the outcomes of our decisions because she already knows the choices we've made."

The witch's haunted expression makes me uneasy. "Urd is wise from the accumulation of history's lessons, and she indeed possesses vast understanding. What is it that you fear her memories will show?"

Monique shivers once more, her head shaking ever so slightly. "Not me. It's Beatrice—" Moniques eyes bulge, glowing bright before turning opaque.

I bolt upright and grab her shoulders. Her head falls back, mouth lolling open, a long, painful moan escaping her throat. "Monique." I shake her. "Monique!"

Haldir bursts through the tent door, fury twisting his features as he kneels next to the witch. "She isn't a seer."

My heart pounds. "She wasn't..." *Until we came to this impossible, miraculous, terrible place.* Chills pick their way along my spine. I send a bolt of a magic through my body to tamp them down. I can't afford the extra waste but I also can't afford to let myself be shaken by this veiled land of twisting destinies.

Rohan and Jofir squeeze into the tent, Rohan still pulling on clothes while Jofir's flushed cheeks make me think of Leah. I dig my fingers into Monique's shoulders. "She's having a vision. I think…"

Jofir nudges Haldir aside. "Let go of her. Let her see what the Norns are gifting her."

"How do you know it's a gift?" My tone draws a warning growl from Rohan but I don't care. "They could be putting her in a comatose state for all any of us know. The Norns haven't exactly been welcoming."

Jofir hits me with a bolt of magic and the shock of her audacity removes my hands from Monique's shoulders. Rohan kneels beside me, eyes narrow, daring me to retaliate against his mate. I grind my teeth. "Control her, or I will."

Before he can respond, Monique's head flings forward and she gasps, holding her throat as a disembodied voice curls over her unmoving lips.

Quiet sanctity once disturbed, echoes through currents of lives upturned. That which haunts you doth now hunt you. Intertwined, present and past, living and dead. Eyes once seeking wisdom now buried in ancient mire, hidden in the place where shadows are drawn. Survive the balance of time and beware that which glows with no fire. Survive, and follow the raven's flight, down into the lair of a dragon's heart.

Monique collapses forward. I catch her body and pry one of her eyes open. "They're back to normal."

"Shh." Haldir's head cocks. My mouth goes dry, Rohan's pale face bleaching white. *That which haunts you doth now hunt you.* The Skarthorn. Mixed within the blustering beat of the wind against the canvas of our tents is a bone-chilling howl, one my brother and I will never forget. One I'll never let hurt my family again. I slide Monique to the ground. "Watch her. This kill is mine."

25

Keela

I sit crouched in the mouth of the cave where Abhartack has been steadfast in his quest to nurture me back to full strength. I am not yet there, but I can no longer see the bones in my hands. They are covered by soft pink skin. Soon enough, the stiffness will go away. As will the discomfort in my arms and legs. What will never leave me is the mental toll of having been inside the Primordial Void. I still hear the otherworldly noises. The clanging. Grinding. I can still feel the rush of air moving past me on my endless fall through the pit of nothing. Worse than all of that is how even as I stand here, tucked into a cave high on the side of this barren mountain, I can still smell Sean Winkle. His scent is faint but no matter where I move within or without the cave, Sean's scent is always here.

It was foolish to believe the fiery human would be so deep within the chasm. That the power I bore witness to as it broke from his body meant that the boy was anything more, or that he would choose to scale a cliff as a means of finding me. Not even *my* allure is strong enough to travers worlds. The void tricked me. And before that, it confused me. Made me feel as if new parts of me were emerging. Parts that desired Abhartack and a life in Dökkbraek. Two things I'm still confused by. I desire the king, more and more each day. And I desire to go home with him...to Draugrkeep.

Abhartack's hands fold over my shoulders. "Come back inside. Another storm is coming and you need to rest."

I reach over my shoulder and place my hand atop his. There is a closeness between us that cannot be blamed on his allure or mine. On his chivalry in saving me. Staying with me. Feeding me from his own veins even when doing so weakens him. Abhartack saved my life at the risk of his own, but not even that can explain how I react to him. Wholly engulfed. It doesn't explain why my heart seizes when he's out hunting for his own nourishment, steadfast in his unwillingness to take even the tiniest drop of blood from me before I fully recover. "We cannot continue to stay here. The mountain is too barren to supply you with food. Each time you leave, you travel greater distances to find even a sip."

He begins to massage my shoulders. "We will leave this mountain once you are fully restored."

I spin underneath his palms and face him. Neither of us knows why the void decided to toss him out unscathed while it left me unconscious and barely clinging to the life I had no hope of regaining for myself. We don't even know *where* we are. All I know is that I care about the king, and it is my turn to protect him. With how much of his blood I have needed and the lack of food on the mountain, he grows weaker by the day. "We must go *now*. Your people probably think you are dead and after what I did to Arsenious, they probably think I..."

He brushes his knuckles over the delicate new skin covering most of my face. "*Our* people are well trained and well organized. They will know that we entered the void, and they will keep Dökkbraek safe while they await our return."

I gently pull his hands away from me. "What if your spot as king is challenged while you're gone? Or the temporary overseer doesn't want to give up his title once you return."

Abhartack frowns. "Dökkbraek's crown is not in danger, but *we* are in danger of getting soaked if you continue to sit here while the storm pours down upon us."

He tugs me forward and I curl my fingers through his, walking to the patch of cave floor now covered in the hides of the animals Abhartack has slain. I cast a glance toward the now brown splotch of moss that he'd first used to cushion my head as I lay barely clinging to life. "What if it takes years to find our way off this mountain?"

He plops onto the hides and pulls me down with him. "Then we have plenty of time for me to tell you a story."

A laugh bubbles out of me. Despite our dire situation, that's been happening a lot lately. "Another one? Will it be scary to match the storm?"

His arms slide around my waist and his cheek rests against mine. "This story is about the reason I once asked if you were familiar with the human concept of a honeymoon."

I heave a sigh. "Please do not liken our unchosen stay on this stormy mountain to a human honeymoon. Humans usually go to beaches."

He groans. "An equally unpleasant location, but I can see the appeal of having your partner wearing nothing but their undergarments." His nose runs along the shell of my ear. "If said partner continues to insist upon wearing clothing."

I smile. Another odd reaction from me. With the way I respond to even his slightest touch, one would think that the king has tamed me into a creature who feels...joy. I relax into the cool warmth of his body. "I admit, I will miss being here. Just the two of us. But we cannot forsake our obligations."

He settles me into the crook of his arm. "I know. But before we discuss leaving, I want to discuss the origins of the Vampir. Do you know how the Vampir came to exist?"

I stare out the cave entrance, watching the rain fall. I've searched for the answer to his question many times throughout the years, all to no avail. As seems to be the case with so many things that are important to me. "I don't even know how *I* came to be, so no, I don't know about the origins of the Vampir other than they...we, are somehow born of Loki."

Abhartack runs his fingers along my chin and brings my face to his. "Most do not know of the true heritage of the Vampir. There are stories, some close to the truth and others wrong in every detail. You being as unique as you are, your story is a little different from that of the others, though."

My breath shallows. "You know...who I am and where I came from?"

His smile is sad. "I do, but before I tell you, I first need to explain what happened so many centuries ago that time itself has forgotten the events." I lock my fingers together on my lap and the king continues his story, a knot forming in my gut with each word. "Many years ago, a horde of demons known as the Lilitu took up residence in Midgard. They feasted on flesh and blood, flying through the night sky with a piercing cry and devouring all mortals who dared to accidentally cross their paths." His eyes go distant. "It was practically impossible to hide form the Lilitu. They were fierce. Terrifying. *Glorious*." His eyes refocus on me, and the corners of his mouth turn up. "They were all female, with bodies resembling those of the most voluptuous of humans. Needless to say, their victims were men."

A lump forms in my throat. "It sounds as if you were there, living during the reign of the demon horde."

He gives a slight nod. "I wasn't there in the beginning, when they first appeared in Midgard, but what I tell you today I witnessed enough of to know the truth of it." He slides a hand to my knee and pulls me closer. "One of the Lilitu fell in love with a mortal man. They spent a decade together before the man neared the end of his mortal life. Up until that time, the Lilitu had only fed on his blood, and in very small quantities. But as the man lay dying, he asked her to take it all."

My brows knit together. "His blood? He wanted her to kill him?"

Abhartack nods, fingers beginning to draw circles over my skin. "It was the last thing he would ever be able to do for her, and her for him. He did not want to suffer through those last days of life any more than she wanted to watch him suffer. They said their goodbyes and then the Lilitu began to feed. Her lover decided to bite her back."

My eyes widen. "A human bit a demon?"

The king smiles. "The Lilitu had tasted her lover's blood many times, but he had never tasted hers. It was his dying wish to know what it felt like to drink from her. So while his demoness drank from him, he bit back, which drove the Lilitu into a frenzy. She slashed her own throat and pressed his mouth against her, demanding he drink. Her ecstasy was great, her feeding violent as she ripped into the flesh of the man she loved, gorging herself while his lips grew ever stronger against her neck."

"Stronger?"

"Yes, Keela, stronger. You see, while she drained every last drop of life from his veins, he had no choice but to swallow her blood as it rushed into his mouth. At some point, he *wanted* her blood. *Needed* to feed from her, the same way she was feeding from him. So he did. While she drained him, he fed from her throat, the lovers locked in this frenzy for three days and three nights. What neither of them realized at the time was that the man was no longer mortal by the end of the first night."

"He became Vampir?"

Abhartack frowns. "Not...exactly. During the second and third days of their frenzy, his flesh burned and ached, but he didn't pull away from his lover because at the very same time, his desire to feed from her was growing as strong as his desire to continue ravishing his Lilitu. On the morning of the fourth day, he finally fell into a deep sleep, waking the very next morning as a new being. A species balanced on the precipice of both life and death. No more a man than he was a demon. He could not fly as his Lilitu could. He could not venture out into the sun's rays as his love did." Abhartack pauses. "This man...the very first of his kind, was my father."

My heart begins to pound. "Your *human* father?"

Abhartack's eyes fix on my stampeding chest. "Yes. It was the demon who took him from my family that I was hunting when you—"

"Me?" I gasp.

His hand tightens on my knee. "Remember when we spoke about the Dearg Dua?"

I nod dumbly. He takes a deep breath. "Before the human girl in the Dearg Dua's story was sold, the girl had been in love with a boy in her village. He was of low birth. Poor. Unable to care for himself, let alone a wife. But he had promised to love the girl as she promised to always love him. He tried to fight for her, but in the end, he did not stop her from the fate of being sold by her own father. So the Dearg Dua hunted down the village boy and ripped out his throat."

"I know," I whisper.

He bites his lip. "Well, the part you don't know is that the low-born village boy was not the girl's true love. Or at least, not the only boy she loved."

My brows knit. "You?"

His head bows. "It has been so long that I barely remember being human, except for those memories I have with you."

I jolt out of his arms, surging to my feet. "Me?"

He swallows. "I was thirteen when you first kissed me. Sixteen when we took each other to bed for the first time. Eighteen when I asked you to marry me, and twenty when I...died."

I sink to my knees. "Your father killed you?"

The king's head shakes, a blood-red tear streaking down his face. "*I* killed *him*. Our family was as wealthy as yours, so our match was a good one in the eyes of everyone. Save for your father. There were rumors about mine, because my father was not an honest man, but neither was yours and my father was hardly ever around. When you said you would marry me and yet your father denied our union, I set out to find my own father. To drag him back and have him make the deal with your father so we could be allowed to wed. Money had to change hands for your father to agree, and my mother and I had no power to execute the deal."

His throat bobs. "What I found was my father bedding a demon. I swore to kill her but the two of them fled, having the time of their lives while I trailed after them, town to town, always too late. My anger consumed me." His eyes close. "I lost two years of my life chasing after my father. Two years that I should have been at home, with you. Instead, I..." He looks at me. "I only caught up with my father because of the illness he developed. Plagues were bad and once he got sick, he never recovered. The Lilitu was by his side, day and night. I knew it was only a matter of time so I waited, planning and plotting the exact moment when the demon would be distracted by his death. That's how I saw what they did to each other. It was...horrifying. Once my father fell into a deep sleep, I lured the Lilitu into a trap and beheaded her."

My hand moves forward of its own volition, wrapping around his. Abhartack's fingers tremble in a way I've never felt before. "I stupidly went to my father, demanding that he go back to our village with me. I thought he could be cured of the demon's blood, or at least be alive long enough to finalize our union with your father. But he was enraged. He knew his Lilitu was dead and he tried to kill me for what I'd done to her. So I...drove my sword through his heart. And since it was well known that the only way to truly kill a demon was by cutting off their head, I severed his."

Sorrow rips through me. "I am sorry."

His fingers tighten on mine. "No, Keela. *I* am sorry. When I finally returned to our village, I heard that you had been sold to a chieftain in a neighboring village. There were rumors that you had fallen in love with another, the field servant, and it was *him* the townspeople looked upon with pity. It was I who was then enraged. I went to the boy and demanded the truth from him. And then I almost killed him. Not because he confirmed that the two of you had planned to run off together, but because he said he tried to stop you from being sold off like cattle but *couldn't.* He was there, doing nothing but working in the field while you..."

My heart aches at the truth in the king's words. His jaw ticks. "I set out for the neighboring village that night but along the way, I encountered another Lilitu." He rubs my hair between his fingers. "Her hair was the same color as mine, and she was certainly beautiful." His hand cups my face. "But not as beautiful as my Keela. A name I put into Rohan's head as soon as I realized who you were because I could not bear to hear you called by any other name but your own."

His eyes shine red with unshed tears. "I am sorry, my love. I tried to get to you, but the demon was too strong. All I could do was what I had witnessed my father doing. I bit down on her and refused to let go. Unlike my father, when I came to, the demon was gone and you were dead. By your own hand." A sob rattles out of him. "I wanted to die, too, but I was rabid. Lost in my bloodlust. I did not want to harm my family so I ran. Fled our country and never looked back. By the time word of the Dearg Dua reached me, it was too late. You were lost to me once more and I mourned you all over again."

"But Odin did not kill me?"

His teeth grind. "A lie I will kill him for telling."

I reach for the threads of memory begging to surface. "The Lilitu, you speak as if they were as common as dogs or cats in Midgard."

He leans his head against the cave wall. "There were 6,659 of them. Counting the one who took my father."

My brows pinch. His laugh is dark. "I hunted them. Killed them all. Save for one."

Realization thunders through me. "The one inside of me."

He studies my face. "She is the one who turned me. And now I know why I could never find her. My guess is that she followed my scent from the scene of where I'd murdered my father's demon. I led her to the outskirts of your new village before she caught up with me. She must have heard your plea and used all of her power to slip beneath your skin while you still teetered on the edge of life." His eyes flick to my chest. "That is how your heart still beats. And me slaughtering the rest of the demons is why you are the only one of your kind."

"Death," I mutter.

"Mi Fagr Dauði," he responds.

I sink to the cave floor, my very bones seeming to deflate. Abhartack moves forward. "Now you know why I hold the power of choice in such esteem. Why I do not allow the humans in Dökkbraek to be prey. I harmed too many innocents after my change and once I got a handle on my bloodlust, I began to seek out those who were already sick or dying. Along the way, I learned that my bite could bestow the gift of eternal life on humans, if I chose to bestow such a gift upon them." A muscle ticks in his jaw. "But you and I both know eternal life isn't always a gift. So I chose wisely, but some of those Vampir also had the power to change humans and before long, there were many more Vampir than there had ever been Lilitu. Being the only *living* original, I am more powerful than all the others, and therefore I became their king. One who has never had need of a queen."

"Because of me?" My voice is small. "Because I betrayed our betrothal?"

His forehead rests on mine. "I left you for two years. I even stopped writing after a while. I...am the one who failed you. I have carried that guilt with me and never let a lover become anything more than that.

I treat them well and I try my best to be...good. Decent. But we are not Loki's spawn, the way the old stories claim. The way I have insisted they be told. Loki was birthed after the void created the cosmos. After Yggdrasil grew and began to give life to all of creation. After the Norns began to weave destinies."

He sits back and stares at me. "The Lilitu were born directly from the chasm, their souls woven from Chaos. The way humans are born of Odin and his brothers. Which makes our history a very long and complicated one, Keela. We are not pure demons. We are not Loki's. And we are not creatures Odin will ever claim because we are only half of what he created. The void is sentient, and we are a product of its primordial forces. Fate is constructed. The Norns try to weave new endings for what the void has preordained, and the gods try to manipulate the outcomes of both for their own gain, but they cannot outwit what created them."

I inhale deeply. "This is why you say Ragnarök will not be the battle we expect."

He touches the gem at the base of his throat. "It is why I *know* it won't. The void is preparing for something. I do not know what or even when, but I feel it drawing more power within itself."

I touch my own gem and his frown deepens. "Mi Dauði, it is the void's claim over the Vampir and over the Dearg Dua that leave the Vampir without the joy of having fate-ordained mates the way the Álfar and so many other kinds do. But there is a way in which bonds can be forged between us. Ones just as powerful as those fate weaves."

I tug at the necklace. "Is this why—"

"No," he cuts me off. "The necklace is not part of the rite."

"What rite?"

"One the void showed me. It is similar to how the Lilitu gave part of her soul to merge with that of her human lover's, the two pieces bonding together inside of him. Similar to the way my Lilitu bonded with me." He stares at my chest. "A rite that all Vampir now hold as sacred, but one in which consent is not necessary to perform."

My body freezes in place. "You bonded me to you. How? When?"

His throat bobs. "When I found you here. Which wasn't easy with you being unconscious but..." He hesitates. "The rite is simple. Each partner feeds from the other until both are drained of their own blood and filled with that of their mate."

"You forced your blood into me?"

Irritation flashes through his features. "You already know I did. To save you. And to get..." He scrubs his hands over his face, smearing the blood trails of his tears. "Trust me, I wanted our mating to be a mutual desire. But a benefit of being mated is that your body could then draw on my strength. Even without feeding, me being near you would strengthen you, so I... I mated you, Keela." His eyes go hollow. "I gave you a wedding vow after all of these centuries, and then we had our honeymoon here, hidden away in this cave."

He looks around. "I asked you about the human honeymoon because Vampir who choose to bond do something similar. They take themselves away to someplace safe where they can perform the rite in peace, because during and directly after, they are too weak to be around others. Their strength returns quickly, though, and over the course of the coming weeks, they develop a heightened awareness of each other." His focus returns to me. "Something I already felt for you. I believe it's the influence of our Lilitu, coupled with the love we had as humans. But you did not feel me from so far away, did you? Not the way I felt you. Not until you were in Dökkbraek."

I glance at the brown moss. Since entering Dökkbraek I have grown closer to the king than I ever thought was possible with anyone. But his confessions... "Is Abhartack your human name?"

He sighs. "No. I gave up that name on the day my terrible choices cost you the life you deserved."

Pain traces through my heart over the crestfallen look on his handsome face. An empathetic response most likely brought on by the mate bond. "It seems that was a very long time ago. You can stop blaming yourself now."

The storm howls, rain beginning to pound down on the mountain. I drag its refreshing scent into my lungs. All Vampir have a heightened sense of smell. One that is superior to that of Fae and Álfar. What I smell rising as quickly as the tempest is more than only Sean. I race to the cave mouth. "Wait," Abhartack shouts. "You were going to die. I had no choice! The fates—"

"Do you smell that?" I growl at him, pulling air into my lungs until they ache. "Do you smell the human? Sean Winkle is nearby. He has to be."

Abhartack's presence looms beside me. "I...am aware that you care for the boy, but you must rest. Hate me or love me as I love you, you must rest."

I whip my head toward the king, "You smell him, too? You smell all of them? Sean, Gelby, Rohan... Tell me you smell them because if you do..."

His nostrils flare. "Yes, mi Dauði, they are near. And they are not alone." He scans my face. "It seems our honeymoon is over. But the boy is not what you think. He is dangerous. So much more dangerous than what you believe me to be."

26

Sean

It's raining again. A light mist falling against the canopy of trees above where Leah is huddled between Collin and me, underneath a rocky overhang that's neither dry nor protecting us from the wind. We've tried to find our way into the heart of the forest but I can still hear the distant sound of the stream. We've moved away from it, but we haven't left it behind. I take another bite of vulture. It's tough and tastes like a mouthful of decaying leaves. Earthy and rotting. Each bite is a struggle but when this one swooped down over us an hour ago, Collin got his massive wolf jaws around the bird's throat and I roasted it. Managing not to cook Collin in the process. Thanks to Leah. She helped me control the dragon fire. It still doesn't always answer when I want it to, especially when the Fae light decides to break free, but I have control that I wouldn't have without Leah. I have answers that I wouldn't have without Leah.

"Do you think there are any more vultures?" she asks Collin. Not me, because despite the agony of this soul-testing journey we've taken together, talking about our *feelings* is what broke us. Not the crocodile, the Fossegrim, or the vultures. Not being physically and mentally drained just trying to survive the marsh. Leah bringing up the past, laying herself bare and changing the truth of my reality is what put the nail in the coffin I was sure I slammed shut long ago.

Collin holds up what's left of his portion of the bird. We were all hungry so eating it only seemed fair. "I think this was the last one. Zara's going to be disappointed that we didn't die."

Fur sprouts along Leah's arms. "I bet dragon tastes a whole lot better than vulture."

Collin grunts his agreement, wary eyes meeting mine overtop Leah's head. We only escaped the vultures because of my...Fae magic. Collin practically turned inside out when the light poured from my hands. Leah laughed, and Collin accused me of being Fae. They both say that's what the light is. Fae magic. "Do fairies have dragon fire?"

Collin's head shakes. "Fairies are different than Fae, and...I don't know. The Fae don't really advertise their abilities, and we don't interact with them much."

"We don't interact with anyone much," Leah mutters.

Collin looks back out at the forest, his features haunted in a way I've never seen on him before. "Because we're not like the others, Leah. And bitterness will consume us all, so knock it off already." He gets to his feet. "I'm going to scout. Zara couldn't have gotten far." Leah reaches for him but Collin growls at her. "Stay here." His eyes flick to mine. "Watch her."

I nod and he shifts, the change even faster than what I've seen Leah do. He stalks through the rain, leaves rustling as he moves through the underbrush, his paws making no sound on the forest floor. Leah pulls her knees up and hugs them to her chest. I swallow. "He knows not to go far."

"Shut up," she snarls.

I snort. "Right. Because you're five years old and not talking to me. Not even when I saved you from a vulture who's about to peck the eyes out of your big, fat, furry head."

The air around her trembles, a rumble rising from deep within her, her wolf clawing its way to the surface. "I don't need you to save me."

I expel a sharp breath or air. "The Fossegrim says otherwise."

A shiver shakes through her, the wolf hair sprouting and disappearing again. Her hands slide down her legs and her eyes glaze over. I reach my arm around her. "I'm sorry, I shouldn't have dredged that memory back up. I'll always be there to protect you, Leah, and I'm right here if you need to talk. We've been through a lot together."

She pushes up and away from me, her movements slow and mechanical. "Collin only outranks me on a technicality, but he's not my alpha so I can fight his orders. I don't need to be stuck here with you."

Her shift is slower than normal but still fast. The rain amps up, turning into a torrential downpour as she lumbers away, slinking through the undergrowth to follow her brother's trail. I close my eyes and breathe, attempting to sort through the weight of everything I'm feeling. Despite Collin's questions, Leah never added anything to what I told her brother. She never told him about Aether putting his fist inside of my chest. I don't know why I didn't tell him, and I don't know what it means that she didn't either. *Loyalty.*

I shake the thought away. Leah's probably only loyal to the fact that I suddenly have power. A lot of it. But if I'm Fae, I don't see how that helps her. I can't be Ulfr *and* Fae. I don't think. I climb to my feet and stomp through the downpour. No matter what I am, I'm not going to sit here letting myself have this level of twisted, mind-bending, heart-wrecking emotions over Leah freaking MacKenzie.

The forest grows denser with each step I take. I'm aware of every rustling leaf and snap of a twig, the trees closing in around me, slowing my progress. "Collin?" I shout. "Leah?" Staying behind was a mistake. I'm probably going to be separated from them now. The way Collin was separated from Nathan, Ethan, Mark, and Lance. He was given Zara, though, the way I got to keep Leah when these Norns decided to separate me from everyone else. And I've never liked Lance. He gives me vibes about as good as the ones Rohan and Gelby give. And Haldir, for that matter. Then there's Jofir. She's full of hatred. So maybe the Norns have been doing us favors. Separating us from those who don't have our best interests at heart while forcing us to be with people who do. Well, except for Zara. She set us up to be killed.

Thunder cracks overhead and the wind picks up, slapping branches across my face. I duck under the branches and beg my beast to help a little more with this night vision trick. I can't see the wolves. "Collin? Leah?"

Guttural growls slither between the trunks, distorted by wind and distance, but unmistakably...dangerous. I charge forward, breaking through limbs and catapulting over rocks. Lightning breaks across the sky, blue and sizzling. A deep-throated rumble rolls toward me, warped by the night and the rain, smothered by a feral snarl I've heard too many times now to mistake it for anything else. I cut through the forest and break out into a field, racing for the outline of Leah's wolf. All around her, a battle is raging. Beasts ten feet tall with thick horns protruding from their heads are leaving a path of destruction in their wake. My mind goes blank, ears assaulted by the sounds erupting from the creatures' throats, the wind and rain being ripped apart by the shouts of the Vasilis. All this time, we've been so close to Gelby and the others.

I drop to my knees and slide through the mud, calling flames to my hands. Leah says I should be able to use it as a projectile but I haven't managed to detach the fire from my body yet. The horned brute towering between her and Collin is still toast, though. Collin raises up on his hind legs, mimicking the beast, and roars. Leah darts around it toward her brother, distracting the animal and giving me the opening I need. I slide between its hairy legs and clamp on. Its dark fur ignites and my hands sink into its charring flesh. The creature topples forward and I thrust myself onto its back, hanging on while it thrashes. Until a coarse vibration echoes through its chest. A death rattle cloaked in rage, but a death rattle all the same. One muffled and carried away by the storm.

I roll off the dead creature and scramble toward Leah and Collin. They're ahead of me and already racing deeper into the battle, where the ground is littered with dozens more of the creatures. Some dead. Some attacking a blazing wall of blue magic surrounding a row of tents. Jofir is holding the shield while Rohan's sizzling magic lashes out, cutting gashes through fur and lobbing off limbs. Haldir is outside of the shield, still in his human form, and slashing out with his blade. Beyond where he fights is Gelby. Surrounded on all sides.

Collin and Leah beat me to the next creature, but not by much. I spin away from a swipe of the creature's claws and it drops to all fours, moving just as comfortably on four limbs as it does on two. Leah's jaws snap at its throat and Collin comes at it from the other side, massive jaw clamping onto the monster's shoulder. They're positioning it for me, but it's too low for me to get underneath. I launch myself toward its head and Leah shifts, a shout ripping from her throat. "No! The horns are poisonous! Don't touch—"

The beast cranks its neck and sends her flying, lifting its clawed foot and peeling Collin off its shoulder like Collin is nothing more than a gnat. I drop and roll, the horn barely missing me as the creature surges forward. Collin regains his ground and leaps at the animal's haunch but it counters, using its massive front arm to knock him away. I suck in a breath. These things are strong. And there are too many of them.

I get to my feet and a cut a path toward Leah. A savage, animalistic roar cuts through the wind, followed by a shrill wail and a high-pitched scream. I look over my shoulder. Haldir is on the ground, a beast standing over him. And...Gelby is on his knees, only a faint blue glow surrounding him. Claws rip through my face and I stab my hands up into the night, grabbing for the arm of the creature. It roars and stumbles away, burning like a torch in the rain. Not enough. Unless I get a good hold on these things, they aren't going to burn.

Another high-pitched scream breaks through the wind and I jump to my feet. This one belongs to Leah.

Keela

Shadows gather around me as I race over rock and earth, streaking like a dark bolt through the howling storm. Heading for the belly of the beast. To my family. To Sean Winkle. Abhartack keeps pace beside me, gathering none of this land's raw energy to himself. He leaves it for me. Or knows he can't take it from me. I can feel him through our bond.

Because that's how these bonds work. Couples feel what their partner feels. Know when they are in danger or at peace. And they develop a hunger for their mate that is fierce and protective. If death separates their souls, the living mate usually finds the torture of living without their partner to be unbearable. But Vampir are already dead, and I was developing a hunger for my king the instant he first touched me—my human soul remembering him, and bound to the demon who created him.

Distant snarls bleed through the rain. I release my shadows. They pour over the land like a mighty flood, swarming ahead, drowning everything in their path. I breathe in sharply, the power intoxicating. "Easy," Abhartack warns, his pace slowing. "I did not bargain for your life to see you throw it away in a desperate attempt to save those who do not deserve the might of your power."

"And I did not ask to be bonded to you," I rebuke. But because he has done this thing, I can now fight for my family with not only my power, but his.

We break over the last crest and leap as one, me inches ahead of my king as we fall to the earth. A sphere of his dark energy bursts out of him, annihilating the three Skarthorns in front of us. "I know your true nature." My king's dark eyes drink me in. "And I love you for it. For who you were and who you are. With no allure to compel me. Do not forget that. You are my queen today, as you have always been."

His words reverberate through the long-abandoned corridors of my heart. He loves me as no other ever has. As no other ever will. I take my king's hand, our power joining. Our footfall shakes the ground as we thunder forward, mowing down beasts and relying on each other as if we have never spent a day apart. My king is my home, and I want eternity with him. But he is not the only one who I crave.

Abhartack

My queen's shadows engulf the battlefield, pulling Skarthorns apart. This is why the void wanted to reclaim her. Why I sacrificed everything, knowing it would be my death, but that she would continue to live. In power. Strength. With the might of my Vampir behind her. Never again will Keela have her choices taken away. Not even by me. I am already weakening. I know she can feel it, but she does not yet understand that I am dying. She simply thinks that I have given her too much, when what I have really given her is *everything*. And I did not agree to let the void take me so that Keela could fall victim to the cowardice of the field hand who betrayed her those many centuries ago. I didn't know his soul still lived until the void revealed the truth to me. Inside of Sean Winkle is the soul of the peasant. My Dearg Dua ripped out his throat once, and this time, it will be me.

"Keela?" The reincarnated fool coughs from the darkness ahead.

My queen's heart begins to pound. I take an exaggerated sniff. The air is thick with the scent of the boy she longs for even when her fangs are lodged in my throat. When I am giving her *everything*. Once upon a time, she loved me and only me. I crush her hand within mine. "Careful, mi Dauði. Do not provoke your king, unless you do not wish to see the boy live."

27

Shock is a fickle thing, wielded by everyone around this campfire in a different way. The Vasilis were barely finished exchanging stories about what had befallen them in this domain of the Norns, where existence is crafted and the lines between reality and dreams are blurred, when the witch had what I am shocked to hear is her second *prophesy*. Hers is not a pure gift. Nor is it natural. I have seen this type of possession before, though, and am truly shocked that whoever is channeling the spirit into the girl has the power to do so at all. And while she is in this domain, no less. Circumventing the weavers right under their noses.

Heed thy plea from present to past, to cherish a moment, mortal and vast. What remorse breaks, threads do forgive. Cosmic whispers. Bonds cast to honor fate. Undying verses. Chanted. Lost to time. Ending rites and pledges made. Clemency screams for balance, mere crumbs given for the forgotten. Many hearts. One face.

I stare at the boy, my presence making him uncomfortable. As it makes all of the others. Had I not come to their aid, and if they were not all drained by their fight with the Skarthorn army, they would have fought more when Keela told them all to heel. But they have heeded my queen's voice, more shocked by the power they witnessed pouring out of her than by my presence at her side. Her might grows as her demon loosens those bonds that Odin placed upon her. *Bonds cast to honor fate.*

Together, the Norns weave their tapestry. Each contributing their unique perspective. Balancing fate. But the possessed witch speaks of remembering the volatile forces at play. Those that formed the past from chaos. Those with the ruinous will of the gods. And those who bow their heads to love. It is no coincidence that fate has brought us all here together. They want to rebalance that which Odin destroyed. *Many hearts. One face.* Keela. And Sean. They both contain many hearts and one face.

The witch tips over, the spirit possession leaving her drained. Gelby Vasilis lifts her into his arms. "Leah, come with me. Monique is in my tent and you can rest in there with her."

Rohan stands, weary eyes meeting mine and flicking to Keela. "We all need to rest. Haldir's tent is free. Sean will stay with us and Collin can join you and...*him*." His eyes glow faintly, narrowing on me.

I remain calm at my queen's side. A harder feat when the boy draws her attention, standing on the other side of the fire, face drawn. "Keela...can we talk?" His eyes never leave hers, his meaning in disrespecting my place in her life clear to everyone. "Someplace quiet and alone?"

My queen's head cocks, turning ever so slightly toward me. I brush my fingers along her lovely cheek. "Do as you wish, mi Dauði. But if he touches my queen, I will kill him where he stands. Him and anyone else."

Haldir, the dragon lurking in the shadows, licking his prideful wounds, lets out a low, gravely growl. He can smell the mate bond, but Keela's allure still drives him mad with want. The boy is different, though. It is the want of the peasant that drives him to clench his teeth and ready his flames. Keela lifts from my side, measuring her steps as she nears him. "Abhartack is my king. I am his queen. Threaten him, and you threaten me." Shadows coil around her, reaching out like a hand to wrap around the boy's throat. "Touch my king, and I will kill you where you stand." Her eyes move around to the others, my words flowing from her lips. "Him and anyone else."

Pride spreads a wide smile across my face. Even though I know her show of force is only because she can feel how weak I am. Feeding will slow the sickness of death, but not by much, and not for long. Keela turns her back on the boy. "We will take Haldir's tent. Alone. The Ulfr can find someplace else to sleep."

I rise, holding my arm out for my queen. Petty as it may be, I take the opportunity to gloat, earning myself a sharp stab through the bond. But even Keela's hit of wrath is a privilege. An honor. In the short amount of time I have left with her, I wish to experience everything that fate has denied us.

"You need to feed." Her face falls into tenderness the moment the tent flap closes behind us.

I lower to the untouched blanket and spread it out for us. "Lucky for me that there are Skarthorn remains in abundance. I will go feed, and then when I return, you will dine on your *very* happy king."

She lowers herself onto my lap, eyes glittering with the adrenaline of a demon who has just slaughtered many. "We will dine now. Together."

My body agrees. The slaughter has restored her, so I lean forward and press a kiss to the corner of her mouth, raking my fangs over her skin. "Thank you, mi Dauði. For choosing me."

She frowns, feeling but not understanding my bone-deep weakness. "You are my king. Bonded to you or not, I would choose you. Now drink." She tilts her head, offering me her neck. "Take what you need, whenever you need. I am yours."

I stroke a finger along her delicious throat. There is so little time left that I should tell her all that I know. Now. Before we embark on our first full union since being bonded. I should tell her that Aether was killed by his father for stealing something powerful from the Fae. An artifact the Unseelie joined with the Seelie to find. So they could stand against Bishop. Against any who would keep them from conquering and controlling. For the first time in history, the Fae royals are in league but instead of telling Keela that, I run my lips along her neck, pulling her body to fit tightly against mine. "Since we first danced under the moon on the summer solstice, I have loved you." I stare into her eyes, repeating the vows I made while she lay dying. "I loved you when we were both human and weak. And I love you in the strength of our death. I take you, Keela, my human love and my Lilitu, to be my mate, bonded by our blood, for *all* eternity."

She smiles, and plunges her teeth into my throat. I shout in ecstasy. For all to hear. And sink my fangs into my queen.

Sean

Abhartack's shout skims across my ears. I break a branch off a tree, shoving farther into the woods, going back into the forest where the smell of Keela doesn't pull me to her. Where I can escape seeing the spot where she stood beside the fire, telling us that she was bonded to Abhartack. Basically *married*. Off the market and not available to anyone else. The second she thundered off the mountain, I could sense the change, but I still wanted to run to her. But that *king*, his hands on her... I hate him. In a deep and visceral way.

"Sean!" Leah pants my name, ragged breaths breathing out of her as she catches up to me. I turn and watch her. The rain stopped as the last Skarthorn died, and we dried by the fire afterward. But the trees in the forest are still wet and as Leah pushes through them, they shed their drops all over her. She stops in front of me, wiping the strands of damp hair from her face. She stares at me, sorrow set deep in her eyes. "Are you okay? That was...Keela was cruel. And I know you hate me because I was too, but...I'm so sorry, Sean. You didn't deserve that. From me or from her. Are you okay?"

Her question makes my heart stop, because the truth is, I am. I've been ready to fight for Keela and I'm still drawn to her, about as much as I despise Abhartack. But Keela isn't who I want to fight for anymore. Not with Leah... I take her face in my hands and kiss her, pouring out everything I wanted to feel that summer when she destroyed any shot I had with her. Leah kisses me back, arms sliding around my neck and hands running through my hair. I lift her off the ground and she wraps her legs around my waist. I groan into her mouth and drag my lips from her chin to her neck. "How much do I need to grovel, Leah? What in the supernatural world do I have to do to finally get my shot with you?"

"Collin is going to kill me." I kiss Leah's cheek, her naked body wrapped around mine. We're on the ground, underneath a canopy of trees. Not a great spot but we've been in worse. And Leah's a wolf. She probably doesn't care that our first time together was on a forest floor.

She splays her hand across my chest and props her chin up, a smile brightening her beautiful face. "My brother is definitely going to break a few of your bones, but you heal fast."

My smile matches hers. For the first time in a long time, I'm genuinely happy. I run my fingers through her hair, working out the few remaining knots. "You're worth some broken bones, even if I don't heal fast."

Her face falls. "You don't really mean that."

I swallow. Because I do mean it. And I wish my mom was still alive so I could tell her that I've found someone. That Leah feels like *the one*. "I see who you are now, Leah. Maybe that's why the Norns stuck us together, so we would be honest with one another."

She sits up. "You mean, so I would be honest with you."

I raise up and slide my arm around her, pressing my lips to her shoulder. "Both of us, Leah. I've always told myself that I only take up for you and care about what's happening with you because you're my best friend's sister. But that's not true. I never stopped carrying a flame for you, I just smothered it. Until now." I call a ball of fire to my hand for emphasis.

She laughs. "Put that away before you burn the forest down."

I snuff it out and kiss her, losing myself in the softness of her lips. She pulls away, pressing a kiss to my nose. "I need to get back before Collin decides to come looking for us. And I want to check on Monique. She looks horrible."

"Unlike you." I follow Leah's lead and stand, watching her casually brush the wet leaves and dirt from her body before putting her clothes back on. "Even covered in mud, you're stunning, Leah. I used to hate how easy you made beautiful look, but now I get to admire you in full."

She rolls her eyes. "I'm a wolf, but I do still like the finer things in life so when we make it out of this land, be prepared to take me on dates to nice places. Rome, perhaps?" She winks. "My treat, because we wolves are also filthy rich. All I need from you is a good...boyfriend?"

That word sounds...perfect. "Collin is going to do more than break a few of my bones."

She runs her hands up my chest, face serious. "I've been in love with you for a long time, Sean, but I know you don't think of me that way. Not yet. So we'll take this slowly. Collin will smell you on me, and me on you. So will the others. We can't hide that. But we don't have to define anything. I know you're still hung up on Kee—"

"Don't." I stop her. "You gave me a shot. *Finally*. So now it's my turn to make sure you don't regret it. To prove that I'm worth being whatever label you want to put on us." I kiss her, deep and full.

She pushes away, a devilish grin on her lips. "Now that I know where a kiss like that leads, I'm looking forward to having no regrets. So get dressed and meet me back at camp. We're going to find these Norns, and then we're going to get back to Midgard and buy a label maker. After I have a long hot shower and get my nails manicured." She sweeps her fingers across my brow, the brevity fading away. "I know how important it was for you to get admitted at Merrymont. Because of your mom. We'll make sure you get to keep attending. It might take you an extra year to graduate because of all of this, but you *will* graduate, Sean. I know you will."

My throat closes up. Leah brushes her lips against mine, winking before shifting back into her wolf and racing out into the forest. I turn and reach for my pants. Leaves crunch behind me. I chuckle. "That didn't take long. Did you miss me already?"

"Yes." Keela's voice is smooth.

I go still, acutely aware of how naked I am. "Where's *your king*? I didn't get the impression that he lets you out of his sight."

She walks around me, eyes scanning my body. I cover my privates with the pants in my hand and the corners of her lips turn up. "My king sleeps."

"Yeah, I'm heading back to get some sleep myself." I say the words but don't move.

Keela steps closer. "Is that what you really want?"

My heart pounds. "Yes." *No.* "I need to find Leah."

Keela trails her fingers up my arm. I want to control the response my body is having to her touch, but I can't, and she can see that I can't. She moves closer, hand sweeping up my neck, fingers pulling tight in my hair. I drop the wad of clothing in my hand, fingers trembling as they dig into her sides. "You're...taken, Keela."

She jerks my neck to the side, fangs extending. "I am a queen, Sean Winkle, and you are my love."

28

I rub my neck. It's as sore as my groin. Keela wasn't gentle and I...wasn't either. Sex with Leah was the opposite. Sweet. Tender. The two of us moving like two people sheltering each other's hearts. And then I... A curse slithers from between my clenched teeth. Like a coward, I spent the night in the forest. Keela had her way with me, and I had mine with her, and then she left. Just like that. Without a word spoken between us. When she was gone, I ached for her, but I couldn't stop thinking about Leah. About how badly I screwed up my one and only shot with her. She'll never forgive me, and Collin isn't going to only figuratively kill me now. He's going to end me for real. I'm surprised he's even let me live this long. Actually, I'm surprised the Vasilis have let me be away from them this long.

I glance at the brightening sky. It'll be dawn soon. I haven't slept. I just sat in the spot where I took both Leah and Keela, and tried to make sense of my thoughts. My actions. I'm not this guy. When I slept with Leah, I really thought I was going to be her sanctuary. That we'd face whatever the future held…together. I *chose* Leah over Keela. And not because Keela is mated off to a vampire every cell in my body instinctively hates. I *chose* Leah. I *want* Leah. But Keela… Gelby told me she would do whatever it took to stay alive, and maybe she mated Abhartack for that reason, which is why she came to me last night in spite of these supposedly magical bonds that the supernaturals have. But that doesn't explain why I let her. I've wanted Keela since the moment I first laid eyes on her and up until I spent time with Leah, I didn't think my attraction to Keela had anything to do with Keela's allure. I thought…I loved her. But Leah…

I punch through the edge of the forest and brace myself for Collin. Leah. All of them. I'm not afraid to admit what I've done, I'm only afraid of how Leah is going to react. These past weeks…I've squandered every minute I could ever hope to have with her.

My foot stubs on a stone with curved edges that have been hewn. It's odd and out of place. I look up, across the valley floor. The tents are gone. So is the valley. In its place is a grove, dotted with trees thick with fruit, their heavy branches stretching overtop fields of flowers. Their colorful petals shift, glittering, as butterflies with iridescent wings flutter among them.

In the center of the grove stands a temple. It's open, the way the rotunda was, its arches covered in creeping vines. In the middle of the temple is a well whose watery reflection casts shimmering shadows over its rim, where three figures stand. They're watching me, their forms shifting between solid and smoke, like water evaporating from a boiling pot. "Come closer," one of them beckons, her gnarled finger curling.

"Your journey was long, seeker," another cackles.

"An anger that threatens both glory and ruin," the third calls, her voice dry and raspy.

The Norns are nothing like I imagined. I take a step toward them, the air around me suddenly filled with whispers, like the leaves of an invisible tree rustling in the wind. I keep walking, hesitating only when I reach the temple's edge. I step up onto the smooth surface of the marbled floor and runes flicker to life all around me, ancient symbols, like the ones Leah tried to decipher in the rotunda.

"Come."

"Seeker."

"Your future awaits."

The three figures glide around the well, their long robes trailing behind them like clouds of mist, their voices harmonizing and breaking apart. I clench my fists. "I'm here for truth, nothing else. The people who brought me here are the ones who *seek* you. Where are they? I'm tired of your games."

My arms begin to burn. My body. Lines like runes cracking open like lava flows, drawing patterns in my skin. The way my blood filled invisible grooves on my skin when the Vasilis were torturing me. Only this time, the pain is blinding. I drop to my knees. "What kind of spell is this? Why did you curse me?" My voice rises, the thin arches of the temple shaking.

"Odin's pawn." The one whose eyes are bottomless pits shoves her hands down into the crystal water of the well.

"Ungrateful, yet worthy." The one with long flowing hair that disappears into the mist of her robe smiles at me, dipping her fingers into the well.

The third studies me, pale lavender eyes distant, as if she's deep in thought. "Protected. And cursed. But not by the weavers."

She plunges her hands down into the well and I scream, burning. The beast retreats into my depths, fire dripping from my lungs, burning lines deep inside my body as this lava scorches me inside and out. "Abomination!" the Norns shout, their voices rumbling like distant thunder. My head falls back, visions dancing in front of my eyes as my body burns. Visions of Keela...with blonde hair and a...human flush to her cheeks. Smiling and waving. Visions of Abhartack...human and enraged. Fae dancing around a fire. Álfar chanting. And...the old man...the one I bumped into my first day at Merrymont. The one I was talking to when the raven clawed my head and...led me to Keela. But the man isn't old. He's...Odin.

"Fire runes." The Norns weave their words into my agony.

"Marked by Odin."

"Hidden from fate."

"One thread pulled."

"And burned into another." Their voices resonate with echoes of the past, and I see it now. Odin purposefully placing himself in my path. To awaken me from the spell he carved into my flesh. Spelled by fire runes, so no one would know what I was until Odin decided it was time...to use me.

Tears slip from my eyes, sizzling as they run over my burning cheeks. What I want in this life has never mattered. I can't have it.

"Brother betrays brother." The voices of fate lower, the fire receding from my body, fleeing with the visions. I lift my head and look toward the well. The Norns stand behind it, their hands clasped together and their faces drawn. "By blood. Not by birth."

A sob rips out of me and they disappear. When the others find out what Aether put inside of me...what's been done to turn me into a vessel capable of containing the Eye of Odin, they'll kill me. Or try to.

I push myself up from the grassy ground. A raw, animalistic snarl slams into me seconds before Abhartack's body does. His fangs scrape my neck and I throw him off, turning straight into a row of knuckles. Collin. He won't use his wolf to fight me. We'll settle this man-to-man.

I duck his next blow, glancing behind him, to where the others are all frozen midstride, whatever magic has been holding them in place wearing off. I was right. They were coming after me last night, but somehow, the Norns decided to give me one more night. To fret and decide for myself what it is I really want. So that when they took it all away from me today, it would hurt even more.

I slam my fist into Collin's stomach, a knot in my throat, tears thick in my eyes. "You are my brother. I love you. And I'm sorry." I throw him to side but he catches me with an uppercut and lands a kick against the side of my knee. Abhartack takes my back, ripping my head to the side and plunging his fangs into the marks Keela left on my neck. But he's weak. I pull him off me as easily as the Skarthorn pulled Collin's wolf from its shoulder. The king swipes at me but he's sluggish. I fling him away and turn back to Collin, stiffening as Keela's feral rumble swallows me in a wave of shadows. I close my eyes. I don't want to die, so I have to fight.

I lift my hands, Fae magic flowing out of me in a bright wave, overtaking Keela's shadows. They fade away with a squeal, and a vine of sizzling blue magic strikes across my chest. Gelby advances, Rohan at his side, lashing out over and over. I throw a ball of fire. If only Leah could be proud of me for that.

Gelby and Rohan scatter apart and I reach to grab Collin's fist. He doubles over, eyes glowing, a deep, guttural growl exploding out of him. Leah screams, tearing away from Monique to get to him. "No! Collin! No!"

Gelby falters, his magic fading as he grabs for Leah. I run toward him, a ball of my fire barely missing his head. Rohan's magic wraps around my neck and slams me to the ground. I land on my back and Abhartack pounces, claws gouging down the side of my face. I shove him into the air and throw him to the side, right into the path of Gelby's magic. The king's head plunks to the ground, his decapitated body following. I search for Keela. Darkness explodes across the valley floor, and she's somewhere in the midst of it.

Haldir runs at me. I jump to my feet and charge to meet him, yelling, "I didn't ask for this!"

A flash of light pops between us and Zara steps out of the portal, wielding the sword Leah and I left behind in the rotunda. I skid to a halt and she raises it over her head, stopping Haldir dead in his tracks. She mutters under her breath, striking too fast for me to counter. The blade plunges deep into my gut, the silver pulling out and arcing wide, slicing across Haldir's abdomen. He falls to his knees and Zara holds the blade at his throat, looking to where Collin is still doubled over, Leah sobbing at his side. "This is where our paths are destined to separate, Collin MacKenzie. Good luck." She slams a stone into the ground, creating another portal, and kicks Haldir through it, the two of them disappearing.

I sink to the valley floor, feeling my life drain away, everything around me happening in slow motion. Keela is an abyss raging toward us. Jofir is racing to Rohan's side, helping him create a shield to guard against Keela. Gelby's hands are outstretched, his body the center of a great blue magical storm. Collin is on all fours, panting in agony, Leah holding him up, heartbroken sobs shaking from her to crumble what's left of me.

"Leah," I whisper her name. She looks up, rage filling her eyes as she holds onto her brother.

A bolt of lightning slams into the ground beside me. Not from Gelby. From the old man. He removes his wide-brimmed hat and transforms into one of the many other faces of Odin. The god extends his hand to me. "East of the sun, west of the moon, my boy. I am The Third, and it is time. You will come with me."

I glance at Monique. She nods. "Many hearts. One face."

I turn to Leah one last time and clamp my fingers around Odin's, closing my eyes so she's the very last thing I see in this life.

Acknowledgements

"Not all those who wander are lost." — J.R.R. Tolkien
This book was a long time coming. Roughly two years off schedule and with a whole heap of life lessons learned between what was to be, and what came to be. In particular, 2024 exploited my every weakness and left me feeling a lot like Sean—powerless to control my own destiny. But I have a bit of magic in my life, too. It manifests in the form of strong hands, a warm heart, and calls itself my husband. Joe, God gave me you for the days of doubt, the ups and downs, and to be the glue that keeps your Aquarian wife stuck in the best place on earth—at your side. Thank you for being tirelessly patient and unwavering in your heartfelt support.

Every book needs an all-powerful eye to scan its jagged edges and soft underbelly. I'm grateful for the guidance and insight of my editor. Thank you, Anita! You're the calming center in a storm of anxiety.

Covers are important but I no longer spend much time thinking about what I want a cover to look like because I have a Seer in my life. Marianne, I'm deeply grateful and forever in awe.

And to my readers—whether you've been with me from the beginning or just discovered my work—thank you. You inspire me. You challenge me. You make every word worth writing. May you find the magic in all the ups and downs throughout the journey of your life.

Lee Dawna

Also By Lee Dawna

Beller Ties – A four-book stand-alone romantic suspense collection.

Something So Beautiful

Now And Always

Dawn Of Devotion

Marked By Forever

Hinton Thriller Series – A serial-killer thriller trilogy.

Descend

Smother

Rise

Sierra: A Modern Psychological Thriller

Eyes of Midgard – Norse fantasy trilogy

Day of the Raven

Join the mailing list for early release news!

About the Author

Lee Dawna is a thriller and suspense author, and host of the Immortal Sunshine Podcast. An avid traveler and outdoorswoman, you may bump into her along a remote trail where a meandering stream whispers her next story.

Visit **LeeDawnaBooks.com** for more on what the author is up to lately and to **join her mailing list** for special announcements.

Find her on YouTube and Patreon.

www.ingramcontent.com/pod-product-compliance
Lightning Source LLC
Chambersburg PA
CBHW061655190726
48289CB00006B/1883